Diamonds & Deception

A Karina Cardinal Mystery (Book 3)

By Ellen Butler

A Karina Cardinal Novel
K.C.

Power to the Pen

Diamonds & Deception Copyright © 2019 by Ellen Butler. All Rights Reserved.

Power to the Pen
PO Box 1474
Woodbridge, VA 22195

Print ISBN 13: 978-0-9984193-8-1
Digital ISBN 13: 978-0-9984193-7-4

Categories: Fiction, Thriller & Suspense, Mystery, Amateur Sleuth, Police Procedurals

Cover Art by: SelfPubBookCovers.com/RLSather

Warning: All Rights Reserved. The unauthorized reproduction or distribution of the copyrighted work is illegal and forbidden without the written permission of the author and publisher; exceptions are made for brief excerpts used in published reviews.

This is a work of fiction. Names, characters, corporations, institutions, organizations, events, or locales in this novel are either the product of the authors imagination or, if real, used fictitiously. The resemblance of any character to actual persons (living or dead) is entirely coincidental.

Prologue

"Mike? Mike, hello? Oh, geez, it's your damn voicemail." My voice shook. "Look, I know you're in the middle of important FBI training, and I promised I wouldn't call you like this, but . . . I could really use your help. It's bad, and I'm scared. Please, call me." I whispered the last and prayed.

Chapter One

One Week Earlier

I slammed the door to my two-bedroom condo and stomped the floor bolt into place. The alarm system beeped at me, and I savagely tapped out my code on the panel, chipping my nail polish in the process. Stalking through my little foyer, I shed my jacket, handbag, and heels, leaving them haphazardly in the hallway on the way to my living room. I debated flopping down onto my comfy suede couch, then decided I had too much pent-up anger to sit still and instead took a few laps around the kitchen island, dragging my fingers along the cool granite countertop as I went. When that didn't help, I pulled my wavy chestnut mane into a ponytail and got out the cleaning supplies. Scrubbing the bathroom floor by hand would surely work out my fit of irritation—no, irritation was too mild a word for my feelings. Angry? Mad? Pissed off? Yes, that was a much better term for my mood—pissed off, a crude but encompassing expression for my current emotions.

My phone rang three times before I picked up. My sister's number displayed across the top. "Hey, Jilly."

"What's up? Did I interrupt something? You don't sound happy."

"Mike and I had a fight."

"Uh-oh. What's wrong?"

It all spilled out. Coherently, for the most part, I think.

****

The humming in my ears drowned out the clank of dishes and drone of noisy conversation, and I withdrew my hand from Mike's, staring at him in disbelief. "Could you repeat that, please?" I asked.

"Would it help if I said I was trying to protect you?"

I looked unseeingly around the restaurant to avoid focusing on Mike while I processed the nuclear revelation he had just dropped in my lap. Old Ebbitt Grill, a Washington, D.C., institution, was filled to overflowing with city power players, normal for a Friday night. A woman at the bar, dressed in a beautiful turquoise dress perfect for the late spring warmth, stood out from the conservative black and gray suits that surrounded her. Three men vied for her attention. I returned my attention to the dark-haired man across from me, a man I'd been friends with since college, and who recently had evolved into my boyfriend and lover. He'd loosened the striped tie at his neck and removed his jacket. His handsome features were drawn into a concerned frown, and the hand I'd abandoned now fidgeted with the salad fork.

"Let me get this straight. You secretly accessed my phone and computer information to . . . clear me of Harper's murder?"

His Adam's apple bobbed as he swallowed and nodded.

"When? Did you and your FBI buddies break into my home? While I was at work?"

Mike's coffee-brown eyes darted away. "I did it when you went to the bathroom."

"When I . . . went to the bathroom? What the . . . ?" My mouth dropped. I swept a lock of hair aside and pressed a pair of fingers to my temple. "Cripes, how long was I in there?"

He didn't answer.

"Here we go." Our waiter had arrived. He placed a glass of pinot grigio in front of me and a tall glass of frothy beer in front of Mike. "Have you decided?"

"Could you give us a few minutes?" Mike asked.

Neither one of us glanced at the guy. He must have felt the tension twanging tight as a bowstring between us, and I'm sure my face displayed my displeasure, because he retreated without another word.

"How many FBI agents culled through my private information?"

"Just one."

I pursed my mouth. "Which one?"

Mike worked for FBI cybercrimes, and a few months ago, I'd had the displeasure of meeting some of his colleagues. Actually, I'm sure his colleagues were amiable folks, but being on the receiving end of an FBI investigation as a possible suspect didn't exactly make for a genial introduction to the crew.

"It doesn't matter."

"It matters to me. Which one?" I demanded, slamming my fist on the table. "Do I know him?"

Mike's jaw flexed once. Twice.

My eyes narrowed.

"Amir," he said in capitulation.

"Amir? Amir. You mean the computer geek? Dark Persian looks? The one from my dining room table? *That* Amir?"

Mike gave a sharp nod. "We go back a long way."

I gave an eyeroll. "So, you're telling me he already knew who I was when he came. He'd already invaded my privacy?"

"K.C., it wasn't like that."

"Don't you 'K.C.' me." I shook my finger at him like one would a naughty child. "After all that crap with Patrick and the tracking app. You *knew*. You *must have known* how I'd feel about such an invasion."

"Yes."

"Yes? You knew? And yet you did it anyway?" Blindly, I snatched up my wine glass and gulped enough to empty half of it before banging the glass back down with a distinct clank. Luckily, the stem didn't snap. "Did you seriously think I'd been involved in Harper's death?"

"No," Mike answered flatly.

His coolness wound me up even more. "Then why *the hell* did you do it?"

"I told you—to clear your name."

"Why didn't you just ask me if I'd had anything to do with it?"

"I did." He stared down, readjusting his napkin. "You would, of course, say no even if you had been guilty."

"You thought I might be guilty?"

"No. But you were with him when he died. *I knew* the FBI was already digging into your background. *You knew* you were a 'person of interest.'"

Breathing deep to regain my composure, I counted backward from ten. "So, you did it on your supervisor's orders?"

He paused. "No, I did it on my own."

I gritted my teeth and clenched my fists, but my response came out in measured tones. "You know how you obtained it was illegal as hell. If you'd uncovered something, it never would have been admissible in court."

"I know." His gaze darted away from mine.

Maybe that's why he did it that way. I couldn't read his expression, or rather, lack thereof: he'd been too well trained. "Why didn't you just ask me for the information?"

"Would you have given it to me if I had?"

"Sure."

He arched a thick brow in disbelief.

I chewed my lip and huffed, "No. I would have told you to get a warrant and talk to my lawyer."

He sat back as though vindicated, a move that shot my simmering blood temperature up to a blistering third-degree burn.

I opened my mouth to blast him, then, catching sight of the waiter heading our way, snapped it shut. My glare sent the server scuttling in the opposite direction, and once again I scanned the restaurant. A thought washed over me. "Why now?"

"What?"

"Why now? Why tell me at all? Harper's case is closed. I invited you into my bedroom a while ago. Why didn't you tell me then? Why . . . now?"

We'd been happily floating in that cloud of bliss, that time period in a relationship where everything was rainbows and unicorns. We held hands when we walked together, even if it was the short distance from the car to the door. We told each other everything and missed out on sleep to talk for hours on the phone. A simple touch from him made me tingle. Our timing finally worked out, and feelings, both emotional and sexual, that we'd repressed or ignored in college were allowed free reign. The best part was, since we were already good friends, there was a comfort level that would usually take other couples weeks or months to achieve.

"It's been weighing on my mind."

I barely listened to him as I stared at the beauty in the turquoise dress. One of the suits seemed to have gained the brunette's attention. He put his hand on her back and guided her to an open bar stool. "And now it's weighing on mine," I murmured.

"I didn't catch that." Mike leaned forward.

When I spoke again, it came out low and even. "You know,

it hasn't escaped my attention that you dropped this explosive piece of information in a public place." I sipped the last bit of my white wine, then folded my arms across my chest. "You even brought me to a restaurant where I might know someone and could be recognized." As a matter of fact, I'd been greeted by another lobbyist and a congressman's staff member when I arrived. "Basically, you did it *here*" —I tapped the table— "so I wouldn't lose my shit."

He didn't deny it, and I gleaned a crack in his composure as regret flashed across his features. "I'm sorry, K.C."

I'll admit when I got worked up, some of my Irish ancestry came out. It usually involved increased voice volume, and, on occasion, volatile hand-waving. Mike and I had had disagreements in the past, but this would be our first fight as a couple. My fists clenched and unclenched as I ruminated on his apology. "I'm not going to lie, I'm hurt. I'm angry."

Mike regarded me, face stricken.

"You know, it's true—what they say—ignorance *is* bliss."

"What do we do now?"

"I'm going to . . . go." I gathered my purse.

Mike laid a hand on my arm. "K.C., don't. Not like this. Talk to me. Don't leave like this."

My eyes flared. "Right now, I don't want to talk to you."

"I've never known you to run away from a fight," he threw at me, withdrawing his hand.

My mouth scrunched up as I held back the invective I longed to throw at him. "Michael Finnegan, let me be clear, I am *not* running away. I am . . . I'm making a tactical retreat." He opened his mouth, but I held up a finger to forestall him. "*Because* I'm afraid, right now, I'm going to say something *so* terrible that I can't take it back."

His challenging look disappeared, and the mask returned.

"Okay." He sipped his beer. "When do you think you'll be ready to talk?"

My mouth flattened. "I don't know."

"You are aware I'm leaving on Sunday to finish the training I missed during the Harper case."

"If you're asking if I will be ready to talk by Sunday—I can't answer. I'm not sure I will be."

"I see." There was definite pain behind that gaze, and it did nothing to calm my temper.

I am the wronged party here, I told myself, irate. To Mike, I said, "I think we need a break."

He cleared his throat. "What kind of break?"

"The kind where I take the week to simmer down. When do you get back into town?"

"Saturday morning."

"Fine. I'll contact you." I scooted to the edge of the booth seat.

"K.C.?"

"Yes?"

"Uh, be careful. Try not to get into any trouble," he implored.

I tilted my head and raised my brows questioningly.

"Every time I go out of town, you seem to get involved in one . . . scrape or another. Just—try to stay out of trouble. I don't think I can handle another one of *those* calls."

Even if that were true, his comment did nothing to improve my mood. "Don't worry. If I do get into a 'scrape,' I'll be sure to call someone else." I pulled the handbag strap over my shoulder and stalked my way through the tables.

"K.C.! That's not what I meant," he exclaimed to my retreating back.

****

"And, that's it," I said to my sister, who'd listened to the entire story in silence.

"Wow. That's a lot."

"I can't *believe* he had the gall to tell me not to get into any scrapes while he was gone," I grumbled. "Like those things were *my* fault. Like I went *looking* for trouble."

"Well . . ."

"Don't you dare." *Did she just giggle?*

"So how long are you going to let him stew?"

"I beg your pardon?" I dropped the scrub brush into the bucket with a small splash and sat back on my heels. I'd scoured the floor as I poured out my story. The tiles sparkled, and if I continued in the same fervor, I'd probably end up scrubbing out the grout.

"You know, how long are you going to let him stew before you make up?"

"Who's to say I'll forgive him?"

"First of all, you're terrible at holding grudges. You'll be rethinking your temper tantrum by tomorrow morning."

"It's not a temper tantrum." I chewed my lip in frustration because she was spot on.

She continued, "Second, this is Mike."

"So?"

"Well, in the inimitable words of Phoebe Buffay, 'he's your lobster,'" she said with a dramatic flair.

My face scrunched in confusion. "What the hell are you talking about? What do crustaceans have to do with it?"

"You know, from *Friends*. I've been binge-watching it on Netflix. Ross and Rachel. That's you and Mike. You guys are made for each other."

I rolled my eyes. "This isn't a television show, Jilly. I'm really pissed." It felt good to say the words out loud.

She tsked. "He was trying to protect you. As far as I can tell, he's always trying to protect you. No—before you interrupt, I want you to just think about some of the crazy scrapes you've been in. It sounds like Mike stuck his neck out for you on more than one occasion. You can't compare him to Patrick."

True.

"Give him a break. The Harper case put him between a rock and a hard place. Did he make a bad decision? Maybe. Come on, like *you* haven't made any bad decisions in your life?"

I blew out a breath. "Okay. Maybe you're right. But I'm still mad."

"You have a right to be. However, to get back to my original question—how long are you going to be mad? How long are you going to punish him by leaving him in limbo?"

She's right. I sighed. "I don't know. Maybe I'll call him *after* he gets back from his trip."

"You're going to leave him hanging for a week?" she asked in disbelief.

"Yup."

Jillian's skeptical snort came across the lines. "Ri-ight. You'll be calling him by Monday."

My sister was probably correct, but I was too stubborn to admit it. "Doubtful."

"Suit yourself. You know the longer you wait, the more you'll tear yourself up inside. You're not just torturing him, you'll be torturing yourself."

This was the second time in recent history Jillian had given me solid relationship advice. It grated on me knowing what she said was true. "Oh, yeah, when did you become the relationship whisperer?" I retorted.

"When I started dating Tony. Everything came into focus for me, Grasshopper," she said.

My sister began seeing Tony Romero, an Alexandria paramedic, about five months ago. Everything seemed to be going swimmingly for them. He reminded me of a Latino Jake Gyllenhaal and, if things continued on their current track, it was simply a matter of time before they announced their engagement.

I rolled my eyes. "Okay, Kung Fu Master. Let's move on. You called me. What's up?"

"Oh, right. Actually, this is good, something to take your mind off your current mood. My girlfriend from work, Sadira, has tickets for a fashion show at Tyson's Galleria tomorrow."

"What kind of fashion show?"

"It's a fundraiser for Ronald McDonald House. A bunch of the stores are participating, including Coach and Lilly Pulitzer."

The moment she said the word 'fundraiser,' I zoned out. My life revolved around fundraisers, primarily for politicians. The D.C. area was a Mecca for raising money—legislators, nonprofits, charities, school activities—you name it, someone always had a hand out. Don't get me wrong, I had no doubt the Ronald McDonald House did good work, and I should probably do my civic duty and go, but I just couldn't muster the strength to attend one more fundraiser this week.

"Rina, you still there?"

I came back to earth. "Yeah. It sounds great. It's just . . . I've got some work to catch up on."

"You are so full of it."

My sister knew me too well. "Fine. I'm kind of in a funk over this thing with Mike and I don't want to drag you down."

"You sure?"

"Maybe next time." I pushed to my feet and picked up the bucket of dirty water.

"All right. We're leaving at eleven. Let me know if you

change your mind before that."

"Gotcha. Thanks for the invitation. We'll talk later."

After we hung up, I considered calling Mike, but once I started thinking about what he did, my blood pressure crept upward and I decided it would be best to wait. Jilly was probably right, I'd forgive him and be calling by Monday. Until then, he could stew. And, in the meantime, my bathroom floors were so clean you could serve high tea off them.

Chapter Two

JILLIAN

Jillian followed behind Sadira's Jimmy Choo stilettos as the usher led them to a pair of seats right in front of the catwalk. A number of gazes followed their progress, which wasn't surprising. Jillian was attractive in the "girl-next-door" way, with long brown hair hanging straight down her back. However, it was Sadira who garnered the most attention. Her hair hung loose in the *au courant* mode of tousled waves, but it wasn't the style, rather the flame-red color from out of the bottle that was so striking against the black and blue designer dress she wore. Sadira was a bit of a fashionista, and besides working as a math teacher at the middle school with Jillian, she held a second job at a jewelry store to "feed her fashion habit," as she once explained.

The usher handed the pair programs before retreating.

Jillian leaned toward Sadira. "How did you score tickets for these front row seats?"

"I have connections." Sadira winked, sweeping a handful of hair over her shoulder. She crossed her legs and tucked the Coach clutch into her lap.

"I think I'm jealous. Can you introduce me?" Jillian quipped.

Sadira delivered a mysterious smile. A camera flashed and the two women shifted their gazes to a man holding a fancy camera.

"Hi, Jared Caddigan, I'm with the Ronald McDonald House marketing department, and we're taking some pictures of the event to send to the local papers and for promotional purposes." He handed Sadira a business card. "Would you two mind signing a release form?"

"Okay," Jillian said.

He handed the girls a sheet of paper and pulled a small pad and pencil from his back pocket. "Can I get your names?"

Sadira smiled at the handsome photographer and leaned forward giving him a gander at her cleavage. "This is my friend Jillian Cardinal, and I'm Sadira Manon. That's S-A-D-I-R-A M-A-N-O-N."

"Sadira." He scribbled on his pad. "That's a pretty name."

She smiled reaching into her purse for a pen. She signed her name on the document, without reading it, and handed the pen to Jillian. "My number's at the bottom. In case you have any questions." Sadira winked, holding her paper out.

"Th-thanks." He blushed as he tucked the papers away. "One more?" he asked, holding up the camera.

Sadira put her arm around Jillian, the two smiled. Jared snapped a few more photos and moved on to get other shots.

"Coming on a little strong, don't you think?" Jillian asked drily.

Sadira laughed and made a swishing motion with her hand. "Maybe. But you know what they say, 'fortune favors the bold.'"

"I suppose." Jillian handed the pen back to Sadira. "By the way, I keep meaning to ask about your name. It's so exotic sounding. What does Sadira mean? How did your parents come up with it?"

"They didn't," Sadira grumbled. "I heard it somewhere and decided it would be a good name. I think it's Arabic."

Jillian's brows drew together. "What do you mean, isn't Sadira your real name?"

"Not the one my parents gave me." She paused, flipping

through the pamphlet. "Long story short, I got a scholarship to college and left the house at eighteen. Haven't looked back. Let's just say, I didn't have an idyllic childhood. After graduating, I legally changed my name."

"Um, wow. You got to pick out your own name?"

"That's how it works."

"What's your original name?"

"Nope, no way." She shook her head. "I don't speak that name."

Taken aback by the repugnance and antipathy in which Sadira supplied that statement, Jillian didn't know how to respond. The awkward moment hung in the air as Sadira perused the program.

"Oh, look at that adorable Lily Pulitzer dress. That would look fab on you." Sadira pointed at a picture of a pink and green sheath dress.

Before Jillian could answer, music blasted out of the two enormous speakers at the foot of the catwalk, and a man wearing skinny red pants, a blue button down, and highly polished black shoes with thick white soles strolled to center stage. The song faded, and his nasal voice welcomed everyone to the fashion show. He thanked a number of the stores sponsoring the event and then explained that a percentage of each piece of clothing purchased today would go toward the charity. Additionally, at the end of the show, a dozen designer handbags would be auctioned off to the highest bidder. The designer purses could be found on the last two pages of their programs, along with a paddle for bidding.

The show began with local school children of all shapes and sizes trotting along the stage. Their hair and makeup had been done by one of the salons in the mall and made them look very mature. A girl with Down's Syndrome strutted her stuff, wearing a pair of pink jeans, red ballet flats, a flowy yellow top, and jaunty hat. Her sunny smile and excited attitude had the audience applauding. The girl stopped mid-strut to wave excitedly at Jillian and Sadira.

"Woohoo, looking good up there, Marissa!" Jillian cheered at the eighth-grader from her school.

The adult clothes were modeled by college students from nearby George Mason University. No professionally paid models walked on the runway today. Sadira madly scribbled on her program, taking note of interesting outfits. Finally, the show wound to its end and the models filled the platform for one last round of applause. After they left the stage, the emcee announced the auction would start in ten minutes. About two-thirds of the audience departed, while those left behind filled in the gaps in the front rows.

Jillian pulled her little cardboard paddle out of the back of her booklet. There was a Coach and a Kate Spade handbag she wanted to bid on. The auctioneer took his place at the podium and a college girl walked out with the first item, a handbag by Cole Haan. Jillian's enthusiasm for the auction deflated as the price for the purse quickly rose to $600. She tucked her paddle beneath her leg.

"You better get that out. Your Kate Spade is up next," Sadira whispered.

Jillian shook her head. "Too rich for my blood. I figured I'd go as high as $200. There's no way I can compete."

Sadira shrugged. "Well, you never know."

Jillian got in the first bid at fifty dollars, but the Kate Spade continued up and up, ending at $575.

"Tough luck," Sadira murmured.

The next handbag, a Dooney and Burke, came out on the shoulder of a lively blonde. Sadira raised her paddle over and over, until she came out the victor at $485.

"Yay! You won!" Jillian high-fived her friend as one of the auction assistants maneuvered her way to Sadira to give her a chit for claiming the purse. "Should we go pay for your prize?"

"Yes, let's. There are a few outfits I'm interested in purchasing too."

An hour later the girls trotted away from the dwindling mass of bodies. Jillian scored a silk Ralph Lauren scarf. She paid $120 for it. Since it was for charity, Jillian didn't mind the splurge. Sadira, on the other hand, carried away almost a thousand-dollars-worth of items.

Jillian enviously eyed the designer bag in her friend's hand. "How much do you make an hour at that jewelry store?"

"Oh, not much."

Jillian figured Sadira would have racked up credit card debt, except she'd seen her pay for the merchandise in cash. "How can you afford all that? Family money?"

"Family money, ha! Not. I . . . uh . . . make a commission on each piece of jewelry I sell," Sadira explained as she took a selfie with the new Dooney and Burke satchel.

"Maybe I should get a job there."

Sadira didn't answer as she posted on her Instagram account.

"Sadira?"

"Hm?" Her friend's big blue eyes stared blankly at Jillian.

"Do you know if the jewelry store is hiring?"

"Oh. No, I'm sorry, they aren't, but I'll let you know if that changes. Actually, I have to run over there to get my paycheck. Do you mind? You don't have to be anywhere immediately, do you?" Sadira asked. Jillian had left her car parked at Sadira's condo, while Sadira had driven them both to the fashion show.

Jillian shook her head. "No, I don't have any plans. Where is it?"

"Across the street in Tyson's Corner Center. We'll drive over, so we don't have to dodge traffic." Sadira rolled her eyes.

"Good idea, getting across can be a bit of a shit-show. Hey, are you thirsty? Let's stop at the Smoothie Shack first. My treat."

The Tyson's Corner Mall complex was basically two malls across a ten-lane road from each other, with few cross walks, constant construction, and an overly aggressive driving population. Right off the Capitol Beltway in McLean, Virginia, the Galleria, where the fashion show had been held, housed expensive designer retailers with two upscale department stores, Saks Fifth Avenue and Nieman Marcus at either end. Tyson's Corner Center had more moderately priced shops—a Macy's, Nordstrom's, and Bloomingdale's. The entire complex was enormous and could be very confusing if you didn't understand the layout, and getting from one mall to the other by foot was akin to chumming shark infested waters, then jumping in without a cage.

Half an hour later, smoothies in hand and their new purchases in the trunk, the girls finally made it over to the other mall and headed to the jewelry store. Sadira's new Dooney & Burke hung jauntily at her elbow. She'd asked Jillian to drive her Audi A4 so she could transfer her stuff into the new bag. She and Jillian had taken another selfie with their drinks, and Sadira was uploading it to Instagram when she came to a sudden halt.

"This is strange," Sadira murmured. The metal security gate at the front of the jewelry store was closed down to knee height. Sadira pulled it up about halfway and ducked under, waving Jillian to follow. "Tazim, what's going on?"

In the back corner, a short, balding middle-eastern man in a peach button-down with a bright white cast on his left arm spoke animatedly to a pair of Fairfax County police officers.

The balding man turned toward them as Sadira led the way to where he stood. He pointed and, with a deep guttural accent, exclaimed, "There she is. That is the woman who stole from me!"

Jillian's stomach dropped, and a sense of foreboding settled there.

"What? What on earth are you talking about, Tazim? What happened to your arm?" Sadira's voice heightened with confusion.

"That is her. Arrest her." Tazim's bushy brows practically met in the middle as he made a shooing motion at the police.

"Miss, is your name Sadira Manon?" one of the police officers asked. His uniform top fit snugly over the bulletproof vest he wore beneath it, and by the wrinkles around his eyes, Jillian guessed his age at late thirties. His partner, a short guy with a buzz cut and young enough he looked like he'd just graduated high school, stared admiringly at Sadira. The name plates on the officers' chests read TORGERSON and CONNELLY.

"Yes. What's the problem, officer?" Sadira responded.

Torgerson cleared his throat. "Mr. Bakir has accused you of stealing."

Sadira laid a hand to her chest. "Stealing! That's—that's ridiculous. Tazim, there must be some mistake."

Tazim blanched but held his ground. "No mistake, girlie. You want to see? I show you." He made an abrupt turn and headed through the open doorway to the back rooms. Sadira followed Tazim, Jillian followed her, and the two cops trooped in line behind Jillian to an office with a couple of monitors that showed the jewelry store's camera feeds. Tazim grabbed the computer mouse and clicked a few times, and then the center monitor displayed a feed that started at 10:17 Thursday night.

Sadira could be seen tapping in a code and then opening the door to the store's walk-in safe. She wheeled out an empty cart and, a few minutes later, returned with the cart full of jewelry. She entered the safe and a few minutes later came back out with the cart empty. She performed this task half a dozen more times. The other monitor screens were broken into fourths, and you could see different angles of the salesfloor as she gathered up the jewelry from the different cases and gently laid the rings, necklaces, watches, and the rest on the cart. Finally, she came out of the safe without the cart, emptyhanded. Sadira closed the safe door, pressed a button on the keypad, and pulled the handle once, as if checking to make sure the door was shut tight. A few seconds later, the lights turned off.

Jillian glanced at her friend, who stood with crossed arms, her normally pale features glowing with a distinct blush.

Tazim tapped the computer and all of the feeds froze in place. "What were you doing in there? You don't have access. You signed in with Monika's code."

"I can explain." Sadira licked her lips. "Monika and I were working that night. She got called away on a family emergency. She couldn't get ahold of you, and I was making an engagement ring sale to a young couple. I've closed with her many times. I told her I could handle it. She gave me her code and left." Sadira spoke in a calm, firm tone.

"So, you admit you were working with a client to sell them a diamond engagement ring." Tazim stuck his head forward as he spoke like an angry turtle with a bad combover.

"Yes, of course."

"And did they buy one?" Tazim asked.

Sadira's face reddened even more. "They ended up not making the purchase, but they said they'd come back this weekend. Pull up the earlier feeds. You'll see them."

"It doesn't matter. You are not authorized to have a code for the safe," Tazim argued, shaking his finger at her.

"Well," Jillian said as she stepped forward, "if anything, I think that tape clears Sadira. I only see her putting jewelry *into* the safe. *Not* taking any out. You can even see it on the showroom floor."

"Who are you?" Tazim demanded, and his beady black eyes glared at Jillian..

"I'm her friend," Jillian replied sternly. "What was stolen, anyway?"

"$100,000 worth of loose diamonds."

Jillian and Sadira jointly sucked wind.

"Do you have any cameras in the safe?" Connelly, the younger officer, asked.

"No!" Tazim said sharply, then pointed his casted arm at Sadira. "You had them out while you were showing the couple the engagement rings. Didn't you?"

"Yes, of course. It's standard to show them different choices of loose diamonds in their price range."

"Wait a minute," Jillian chimed in, "was that the green box with all those tiny cubbies? I saw that go on the cart and into the safe. Rewind the tape."

Tazim made a dismissive gesture. "Yes, yes, little girl. We *all* saw that. What you didn't see—she dropped a dozen practically flawless stones into her pocket while she was in the safe." He delivered the charge vehemently, but his eyes darted all over the room—at the cops, Jillian, the monitors, everywhere but at Sadira, whom he accused.

Sadira drew in a breath and screwed her mouth up tightly. "How dare you!"

"You have no evidence of that!" Jillian cried. "Where is the recording?"

"There are no cameras in the safe," Sadira and Tazim said as one.

"You were the last one to handle the diamonds," Tazim alleged. "And the diamonds are so small." He held up his thumb and pointer finger to demonstrate the tininess of the jewels. "'Who would notice?' you probably said to yourself. Tazim, that's who." He thumped his chest and stuck his hand in his pocket.

"It's Saturday," Sadira uttered. "Surely someone handled the loose diamond box between Thursday and now."

"Monika called in sick on Friday. I worked, by myself, all day. Your couple returned today. When I opened the box—I discovered they were missing."

Sadira swallowed.

Torgerson stepped forward. "I'm afraid, ma'am, we need to take you in for questioning."

Sadira spun around. "What? Take me in? Are you joking?"

"I'm afraid not." He hooked his thumbs in his utility belt.

Her eyes widened in panic. "What if I said right now is not convenient?"

The cop ran a hand through his short locks. "It would be best if you cooperated."

"You have absolutely *no* proof *I* took those diamonds. Only what he says." Sadira made a derisive gesture toward Tazim.

"She has them! Check her purse! Check her purse!" Tazim pulled his hand out of his pocket and, with a sweeping gesture, knocked Sadira's purse off the table. The new bag fell to the floor on its side, spilling contents willy-nilly.

"Oh, for Pete's sake, that's my new bag," Sadira said irritably, and bent to pick up her belongings.

Jillian started to come around the desk to help but was halted by Torgerson's authoritative voice. "Miss, stop what you're doing and step back from the purse."

Sadira rose up. The officer, pulling a rubber glove from his pocket, leaned past Sadira to pick something off the floor at her feet.

"That's not mine!" Sadira exclaimed.

"Mr. Bakir, is this one of the diamonds you're missing?" Torgerson held the sparkling jewel between his thumb and forefinger.

"Maybe. Let me get a loupe." Tazim scrabbled through his desk drawer for a jeweler's small magnifying glass and held out his hand.

"I'm afraid I can't let you touch it," the officer said.

"I'll use the tweezers." Tazim turned on a bright light at his desk and examined the diamond.

It looked to be a carat in size, and while Jillian anxiously hopped from foot to foot, Sadira remained in place with a pinched mouth and narrowed eyes.

"Yes, this is one of the missing diamonds," Tazim announced.

"*You* planted that! *You* threw it on the floor when you knocked down my purse!" Sadira snarled.

Torgerson pulled a pair of cuffs out of a pocket on his utility belt. "Connelly, can you please read the lady her rights."

The kid, who'd watched in fascinated silence, straightened up. "You have the right to remain silent—"

As Officer Connelly reeled off the Miranda rights, Sadira passed Jillian a frightened look. Her eyes shone with tears. "You've got to believe me, Jilly. I had nothing to do with this."

"I know," Jillian assured her friend. "My sister's a lawyer. I'll call her. She can help." Jillian bent to gather Sadira's stuff from the floor.

"Don't touch that. It's evidence," Torgerson barked.

Jillian put up her hands and stepped back.

"You remember where we parked?" Sadira's voice wobbled. "Meet me at the police station."

"I will." Jillian nodded, realizing, thankfully, she still had Sadira's car keys in her pocket. "Don't worry. I'll help straighten this out."

"Please step back, ma'am." Connelly held out his arm to bar Jillian from getting closer to her friend.

Torgerson directed his younger counterpart to take Sadira to the cruiser and call it in while he bagged the evidence. Jillian trailed them into the showroom, watching as the cop raised the security gate to escort Sadira into the mall. Glancing back over her shoulder, she found the shifty little owner blotting his sweaty forehead with a handkerchief. She fixed him with a squinty-eyed glare before huffing out of the store, phone in hand.

Chapter Three

"Okay, that's enough with the punching and kicking." Josh stepped back and tugged off the padded boxing-style helmet. "You seem aggressive, almost vicious, today."

"So?" I grabbed a white towel and swiped my sweaty brow.

"Not that it's bad." He removed the padding covering his torso and family jewels. "But I'm wondering where it's coming from."

"Mike and I had a fight."

"Your FBI guy?"

"The very one." I gulped down some water from my pink bottle.

"That explains it."

"Explains what?"

"Why you called for a class today. Good way to blow off some steam. What'd he do? Cheat on you?"

I scrutinized Josh, one of my self-defense trainers. I'd met him and some of his colleagues when I'd gotten mixed up in an old art heist that included deadly mafia connections. Josh worked for Silverthorne Security and had been hired to protect me. They were a group of well-trained, ex-military types that provided private security to diplomats, corporations working in warzones, and though it didn't specify on their website, I guessed they were also available for hire by the CIA and other three-lettered organizations. As Mike had put it, you hired

Silverthorne when you needed a private army to create a small country coup d'etat. Needless to say, Mike had his reservations about Silverthorne. I had no such reservations. Josh was a former SEAL and looked like a big, blond, burly male himbo—all muscle and cute dimples. I'd learned not to underestimate those dimples—Josh was intelligent and watched out for me as one would a little sister.

"No," I huffed as I tossed the towel aside.

Josh eyed me.

"I don't want to talk about it."

One dimple peeked through the full beard—a new addition since I'd last seen him. "Okay. Let's work on an attack from behind."

I rejoined him at the center of the practice mat, which was the center of the entire gym at the Silverthorne facility. Treadmills, a pair of stationary bikes, various free-weights, weight machines, and a pair of thick ropes large enough to tie a Carnival Cruise liner to the dock surrounded the mat area. The place smelled of sweat socks and pine fresh deodorizer.

"Now, I don't think we've done this before, but if you stand here, and I wrap my arms around you from behind like this—"

Josh and I may not have worked on this move, but Jin, another Silverthorne specialist, and I had done so last week. As soon as I felt his body pushing down on me, I grabbed his upper arm, dropped to one knee, tucked my head, and, with his weight off balance, Josh flew over my shoulder, landing flat on his back.

I laid a sneaker against his trachea. "Do you yield?"

His stunned blue gaze stared up at me.

I stepped back and held out a hand. "Jin and I worked on that move last week. It's tough on the knees, and, wow, you went over much harder than Jin. If you'd landed on me, I think you would've crushed me."

Josh gripped my hand and got to his feet. "That wasn't bad. But if I'd held you in a headlock, you could have broken your neck. We need to work on your technique." He continued his tight hold on my hand as he spoke.

In an instant, I pivoted, turning to my left and rotating Josh's arm as I went. He dropped down to one knee with a gurgle of pain. "Christ, I see Jin has been busy."

"Sorry, I thought you were testing me." I released him, delivering a cheeky grin and peace sign toward one of the security cameras. "You've been away for a few weeks. If you don't stick around, you're going to miss some things."

"I'll keep that in mind." He shook his wrist and stood.

"You look like you got some sun. Where have you been?" I asked, figuring I had a fifty-fifty chance Josh would actually divulge that information.

"Let's work on that attack from behind again," he intoned with zero inflection, patently ignoring my question.

Josh's techniques tended to use more brute force, whereas, Jin, a master at a multitude of martial arts whose Vietnamese stature was smaller and more compact than Josh, used techniques with a fluidity of movement that was probably better suited to the female shape and strength. Working with Josh was like wrestling a bear and strained every muscle in my body, whereas, Jin moved with the speed and agility of Jackie Chan and exhausted my mind and reflexes. I wouldn't dare tell Josh any of this. They both had their strengths and I was lucky they continued to train me.

At the end of the hour, my T-shirt was drenched and my sagging ponytail stuck to the sweat on the back of my neck. I finished the water in the bottle I brought, and Josh tossed me another from a small refrigerator at the back of the room.

"Rick said he wanted to talk to you before you left today."

The cap made a small snapping sound as I twisted the lid. "About what? Am I in trouble?"

"Not that I know of." Water dripped down Josh's beard as he upturned his bottle and gulped.

"Is Jin in today?"

He wiped the wetness away with the back of his hand. "Not sure. Why?"

"Just wondering. Is anyone still betting against me?" I crossed my arms and wiggled my brows. The Silverthorne boys entertained themselves by making bets about me—whether I'd land a punch on my trainer, take him down, or maybe make Jin laugh.

"I've stopped taking their bets." Josh crushed the bottle with one hand. "You'll have to ask Jin."

Speak of the devil, Jin opened the door, and a whoosh of welcome, cold air swept over me.

"Hey, Jin." I finger-waved. "You win any money today?"

He grinned, and the long scar running from his temple to his chin puckered. "I won twenty bucks off Hernandez when you threw Josh over your shoulder. After that, no one would take my bets."

"You know, I think I should start taking a cut from these little side bets you guys are making."

Jin winked, then turned to Josh. "You got a call. The prince is coming to town and wants you again."

Josh tossed the bottle in a blue recycling bin and waved at me on his way out. "Take it easy, Karina."

"Later." I turned to Jin. "Prince? Like from England?"

He shook his head. "Saudi Arabia."

I didn't probe. There were literally hundreds of Saudi princes. I doubted he would tell me more anyway. "Josh said

Rick wanted to see me."

"He does, but he's in the middle of a meeting right now. Were you planning to shower here?"

"I hadn't thought about it. I've got some extra clothes in my bag. I suppose I could."

"You have time. You remember where the ladies' shower is?" Jin asked.

"Yes, but I don't have a badge for the elevator."

"C'mon. I'll take you up."

I seized my pink and white duffle, tossing my phone and handbag inside, and followed Jin to the pair of elevators at the end of the long, beige hallway. We passed half a dozen closed doors. I knew one of them housed the IT and security center but had no idea what was behind the rest of them.

Jin swiped his ID badge down the card reader next to the elevator; once the LED flashed green, he pressed the UP button. "You can take the elevator back down to the first floor without an access card when you're done. Take care, Cardinal."

Exiting on the second floor, I went to my left, around the corner and entered the bathroom marked *Ladies*. It held a sink, one toilet, and a shower. There was a doorway to the men's locker room in the gym, but not one for women. I had a feeling Silverthorne rarely hired women, and if they did, it was on a short-term basis. I'd never trained with a female, nor had I ever seen one wandering the halls. Very un-PC if you asked me, especially in such a political town. If I wanted to make a stink about it, I'm sure I could, but it would be a piss-poor way to thank a group of folks who'd literally saved my life. Moreover, they'd always treated me with respect, so I had no firsthand knowledge that Silverthorne was actively biased against women.

I took a long, cold shower and spent some time blow drying my wavy hair into submission. A dash of eyeliner and mascara made my green eyes stand out, and a touch of lipstick finished the look. *Not too shabby.*

I pulled on a pair of jeans, adjusted the dark green V-neck knit top and headed out. Swinging around the corner, I ran into a large chest.

"Cripes! Sorry, I didn't see you there . . . Rick?" Rick, the head honcho, a.k.a. Batman because of how he swooped in and out of my life, leaned against the wall with crossed arms. "Gee, I barely recognize you. What's with the beard?"

Like Josh, he sported a new beard. However, whereas Josh had groomed his, Rick's resembled mountain man chic. His normally short-clipped hair had grown longer and shaggy, which made the salt in his pepper stand out more. The plaid button-down and jeans only enhanced the mountain man appearance. I could barely discern his to-die-for cheekbones, but that blue-gray gaze was unmistakable.

"I've been on assignment. It's better to blend in with the locals," he said.

"Oh, yeah? What locals?"

He didn't deign to answer, instead he pushed the button for the elevator.

Knowing Rick spoke Hebrew, and guessing he spoke either Farsi or some other Arabic language, I surmised he'd been somewhere in the Middle East. The elevator arrived, and I preceded him onboard. "Josh said you needed to talk to me. What's up?"

"I do." He pushed the button for the first floor. "How have you been?"

"Fiiine. . . ." I drew out the word, surprised by Rick's efforts at small talk.

"No more murders? Mafia thugs? Stolen art work?"

I delivered an arch look as the doors opened on the first

floor.

"Follow me." Rick led me halfway down the hall, stopping at a door I'd never entered. He swiped his card, tapped in a nine-digit code, then pressed his finger against the touchscreen.

"What, no retinal scan?" I asked sardonically.

"Not this time," he deadpanned, holding the door for me.

It was a small, boxlike room with a wooden table and four chairs. The walls were padded with black soundproofing, and when Rick shut the door there was a sucking sound. I could literally hear no outside noise—no hum of the air conditioning nor tick of a clock, just our breathing and the crush of cloth as we moved.

My instincts went on alert. I put the table between us. "What's going on?"

"Have a seat."

"You first."

Rick flipped a chair backward and straddled it. "It's nothing bad."

I sat tentatively across from him, still kind of weirded out by the room and how our voices sounded flat and inert.

He pulled an envelope out of his back pocket and laid it on the table. "This is yours."

Inside the envelope was a check from Silverthorne Security made out to me for $200,000. "What the hell is this?"

"That's your cut from the bounty on Rivkin."

I dropped the check as if it had burst into flames. Naftali Rivkin, a rogue Mossad agent who'd put my coworker and me on his hitlist, had been captured by Silverthorne. They used us as bait to trap him. The Israeli had a bounty on his head for a million dollars. However, we hadn't been able to collect. The FBI took him into custody, and, while in a holding cell, someone had been able to get through security and slit his throat. Though Mike never talked about it, I'd gathered it was a huge breach and some folks in high places got canned.

"You promised me you had nothing to do with his death," I uttered.

"We didn't." Rick stroked his beard. "Apparently, Rivkin stole a shipment from a Chechen gunrunner and sold it to a Libyan warlord. The Chechens weren't happy."

"So why didn't the Israelis pay the gunrunner?"

"They have no interest in giving the money to a Chechen gunrunner."

"Why'd they give it to *you,* then?"

"I convinced them if it hadn't been for our capturing Rivkin, he never would have been brought to justice." His straight, white teeth flashed at me.

"He wasn't brought to justice. He was murdered." I tapped the table. "In FBI custody, no less."

"According to Mossad, justice was served."

I licked my lips as I digested that. "An-eye-for-an-eye and all that business?"

Rick shrugged, his expression flat.

I grimaced and scrutinized the check. "Please tell me you didn't notify the Chechens of Rivkin's arrest."

"*I* didn't notify the Chechens." The *way* he said it made me feel like he wasn't lying per se, but that there was more to the story—like someone told someone, who told someone, who told the Chechens. "Karina, he was a bad dude."

I sighed. Rick was not known for windy explanations or exposition, and his single sentence cut to the heart of the matter. I hadn't shed any tears, and was frankly relieved, when I found out Rivkin was dead. He had threatened me before the FBI hauled him off, and I believed him. If he'd ever gotten out, I never would have had a decent night's sleep again.

"What am I supposed to do with this?" I pointed to the check. "How do I claim it on my taxes? Is there a line item for illegal bounty income?"

His mouth curled inward before he spoke. "I could show you how to . . . invest it—offshore, let's say."

I scowled.

"Otherwise, you can claim it as a gift and the government will take half."

Chewing my lip, I debated my options. If I took Rick's advice and put it in an offshore account, $200,000 would go a long way. I could pay off my college loans and buy a new car that didn't have a dent in the bumper. Unfortunately, even though it sounded good, I'd never be able to live with myself. I'd crossed some lines into gray areas in the past, but this was one line I simply wasn't willing to cross. Claiming it legally would likely send up a red flag at the IRS and could get me into a different kind of trouble. Rick's company would have an easier time absorbing the dollars.

Sighing, I put the check back in the envelope and pushed it across the table. "I can't take it. It's blood money."

Rick placed a hand over the envelope. "You're sure?"

I took a beat before answering, "I'm sure."

"Tell you what, here's what I can do, I'll open a line of credit. Your self-defense classes will come out of it and should you or a family member need our services in the future, it'll be covered."

I considered his suggestion. The last time Silverthorne helped me was because Rick owed me a favor. Getting Rivkin off the streets, and me out of his crosshairs, had repaid that favor and then some. "I have a sister. Can I bring her in for classes?"

"Absolutely."

"Ok-ay. In reality, I hope I never have to take you up on your offer." My shoulders slumped as I thought about the times I'd already relied on the Silverthorne boys. "But I suppose it's worth having an insurance policy—just in case."

He pocketed the check. "Good choice."

"Thank you."

"No problem." Rick rose.

I followed his cue. "Why did you want to talk to me here, in this weird little room?"

"No cameras. No recording devices. No wi-fi. No cell service." He flipped the chair around and pushed it in.

"So, we're . . . off the grid? In a dead zone? Like a Faraday cage?"

"Exactly."

I didn't want to know the reason Silverthorne needed such a room. My imagination conjured up too many to count. "So, this conversation never happened?"

"No, it happened. I just never told you anything about putting the money into an untraceable offshore account. You chose to leave the money with me in exchange for our services."

"Gotcha."

When I got to my car, I checked my phone to find three voicemails and four text messages from my sister over the past hour. The topic of all of them were pretty much the same—call her immediately! Someone she knew was in trouble and needed my help. I put in my earpiece, dialed, then backed out of the parking space.

She answered in the middle of the first ring. "Karina! Where have you *been*? I've been trying to reach you for *hours*!"

"I took a class and the phone was buried at the bottom of my gym bag." The metal security gate slowly drew back and I pulled out onto the street. "What's up?"

Jillian described a rather bizarre story about her work friend who was arrested for stealing $100,000 worth of diamonds from the jewelry store she moonlighted at on the weekends.

"Did she do it?" I asked.

"Of *course not!* Sadira's a scapegoat," my sister defended.

"But you said there was video."

"Not of her actually *stealing* the diamonds. The owner claims she was the last to handle them, but that guy is kind of shifty. I think there's something more to this."

"Okay. What do you want me to do about it?" I rolled to a stop at a red light.

"Well, first of all, you need to come to the station and be her attorney for the arraignment."

"Uh, Jillian. You know I'm not that kind of attorney. I'm a lobbyist, I'm not skilled in criminal trial law."

"You've got to be better than any public defender," Jillian pleaded.

"Not necessarily." I drew the car to a halt. A large dump truck was stalled in my lane and half a dozen cars had lined up as each driver waited for a break in traffic to navigate around it on the two-lane road.

"You're licensed in Virginia, right?"

"I am. But, Jilly, you're not listening. I'm not that type of lawyer. I could end up making it worse for your friend."

"Nonsense. It's an arraignment. How hard can it be? Besides, you *owe* me. I'm calling in my chip."

I inhaled sharply.

My sister continued with a new edge to her tone, "That's how this works with your politicians, right? When someone owes you and you need a favor, you tell them you're calling in your chip? Well, that's what I'm doing now. It's time to pay up."

"Whoa, Jilly, take a breath. You don't need to call in your

'chip.' I didn't say I wouldn't help. What I'm saying—I may not be the best person *to* help your friend. When is the arraignment?"

"Lord only knows. This place seems to work at snail speed. They said an hour, but that was almost an hour ago. How soon can you get here?"

"Where are you?" I tailed a large white Cadillac around the truck.

"Fairfax police station off Route 50. Where are you?"

"I'm in D.C. Oh, come *on! Move it, slowpoke!*" I hollered, gripping the steering wheel as the white car puttered ahead of me below the speed limit. "It'll take me a while to get out there. Here's what I can do—I'll help her with the arraignment and get her bonded out. Then, I have a good attorney who handles criminal cases that I can put your friend in contact with, because, beyond the arraignment, I am way out my league."

"Okay, that sounds like a good plan," Jillian conceded.

"Why don't you text me the address, and I'll get there as soon as possible. If they call her for arraignment, make sure she tells them that her lawyer is on the way and request extra time."

"Will do. See you soon."

Chapter Four

Jillian rushed at me, her straight, dark hair flying, as I walked through the precinct door. "You are not going to believe this." She grabbed my arm, spun me around, and escorted me back out the door, finally stopping beneath a large oak tree.

"What's up? Did I miss the arraignment?"

"No. She's not getting arraigned today. The diamonds are worth too much. It's a case of felony larceny or some such nonsense, and she's going to have to wait until Monday to see the judge, in court."

I grimaced. "I was afraid of that."

"You knew?"

"Not exactly, but one hundred K is a lot of dough. Have the police found the diamonds yet?"

Jillian explained how one of the "supposedly" missing diamonds had been found on the ground at Sadira's feet. "But I'm not so sure Sadira's accusation was incorrect. That Tazim guy seems a little squirrelly to me. And it did seem like he deliberately knocked her bag to the floor."

"Have they let you speak to her?"

Jillian shook her head. "Lawyers only."

"Okay. I'll go in and see what I can find out."

Once I established myself as Sadira's lawyer, a tall, blonde officer with a nametag that read Shandlin led me through a maze of cubes to a heavy black door. The woman knocked twice.

A silver-haired detective in a black button-down with his

badge clipped onto a pair of gray dress slacks opened the door to the interrogation room. "Officer Shandlin?"

"This lady is her lawyer," the officer said.

His gaze flicked up and down, taking in my jeans and T-shirt.

"Hi, detective." I held out my hand. "Karina Cardinal. I'd like to speak with my client."

The detective gave me an abrupt handshake and opened the door wide, allowing me to enter.

I found Jillian's fashionably dressed friend cuffed to the metal table. "Are those really necessary? She's not been charged with a violent crime."

The detective removed the cuffs and remained standing next to the table.

"I'd like to speak with my client. Alone."

"You've got ten minutes." The detective pulled open the door.

"She's my client. I'll take as long as I need," I replied imperiously.

"Okay, but the next guy we're bringing in is here on murder two charges. It might get crowded."

My jaw dropped as the door slammed shut. With a shake of my shoulders, I turned to my client. "Hi, Sadira. I'm Jillian's sister, Karina Cardinal." Placing my phone on the table, I slipped into the seat opposite Sadira.

"Thank the lord you're here." She rubbed her wrists. My first impressions were of an exotic-looking young woman. Her eye makeup was smudged, and her red-rimmed eyes looked as though she'd been crying. "They k-kept asking me all these questions about the d-diamonds," she sniffed.

"Did you answer them?"

Her foot jiggled and she shook her head. "Nope. They kept

saying it would go better for me if-if I cooperated. But I-I asked for a lawyer and kept my mouth shut." The stutter seemed to be a direct result of her anxiety.

I ground my teeth. They should have stopped asking questions as soon as she requested a lawyer. "Good for you. My sister told me a little about your situation. Can you explain the diamond that fell out of your purse?"

She frowned. "It didn't 'fall out' of my purse. I'm pretty sure Tazim dropped it when he knocked my purse to the floor."

"Why would he do that? Does he hold a grudge against you?"

"I have no idea why he would do it." The stutter disappeared with Sadira's anger. "I really don't know all that much about my boss. He comes in, we work, we leave. That's it." She made a slashing motion with her hand. "It's not like he's a great conversationalist."

"Do you have any priors?" I asked.

The jiggling stopped. She tucked her hands beneath her thighs and stared down at the table.

"Sadira?"

Her hair fell, blocking her face. "I've got some traffic violations."

"Such as?"

"Speeding. Running a red light." She continued to gaze down. "It was D.C., you know how hard it is sometimes when you're used to seeing traffic lights above, not on the street corners."

Indeed, I did. I'd accidentally run a red light or two in D.C., but had never been caught. "Well, I wouldn't worry about that. Now, listen, I have some news. The weekend magistrate will not be able to set bail. Which means you'll have to wait until Monday when court is in session."

Her head flew up at my statement. "You mean I've got to stay here? All weekend?" she squeaked.

"I'm afraid so," I said sympathetically.

"It smells."

"I beg your pardon?"

"The jail cell, it smells like pee and body odor. Isn't there anything you can do to get me out sooner?"

My nose scrunched at the thought of spending a night in a stinky jail cell. "I'm sorry. I can't."

"But what about innocent until proven guilty and all that? What about my job? I'm a schoolteacher. They'll fire me over this. Can they really keep me here until Monday?"

"I'm afraid so. The diamond the officer found at your feet is enough to hold you."

She shivered.

I didn't blame her. Spending a couple nights in jail wouldn't be on my list of 'fun things to do' either. Unfortunately, her assessment of the situation was correct, felony charges against a teacher working with kids could absolutely get her fired. At minimum, she'd be put on leave until after the trial. I didn't tell her, but there was a decent chance the press would get ahold of her arrest. "The good news is I've put in a call to a top-notch criminal attorney, who I'm going to try my hardest to get here for your arraignment. Her name is Jessica Williams."

"What about you?"

I shook my head. "I'm not a criminal attorney. I told Jillian I'd help with the arraignment today, but since it's not happening this weekend, you're better off if Jessica, or one of her associates, handles your case. Jessica can also advise you on your job situation."

"Okay, I guess." She picked at a hangnail.

I squeezed her hand. "Don't worry, everything will be all

right."

"Who's going to take care of my cat?"

"You have a cat?"

She pushed a hank of scarlet hair away from her face. "Smokey."

"Is there a neighbor who can watch him for you?"

She shook her head. "Not that I know of. I mean, I'm friendly with my neighbors, but I'm not friends with any of them."

I liked dogs. I was not a cat person. My sister, on the other hand, loved all kids and animals as long as they didn't slither or walk on eight legs. "I'll see if Jilly can take care of Smokey."

"I'd appreciate that."

"Why don't you write down your address and instructions for feeding Smokey." I dug into my purse for a pen and paper. "Does someone have a set of spare keys to your home?"

"Jillian has my keys and she knows where I live."

"Okay. Then we'll take care of that for you. Trust me, you'll be in good hands with Jessica." I patted her shoulder while she wrote down instructions for the cat.

"Thanks."

I let myself out of the interrogation room and found the gray-haired detective lurking nearby, a fresh cup of coffee in hand.

"Well, hello, detective . . . ?"

"Clark," he filled in, handing me a business card.

"Detective Clark, have you found any of the other diamonds my client allegedly stole?"

He took a long swig of coffee. "Not yet."

"Not yet? One diamond—possibly planted by the jeweler—seems a little thin." I crossed my arms and gave him the stink-eye.

"We'll find more."

"Find them where?" I allowed a skeptical brow to peak. "You've got her handbag. I'm assuming you didn't find any more in there."

"You'd be correct."

"Where do you think you'll find them?"

He shrugged. "Maybe her apartment."

My Spidey sense went on alert. "Did you get a warrant?"

A slow smile spread across his features. "We did."

"May I see it?" I held out a hand.

"The detective on site has it." He glanced at his watch. "If you hurry, you can probably meet him at her apartment," he said triumphantly.

I jogged past Clark, hustling my way through the maze of cube-world and into the lobby where Jillian impatiently paced. "Jillian, c'mon," I barked. "Time to go."

"What? What's the matter?" Jillian's steps dogged mine.

"They've got a warrant. They're searching her house. You'll need to direct me to her place."

"You can follow me. Where are you parked?"

"Over there, by the dumpster."

"Me too." Jillian pulled out her keys and the black Audi next to my beat-up Honda chirped. She pulled the car door open.

"Wait. What is *that*? Did you get a new car?"

"No, it's Sadira's." She started to climb into the car.

"Stop!" I exclaimed.

My sister halted mid-movement.

"Why are you driving Sadira's car?"

"She drove us over to the fashion show. I left my car at her apartment," she explained.

That's why my sister had her keys. I did some fast thinking. The warrant probably included Sadira's car. "Get in my car.

Leave Sadira's here."

"Are you sure?" Jillian's face fell with confusion.

"Yes." If they asked about her car, I wouldn't lie, but I also didn't feel as if I needed to deliver it to them on a silver tray. Besides, if there were diamonds hidden in the vehicle, I didn't want my sister to get caught driving around in it.

By the time we got to The Sargetti, Sadira's condo complex in McLean, there was no sign of any police presence. I wondered if we'd beat them there. However, letting ourselves in to the apartment, we realized they'd already come and gone. The place wasn't completely upended, but drawers were pulled halfway out, kitchen cabinets hung open, dishes and glasses were spread across the countertops, and the couch cushions were stacked in a corner. Even the mirror in the half bath hung crookedly, as if the searchers had removed it to check behind it. Smokey greeted us with a timid meow as we walked into Sadira's bedroom.

"Hello, kitty." My sister scooped up the silky gray Siamese.

"That must be Smokey. Sadira asked if you could take care of him until she's released."

"Of course." She rubbed her nose against the cat's neck.

The apartment matched the elegant creature—soft gray tones on the walls, modern, simple furniture, and hand-scraped hardwoods throughout. I could tell, even through the messiness left behind by the police, that Sadira like things neat, clean, and expensive. A visit into her closet revealed more of Sadira's upscale taste. Designer shoes rose to the ceiling of the back wall, haphazardly stacked on the shelving as if the police had checked each pair for the missing jewels. Dresses, pants, tops, skirts, and other clothing items hung crookedly on hangers, with a few pieces left on the floor. All of it filled a closet large enough for a couple to share with space left over.

"Your friend likes nice things," I commented drily, fingering a Marc Jacobs dress.

Jilly came into the closet carrying Smokey over her shoulder. "I know. Wouldn't you kill for her shoes?"

"Mm." Frowning, I read some of the labels—Prada, Choo, Ferragamo. "She's just a schoolteacher like you, right?"

"Yup." The cat became fidgety and Jillian returned him to the floor where he began cleaning himself.

"Jilly, this is a *very* nice condo, she's got thousands of dollars' worth of clothes in here, and she drives an Audi. This" —I indicated the wall of shoes— "screams living beyond her means. She must be up to her eyeballs in debt. Are you sure she didn't steal the diamonds?"

"I know, right? I asked her about it. She said she makes a commission off her jewelry store sales."

My gaze scrolled through the room again. "She must be a damn good saleswoman."

"I suspect so. She can be very charming. And she's quite beautiful." Smokey began stropping himself against my sister's legs.

I didn't agree with her assessment. Sadira held an appeal, but not that of a beauty in the classic sense. Her nose was too wide, eyes a bit small, and forehead too tall; however, with her skilled use of makeup and eye-catching hair color, she made for a striking specimen. "Let's get Smokey's supplies and go."

"Do you think we should clean this place up?"

"Nope." I trooped past my sister to the kitchen and found Smokey's food in the cabinet next to the refrigerator.

Back in my car, Jillian sat in the passenger seat with Smokey on her lap, trying to convince me to agree to her whack-a-doodle idea.

"But you can help investigate the theft," she implored.

I slanted my eyes at her. "I beg your pardon?"

"Yeah, you and me together, like Cagney and Lacey. Rizzoli and Isles."

"Jillian—we're not private investigators. You're a schoolteacher. I work for a healthcare advocacy organization."

"I *know* that! But you solved that art case."

"I have no idea what you're talking about," I said without inflection, and stared out the windshield.

She harrumphed. "Don't bullshit me, Rina. Like I said, I'm calling in my chip and we're investigating."

"How?" I turned with my palms up. "Where would we even start?"

"I want to talk with some of the other employees at the store."

"I imagine the police are already doing that." My hands dropped.

"Yes, but they aren't doing it to help Sadira," Jillian whined. "They'll do it to make sure she goes to jail."

I directed a gusty sigh heavenward, causing my bangs to flutter up. "Mike would consider this snooping." Besides that, considering what I just witnessed in Sadira's home, I wasn't so sure she was innocent of the charges. I feared, not only would the police find evidence to convict her, what would happen if Jillian and I found evidence of the same thing? Technically, as her lawyer, I couldn't testify against her—but Jillian could be forced to.

"Yeah, but he's out of town, and you're mad at him right now anyway. What he doesn't know . . ." She stroked the purring cat and grinned at me.

Shifting, I turned to face my sister so I could look her straight in those baby blues. "You seriously believe Sadira is innocent of this theft?"

Jillian made a crossing motion against her chest and held up two fingers. "Scout's honor, I believe she didn't do it."

"Girl Scouts use three fingers," I muttered.

She flipped up a third finger.

I sighed. "Okay, we can make some inquiries." Jillian reached for the door handle. "But not today. This Tazim guy will surely be around, and he knows you. Not to mention the police. We'll go tomorrow."

"Good idea. When do you want to go?"

"Let me see what time they close." I started to do a web search of the hours on my phone.

"Tyson's closes at seven on Sundays," Jillian supplied.

I should have known my sister would be familiar with the mall's hours. "I'll pick you up at five."

"See you then." Jillian and the cat exited. Smokey slipped out of her arms onto the passenger seat of her Hyundai sedan, and I waited for her to drive out of the complex before phoning Jessica again.

"Karina Cardinal," she answered. It sounded like a cocktail party going on in the background. "Hold on, let me get somewhere quiet." The party sounds decreased and I heard a definitive thunk, as though Jessica closed a door. "What trouble are you into now?"

"Why on earth do you assume I'm in trouble?"

She snorted. "It happens."

"Well, as a matter of fact, I've got a new client for you." I ran down the stats on Sadira's arrest.

"I'm out of town for the weekend, but I'll have one of my associates meet with her and take care of the arraignment."

There was a burst of noise on Jessica's end and a giggling girl's voice said, "Oops, sorry. Didn't know it was occupied."

"Where are you?" I asked.

"Hamptons," Jessica replied.

"Lucky duck. How much do you think her bail will be for a crime like this?"

"Not sure. Depends on the judge. If she's got no priors, and they didn't find anything at the apartment, she's not violent. . . . They'll probably set it at fifty thousand, but the judge might set it at one hundred—the price of the diamonds. That makes her bond ten grand. Do you think she'll be able to afford it?"

I considered all the designer tags in her closet. "Probably. Do you have a bail bondsman you use?"

"We have a few."

"At minimum she's got some property she could use for collateral."

"We'll use one that can work with her situation." Another burst of laughter filtered through the closed door.

"I'll let you get back to your party. Thanks for taking my call, Jessica."

"Anytime, Karina."

I disconnected and rolled out of the parking lot. Jillian seemed certain Sadira didn't take the diamonds. However, her home, car, and lavish clothing seemed a bit much, even if she did make a commission on her jewelry sales. I wondered if she carried a lot of credit card debt. Jillian said Sadira had paid for her purchases today in cash. There was such a thing as cash advances for credit cards. Those advances had gotten a number of people into a world of financial trouble. I made a mental note to suggest Jessica look further into her new client's finances.

Chapter Five

The downy clouds shifted overhead, blotting out the sun one moment and revealing it the next. A plastic bag blew past our feet, and I pulled wisps of hair out of my lipstick as Jillian and I hurried through the glass doors of the mall into the food court on the ground level. On the drive over, my sister explained her plan to approach the jewelry store and gain information. Since Tazim didn't know me from Adam, I was in charge of recon while Jilly waited in a nearby store. If Tazim was on the floor, as I suspected he would be, my mission was to identify another coworker who we could approach after closing when he wasn't around.

"You mean stalk her?" I drawled.

"No, not stalk! Accidentally bump into her after she leaves."

"And how do you propose we do this 'accidental' meeting?"

"I haven't gotten that far yet. Let's just see what we see." Jillian swished her hand dismissively.

"Fine. I need something to drink before heading into the lion's den." I pulled my sister over to a Chinese chain and ordered two diet sodas.

Sucking down the caffeine in hopes of obtaining motivation, I followed Jillian to the second floor, past dozens of glass window dressings designed to entice shoppers. The closer we got to the jewelry store, the louder my instincts bellowed that this was a bad idea. What I'd decided, but hadn't told my sister, was if Tazim was the only one on the floor, the mission would be aborted. This entire harebrained scheme seemed ridiculous, and if I didn't owe her one, I'd be home doing something useful with my time.

On second thought, maybe I'd be stewing over my fight with Mike. I sighed as we passed the Victoria's Secret and had to give Jillian credit—at least this little trip got me out of the house and my mind off my own troubles by focusing it on someone else's.

"Come in here, quick." My sister abruptly pulled me into a shoe store.

"What are we—oh . . ." I fingered a handsome navy-blue stiletto sandal that caught my eye. "Aren't these adorable? I've got a polka dot dress that would be perfect with these."

"Put those down." Jillian snatched the shoe out of my hand.

"Hey," I protested.

"We're not here to shop," she hissed. "The jewelry store is diagonally across the way." She made a jerking motion with her head and I glanced across the wide pedestrian avenue at the narrow entryway of the jewelry store. "I can't see him, so you should go now. I'll stay here and cover you."

I wasn't sure my sister understood exactly what it meant to "cover" your partner, but I didn't feel now was the time to point this out. Jillian seemed to be having too much fun with her covert op. "You might want to hide behind that stack of shoes over there," I told her. "He may be behind that window display. Or if he comes out of the back room, he'll be able to see you."

"Good idea." She ducked behind the boxes and pretended to become engrossed with a pair of running shoes.

Sighing, I trotted obediently across the avenue to the jewelry store. The front windows displayed some beautiful matching earring and necklace sets that were far beyond my means. After admiring a sapphire and diamond collection, I entered the store. Glass display cases to my left and right ran the length of the store, connected by a perpendicular case at the end, creating a U-shape. A small island featuring an array of watches stood in the center of the floor. The store appeared empty, not only of Tazim, but of anyone. I strolled over to a display of opal jewelry, and a movement from the back had me glancing up. A young woman, perhaps in her early twenties, approached me. I quickly assessed her. She was of average height, perhaps a little on the plump side, but she dressed nicely in a yellow dress that highlighted the golden tones of her dirty-blonde hair. As she came to a stop in front of me, her thin, gold nose ring glittered in the light reflecting off the glass counter.

"Hello," she said with a smile. "Are you looking for anything in particular?"

"Not really, window shopping." I sipped my soda. "Those are very pretty." I pointed to a pair of opal earrings.

She reached beneath the cabinet and pulled them out. "I love our opal jewelry, the variety of colors from blues to turquoise to green and white all melding together."

"Yeah, they make quite a splash, don't they?" I held one up to get a closer look. "I understand they're very soft though, and prone to cracking."

"They can, but it's all in how you take care of your opals."

I returned the earring back to its black velvet holder. "I heard you all had some excitement yesterday."

The salesgirl shot me a wary look.

Chewing on my drink straw, I asked in a confiding manner, "Do you think she did it?"

Blondie replaced the earrings. "Have you seen our ruby selection? We're running a special this week, fifteen percent off." She moved further down the display counter, closer to the door. She reached into the case and pulled out a tray of diamond and ruby bracelets.

I followed dutifully, admiring the display. "Did you ever work with Sadira?"

Her eyes widened at the mention of Sadira's name. She picked up one of the bracelets and spread it across her palm. "Not here," she murmured, keeping her eyes down.

I took the bracelet off her hand, laid it across my wrist, and whispered, "You know something, don't you?"

"Are you a cop?"

"No, just a friend of Sadira's. She's really scared," I muttered.

Her eyes darted to the back room doorway before answering. "Meet me at the T.G.I. Friday's in an hour."

"Okay," I said in a normal voice, handing the jewelry back to her. "Thanks, I'll think about it. How long did you say the sale was running?"

"Until Saturday." She too spoke in louder tones.

"Great."

"If you come back, ask for Misty."

"Sure thing, Misty." I meandered out of the store and turned toward Macy's.

Jillian joined me. "Did you find out anything?"

"We are meeting Misty at the T.G.I. Friday's in an hour." A trash can came up on the left, and I chucked my empty cup in it.

"Does she know something?"

"Dunno. She was hesitant to say anything. I think Tazim might have been in back."

"Hmm . . . interesting. What shall we do in the meantime?" Jillian's cup followed mine.

"Destination—Macy's. I need to look for a new black belt."

An hour later, Jillian and I sat at a high-top table in the bar area at Friday's. Jillian nursed a beer while I flicked salt off the rim of a very weak margarita.

"She's late." Jillian restlessly shifted on her stool.

"Give it time. Maybe closing is taking longer than she anticipated."

"What if she doesn't show up?"

"Then we're no better or worse off than we were before."

Jillian scanned the room again. "I have to go to the bathroom."

"Then go."

"I don't want to miss her."

I rolled my eyes. "Oh, for crying out loud, just go."

Jillian slid off the stool and hustled to the back of the restaurant.

"Hi," a voice chirped at my shoulder. Just like a watched pot—Misty arrived when we weren't looking.

"Hi, Misty." I delivered the hearty greeting with a big, fake smile. "Have a seat."

"What would you like to drink?" The cocktail waitress placed a napkin in front of Misty, and she requested a beer.

"Have you already ordered your dinner?" Misty asked after the waitress left.

I shook my head and handed her a menu. "No, my sister and I were waiting for you to arrive."

She perused the options. "Gosh, I'm starving. I think I'll get a hamburger."

"Sounds good."

Jillian spotted us from across the room and speed-walked her way back to our table. "Hi," she waved, "I'm Jillian."

"Misty." They shook hands. Misty turned back to me. "I didn't get your name."

"Karina," I supplied.

The server arrived with Misty's beer. "What can I get for you folks?"

After ordering, we all took a drink and an awkward silence settled over the table. Jillian stared down, picking at her napkin, so I decided to get the ball rolling. "I appreciate you meeting with us. It seemed you had something to say back at the shop, but I suspect Tazim was nearby."

"Yeah." She flipped her hair and let out a puff. "I don't think Sadira stole those diamonds at all."

"Really?" My surprise was not false. "Who do you think stole them?"

"Tazim."

"Tazim?" Jillian exclaimed. "But—he owns the store. Why would he steal from his own stock?"

I took a stab at the answer. "For the insurance?"

Misty clicked her tongue and pointed at me. "Ding-ding."

"Why would he need the insurance?" Jillian leaned forward on her elbows.

"Tazim has a gambling problem."

"Really." My sister rested so close she practically put her chin in my margarita.

I shifted the drink out of danger. "Tell us more."

"He gambles at the MGM National Harbor. I can always tell when he's winning because he bounces around the store, practically jubilant. But when he's losing—" Misty made a thumbs-down motion. "He's cranky and short with everyone. He won't even go out front to talk with the customers because he's in such a bad mood."

"How do you know this?" I asked.

"Last year he had to take on a silent partner. I've only seen him in the store a few times. His name is Vijay. One day about a year ago, I came in early. I wasn't expecting anyone to be there, but to my surprise the gate was up, so I walked in. I could hear them arguing in the back, so I eavesdropped." Misty winked.

"Vijay was chewing Tazim out. I remember him telling Tazim that he wouldn't be there if Tazim could control his gambling habit. But now that Vijay was there, Tazim had better straighten up. Vijay said he was bringing in a third party to go through the books and take a full inventory, and everything'd better be in order and stay that way."

Jillian sat back in her chair with a triumphant grin on her face. "How did you know Tazim gambles at the MGM?"

Misty lifted a shoulder. "A few months before Vijay came on, Tazim asked me if I knew how to get to the MGM. I told him I did, and also told him the best place to park. He wrote it all down. You see, at that time, I dated a guy who worked the craps tables. He said he saw Tazim a number of times. Apparently, he even played in the high rollers room. After Vijay came on, things changed, Tazim was never late to the store, paid attention to the customers, the black moods vanished. My boyfriend said he didn't see Tazim anymore."

"Then how do you know he's still gambling? Has your friend seen him recently?" I asked.

"We broke up." Misty shrugged. "Tazim's gambling is a hunch. The black moods returned a few weeks ago. He's been snappish, ordering the staff to do things rather than asking, and he's barely been out front to meet potential customers. The last shift I worked before today was Wednesday. Today, I see Tazim. He's got a cast on his arm and Sadira's been accused of stealing a bunch of diamonds. It doesn't take an Einstein to put two-and-two together. You want to know what I think?"

Jillian and I nodded.

Misty put her arm on the table and leaned forward. "I think he's been gambling. And I bet he lost a bundle. Panicked. Went to a loan shark thinking he could win back his money—but we all know what happens when you go down that rabbit hole."

She tsked. "Stupid. I'd wager the loan is due, and whomever lent him money sent in some muscle to rough up Tazim. That's what happened to his arm." She tapped her temple with a black painted fingernail.

I sat back, contemplating my watery margarita. "Did the police come by to speak with you today?"

"Yup."

"And you told them all of this?" Jillian asked.

Misty's head moved side-to-side. "It's just my guess."

I swallowed the last of the margarita. "But the conversation you heard between Vijay and Tazim. You told them about that?"

"Nope." She sat back and sipped her beer. "They never asked. It was all about Sadira. Sadira this, Sadira that. How long had I worked with her? When was the last time I worked with her? What did I know about the diamonds? Were they there when I worked on Wednesday? You know, that sort of stuff."

Jillian grabbed my thigh and shot me a wide-eyed look. She'd been right about the police simply seeking to hang the theft around Sadira's neck without investigating further.

I pushed Jillian's hand away and asked Misty, "Has the insurance adjustor been in yet?"

"Not yet." Misty drew lines in the condensation on her glass. "Tazim told Vijay that the adjustor would be in on Monday."

"So you saw Vijay today?" Jillian asked.

"Yeah, he came in to talk to the detective. And I'll tell you what—I'm not sure Vijay is buying Tazim's story either." Her eyebrows waggled at the declaration.

"Why do you think that?" I took the bait.

"The way he watched Tazim as he spoke to the detective. His eyes were kind of narrowed and he scrutinized his partner as one would a bug beneath a microscope lens." Misty demonstrated, squinting her eyes and crumpling her face. "After the detective left, Vijay told me to man the front while he and Tazim disappeared for an hour in back. Let's just say, Vijay did *not* look happy when he finally left. A little while later, Tazim came out and told me he needed me to work Monika's shifts the rest of the week."

Our waitress arrived with our meals. Jillian helped sort the dishes to the appropriate person, and after assuring her that we had everything we needed, the server retreated.

"So, he fired Monika," I said, returning to our discussion.

"Yeah." Misty munched on a fry. "If she really did give Sadira her code to the safe—that *is totally* a fire-able offense. It's, like, store policy 101. You don't share any passwords, safe codes, or cash register logins. Monika should have closed the shop. There are all sorts of insurance ramifications for what she did. And if the diamonds don't turn up, I bet they could prosecute her too."

Jillian gasped. "That's terrible."

Misty shrugged and bit into her hamburger.

"Why do you think he took the loose diamonds rather than a necklace or fancy bracelet?" Jillian asked, absentmindedly spearing a piece of chicken with her fork.

"Easier to fence. Each piece in that store has been photographed and would be identifiable."

I swallowed a mouthful of rice pilaf and asked, "But haven't the diamonds been photographed and identified by the four C's?"

"Yes. However, it's not like they've been marked in any other way. Without paperwork, it's just another diamond."

My sister wiped a drip of BBQ sauce off her mouth with a napkin. "So, what? He paid off his debts in diamonds?"

"Either that, or he's trying to sell them on the black market for cash to pay it off."

I chewed a bite of my salmon steak and observed Misty. "Why are you telling us all of this?"

Misty laid down her hamburger and wiped her fingers and mouth with the napkin before speaking. "Because it could have been me in Sadira's shoes. If I'd been the one to close that night, he would have blamed me. It was dumb luck that Monika broke protocol and gave Sadira her code. Tazim found his scapegoat."

"Why don't you tell the police?"

"I told you, it's all just a guess. I don't have any proof. And I need this job. If I tell the police and I'm wrong—Tazim will fire me. I'm an assistant manager. With Monika gone, Tazim will *have* to make me a manager." She muttered the last part so quietly I almost missed it.

"Yeah, but knowing what you think you know" —Jillian pointed her fork at Misty— "aren't you worried that Tazim will do the same to you if he gets in debt again?"

Misty shook her head. "I don't think he'd be stupid enough to pull off the same stunt twice. I also think that Vijay is no longer going to be a silent partner. On his way out, he said he'd see me tomorrow. If he's around, I definitely want to keep working there."

"You think he'll put Tazim on the straight and narrow?" Jillian asked.

"I don't know. But—Vijay's hot too." Misty licked her lips and grinned. "He's over six feet tall, dark hair, mahogany skin with these lashes . . . oh so thick. His nose is kind of crooked, but who cares? If he's going to be in the shop more often, it'll be worth it to stay."

"Is he married?"

Misty glanced at us from beneath her mascaraed lashes. "He doesn't wear a wedding ring if he is."

"And, of course, the money's good," Jillian piped in.

Misty gave a half shrug. "Eh, could be worse."

"Sadira made a lot of money," I commented drily.

"I don't know about that. She could have made more if she'd picked up additional shifts."

"But with the commissions she did well," Jillian said enviously.

Misty's brows drew down. "Commission? She didn't make commission on her sales."

My sister frowned in confusion. "She didn't?"

"Nope. Only store managers make commission. Even as an assistant manager, I don't make a commission. If we sell a certain amount, I get a bonus at the end of the month. But it's nothing to write home about. Especially after the government gets their cut."

"But—"

I kicked Jillian beneath the table to shut her up.

"Ow!" she cried, and rubbed her shin.

"Sorry," I muttered. "You were saying you thought Vijay will be taking on a larger role?"

Misty wiped burger juice off her chin with a napkin. "I hope so."

"Do you think he'll look into Tazim?"

"Dunno." Misty shrugged and took a deep pull on her beer. "Maybe. Or maybe he'll be content to get the insurance pay out."

"They won't get paid until there's been a thorough investigation," I stated drily.

"Well, if Sadira, *does* have the diamonds, they're bound to find them. Right?" Misty's blue eyes widened. "If it's Tazim . . ."

She cocked her head and left the comment hanging.

The money is as good as gone. Nobody said the words out loud, but we all thought it.

Eric Clapton played in the background as I drove Jillian back to her apartment. Both of us remained quiet as the events of the day spun around in my head. Tazim was certainly a suspect. And if Misty was correct, he had a motive for stealing his own merchandise.

"Why do you think Sadira lied to me?" Jillian broke the peace.

"I've been wondering that myself. When did she tell you that she got a commission on her sales?"

"Yesterday. Right after the big fashion show. I asked about her wages at the jewelry store. I thought I might want to work there."

"I think that's a hard 'no.'"

Jillian snorted. "Yeah, *now* it is."

"So, where is she getting her money? And if she lied to you about the commission—"

"What else is she lying about?" My sister completed my thought.

"Do you think . . . nah."

"What? Throw it out there."

I chewed my lip. "Could she and Tazim be . . . working together?"

Jillian didn't respond. Presently another car's headlights lit up the windshield, and I saw my sister's face pulled in concentration.

"Look, I don't know this woman at all," I said. "You've been working with her for how many years?"

"Let me see." She tapped her knee, silently counting. "Three."

"You met Tazim. Was there an undercurrent between the two of them? Do you think she could have pulled this off?"

Jillian pinched her lip in thought. "Two hours ago, I would have answered with a resounding '*no.*' But, two hours ago, I didn't know my friend had lied to me about where her money comes from."

"So, do you think they're . . . romantically involved?"

"No-o." Her hair slid over her shoulder as she shook her head. "I have a real problem imagining she and Tazim are in on something together. And I can't imagine she'd spend a couple of nights in jail for him. Not to mention, risk her teaching position."

"Maybe she's over her head in credit card debt and needs the cash." I voiced the thought that'd been on my mind ever since I saw her closet.

"That was my initial thought as well."

I rolled to a stop at a red light. "If she didn't steal the diamonds, credit cards could be our answer. Unless she had a rich uncle die and leave her a bunch of money."

"Hm," was the limited response Jillian gave.

Tomorrow was Monday. I was almost glad I had work to do which would take my mind off the Sadira Diamond Heist. Almost.

Chapter Six

Monday morning dawned about as well as Monday mornings do. There is not enough coffee in the world to make me excited about getting up at the crack-o-dark to go anywhere on Monday morning. Don't get me wrong, I love my job as a lobbyist for National Health Advocacy Alliance, or NHAA, but this morning I had a seven o'clock. professional development breakfast to attend. Which meant full makeup, hair, suit, and heels had to be in place by a quarter after six so I could roll into D.C. metro traffic to get to the venue on time. I headed out of my Alexandria condo complex's parking lot and found said traffic fifty feet down the road.

Note to self, do not agree to attend any event before nine—a sensible if not unreasonable thought. Sucking down a large gulp of Colombian roast nectar of the gods out of a to-go mug, I crawled along with the rest of the commuting grunts.

Since I have to sit in traffic, I might as well get some work done. Tucking my Bluetooth earbud in, I stated clearly, "Call Jessica, office." I didn't expect her to be in the office, especially since she'd spent her weekend in the Hamptons, but if I figured I'd get the ball rolling and leave a message.

She picked up on the fourth ring. "Hello?"

"Jessica? It's Karina. I—I didn't expect you to be in yet."

"I'm not. My work phone is forwarded to my cell."

"I didn't wake you, did I?"

"No, I'm up. I've got a seven thirty flight out of Islip. What's going on? You're not in jail, are you?"

"Ha-ha," I said wryly, "no. I wanted to tell you about an interesting conversation Jillian and I had with one of Sadira's coworkers last night." I went on to describe our meeting with Misty and her allegations about Tazim. "And that's it." I waited for a response. "Jessica, are you still there?"

A windy sigh met my question.

I cringed. "Sorry to hit you with it so early. It—it could be nothing, but I thought you ought to know."

"I do. I've got an investigator I can put on it."

"Let him know that Misty will not want to talk to him in or around the store."

"Noted."

"Who are you sending to the arraignment?" I moved into the lane on the right and my speed went from snail to turtle.

"Bernard Theodore Evans the third . . . Esquire," Jessica drawled in a snooty sort of accent.

"Wow, that sounds . . ."

"Pretentious? He is. But, he's excellent with the details, well-spoken in court, and one of my best up-and-coming associates. He'll probably make partner in the next few years." Jessica's voice held a definite edge of irritation.

"Sounds like Sadira is in good hands."

"She is."

I waited because it felt like Jessica had more to say.

"Karina, would I be wasting my breath if I told you, in the politest of ways, to butt out?"

"Uh—"

"I don't know where this case is going to lead, but it seems any time you're involved, things get—"

"A little hairy?"

"Precisely."

"Got it. Honestly, my sister dragged me into this, and the

more I learn about Sadira, the more I want her to get away from whatever this is," I assured Jessica.

"*This* is either—she did it, in which case, your meddling could put you in a bad position and your sister on the stand to testify for the prosecution. *Or* she didn't, and your meddling could put you in the crosshairs of something more dangerous."

"Oh, I don't think we're dealing with criminal masterminds here," I scoffed.

"Karina, if your friend Misty is right, they broke Tazim's arm." Her tone possessed a warning note.

"Okay, okay. I get it. I'm out." Even though she couldn't see me, I held up a hand in surrender.

"And take your sister with you."

I couldn't help the chuckle that escaped. "Very well, I'll take Jillian with me."

"I've got to run. We'll talk later." She hung up, and I took a left onto a street with traffic moving at the speed of an old basset hound on his way to bed.

****

I returned to my workplace close to eleven. Rodrigo, my colleague, joined me as I strode down the hall toward my office. He must not have had any meetings on the Hill today, because he wasn't wearing one of his snazzy suits. Instead he wore a pair of gray slacks, a lavender dress shirt with a black vest, and no tie. The shirt complemented his young, dark Puerto Rican skin tones. He greeted me with, "You missed the morning meeting."

"I know. Professional development seminar. What did I miss?" We reached my triangular-shaped office space and I pulled the laptop out of my computer bag.

Rodrigo placed a handful of newspapers on my desk with *The Washington Post* on top. "Budget cuts. We have to share newspapers now. I offered to buddy up with you. Since you weren't in, I took first crack at them. I've highlighted a number of articles you'll probably want to read."

"Seriously? We can't afford newspapers for everyone who needs them in the office?" I shuffled through the stack.

"Apparently, too many people who don't need them were getting subscriptions. We were dumping piles of papers every day. Hasina has decided this isn't just a budget issue, but also an environmental one as well. The company will pay for more online subscriptions."

"I already have all the online subscriptions that I need, and while I do understand the environmental issues . . . Actually—" I flipped open the *New York Times*. Rodrigo had folded down the top corner and outlined in pink highlighter an article about the closing of a large hospital conglomerate in the Midwest. "—this is great. If you're going to do this, you can have first crack at them every morning."

"Sure thing, boss lady." He snapped a haughty salute.

"I'm not your boss," I responded mildly and changed topic. "How is Alphonse doing?"

Alphonse was Rodrigo's partner and a head chef at a five-star French restaurant in D.C. Last week he woke at four in the morning with lower stomach pain. Rodrigo rushed him to the hospital where tests revealed appendicitis, which led to an emergency appendectomy.

"He's got a doctor's appointment today, and I sincerely hope the doc clears him to return to work because he's becoming a pain in my ass. I've practically had to chain him to the plumbing to keep him away from the restaurant," Rodrigo complained.

"It's his baby. You'd do the same thing."

"No, I wouldn't. I'd read and watch trashy reality cable shows."

I arched a single disbelieving brow.

"What? I would." He sniffed and crossed his arms.

"Give him my best, will you?" My desk phone rang, and Rodrigo retreated to his cubicle.

The call turned out to be a telemarketer, and, after hanging up, I sorted through the newspapers. I finished perusing the *Wall Street Journal*, then pulled *The Washington Post* to the top of the pile. The article popped out at me from the front page of the Metro section. The photo they used must have come from a social media account instead of the police mugshot. That and the fact it was below the fold were the only silver linings I could identify. The headline alone would doom Sadira—"Diamond Theft! Fairfax County Teacher Arrested." The article went on to describe the facts of the case, including information that the county school superintendent had put her on leave pending further investigation. Jessica's firm, speaking on their client's behalf, provided a "no comment," to the press.

I wondered if Jillian had seen the piece. Now, more than ever, it would be prudent to take Jessica's directive and stay out of it. I made a note on my calendar to contact Jillian after school to bring her up to date on the current situation.

Chapter Seven

JILLIAN

School ended at 2:20 p.m. Jillian bolted to her car and headed out of the parking lot by three thirty. Sadira hadn't answered any of the texts Jillian sent today and, not knowing what time the arraignment would be, she supposed either Sadira was still waiting or she'd already been released.

Jillian decided to dial her sister's office.

"Hello," Karina answered.

"Hey, it's me. Have you heard anything about Sadira's arraignment today? Do you know if she's out?"

"I haven't. I spoke with Jessica this morning and she's put her best associate on the job."

"Well, Sadira hasn't returned any of my texts or calls." Jillian pulled to a stop behind a school bus releasing its cargo. "I'm headed over to her place to make sure she's not standing outside."

"I'm sure the apartment's superintendent could let her in. It's also possible that she is not yet out. There will be processing to get through after she's arraigned. She'll need to fill out the paperwork for the lawyer, the bondsman, probably the court system."

"So she's probably still at the courthouse?"

"That would be my guess."

The opposite lane showed a surprising break in traffic, the bus rolled on, and Jillian wheeled her sedan around in a sharp U-turn. "Okay, I'll head there."

"Jillian, wait. There are a couple of things I need to tell you. I'm assuming you didn't see the paper this morning?"

"I don't get the paper anymore. Why?"

Her sister sighed. "There's an article in the Metro section about Sadira's arrest."

"Oh. My. God." Jillian paused between each syllable. "That's horrible."

"It is. But not unexpected. It's a juicy story. I wouldn't be surprised if the local TV news stations pick it up," Karina explained.

"How terrible for Sadira."

"That's not the only thing, I told Jessica about our little sleuthing trip yesterday, and although she was appreciative of the information we provided, she asked us to take a step back from our— well, meddling, as she put it."

"But—"

"Listen." Karina cut her off. "Jessica said she'd put one of her own investigators on the case to find out if Misty's theory held water."

"So you don't think I should go to the courthouse to show my friend some moral support?" Jillian asked rather snippily.

"No, that's not at all what I mean. I know this girl is your friend, and you want to help. However, the Cagney and Lacey routine *is* over. If we stumbled across the wrong information, we could end up making things worse for Sadira," Karina cautioned.

"Fine," Jillian sighed. "I didn't have any more leads for us to follow anyway."

"Good. If I were you, I'd stay out of her business at work as well. The paper said she'd been put on leave pending investigation. I'm not sure what this arrest will mean for her job in the long run—"

"Nothing good. You can believe that."

"So, it might be better if you didn't gossip with your other coworkers about your part in it."

"I don't gossip," Jillian bleated defensively.

Karina let the silence hang between them.

"Okay, okay," Jillian groused. "Mum's the word. I know nothing."

"Good girl."

Jillian gave a sarcastic snort. "Whatever. I'll let you know what I find at the courthouse."

"I'll be waiting with bated breath," Karina responded in acerbic tones before hanging up.

Jillian's watch read quarter past four by the time she found the correct courtroom. Entering through the open door, she found the compact chamber relatively quiet. A few reporters were scattered through the gallery, and on her left, four suited, lawyerly-looking folks sat in the front two rows, surrounded by boxes of file folders. The judge, a balding man in his black robe, a pair of glasses sitting on his nose, stared down, reading the documents in front of him.

At the back corner, Jillian caught a glimpse of Sadira's flame red hair as a bailiff escorted her out of the courtroom in handcuffs. Between the defense and prosecution tables, a sharply dressed lawyer of average height with thinning sandy hair spoke in quick undertones to another lawyer, whom Jillian assumed was the district attorney. She wore a black suit that hung off her tall, thin figure, as if she'd recently lost weight and hadn't taken time to have it properly tailored. The DA shook her head and gave her counterpart a stern glare before returning to the mound of paperwork at her table. The other lawyer pushed through the swinging door into the gallery area as the bailiff called the next case.

"Excuse me." Jillian stopped the sandy-haired lawyer. "Are you Sadira Manon's lawyer?"

"Are you a reporter?" He gazed down his long patrician nose at her as though she was a pesky bug.

"No, a friend." Jillian's hackles rose. "I was with her when she got arrested. I just arrived. What happened? Is she getting out today?"

The supercilious look faded slightly. "Follow me. We'll converse somewhere quiet." He took Jillian's elbow, escorted her into the tiled hallway, and led her to an unoccupied corner.

"What's going on?" Jillian asked in low tones.

"Did you know your friend purchased airline tickets this week to Argentina?"

"No." She shook her head. "School is almost out. Many of us travel in the summertime. What does that have to do with anything?"

"Argentina has no extradition treaties with the US."

"So?" Jillian put her hands on her hips.

"The DA argued your friend was a flight risk."

"Uh-oh." Her hands dropped. "I don't suppose that went well."

"No." He glanced past Jillian as if checking to make sure no one listened.

"So she's not getting bailed out?"

"No, I was able to get the judge to set bail. However, due to the DA's arguments and the fact that the diamonds have not yet been found, he set bail at $200,000, your friend must surrender her passport, *and* she'll have to wear a tracking anklet."

"Two hundred! How much will she have to pay a bail bondsman?"

"Ten percent."

Jillian whistled. "I wonder if she can afford it."

The lawyer scrutinized Jillian. "She assured me she could. Why? Don't you think she'll be able to?"

"No, no, if Sadira said she could pay it, I'm sure she can," Jillian replied in an overly jovial manner. Her smile fell as the lawyer continued to study her through his small rectangular black glasses. "So—where is her passport?"

"I'm not sure. I need to speak with my client before they transport her back to county lockup."

"I have a set of her housekeys if that helps," Jillian offered.

He finally looked interested in something she said. "It might."

"Do you think I could talk to her before she goes?"

"Doubtful, but" —the lawyer's phone beeped, and he glanced at it distractedly— "I'll see what I can arrange."

"Oh, by the way, my name is Jillian Cardinal." She held out her hand. He ignored it, his attention focused on the phone, and Jillian began to wonder if the haughty mien was simply his resting face.

"Bernard Evans." He pronounced his first name *Ber-nerd*, in the English manner, rather than the Americanized way of *Burr-naard*. "Esquire," he added while tapping on the mobile.

Did he just esquire *me?* Jillian rolled her eyes and crossed her arms, waiting for *Ber-nerd* to finish his message.

"Follow me," he said with an abrupt turn, still staring at his phone.

Bernard was able to get Jillian in with Sadira. "Against my recommendations, she wants to talk to you—without me." His stiff demeanor bent into a deep frown. "She'll tell you where to find the passport. You're not her lawyer. Your conversation is not confidential, and an officer will be in the room with you."

Jillian nodded, and Bernard held open the door for her.

The miniature room held a metal table, but Sadira wasn't

handcuffed to it. The bright orange jumpsuit turned her skin tones sallow and, without any makeup, Sadira's face resembled melted wax, shiny and pale. Her eyes were red-rimmed from lack of sleep or possibly crying. A barrel-chested police officer entered the room behind Jillian and posted himself in the corner.

"Hey, Sadira, how are you holding up?" Jillian reached out to place a reassuring hand on her friend's.

"No touching," the officer barked.

Jillian pulled her arm back as if dodging a cobra strike.

"I'm holding up." Sadira delivered a wobbly half-smile. "My lawyer said the school system put me on leave for the rest of the year."

"You mean Ber-nerd?" Jillian's mouth twisted.

Sadira nodded, and her eyes shined over. "He seems like he knows what he's doing."

"Don't worry. Once this gets straightened out, they'll have to let you come back in the fall. Besides, summer break is only two and a half weeks away. Testing is almost done. The kids are checked out. You're not missing anything."

"Nothing but the field trip, I suppose. And I won't get to say goodbye," she sniffed.

Jillian leaned forward and whispered, "Listen, we don't have much time. I heard about your bail. Are you going to be able swing it? I could start a Go Fund Me page. . . ."

Sadira shook her head and mumbled, "I'll figure it out."

"What about your passport? Is it at the apartment? Can I get it for you?"

"That . . . could be a problem." Sadira frowned and her gaze shifted sideways. "I'm not sure where I left it."

"Okay, why don't you tell me where you *think* it might be."

Sadira listed off half a dozen different locations for Jillian to search. "One last thing, can you pick up and deliver a package for me?"

"Deliver a package?" Jillian's brows drew down in confusion.

"Yeah, I provide courier services—kind of like Uber. It's one of the ways I make extra money."

This reminded Jillian of the entire reason she wanted to speak to Sadira. "Right, because you don't actually make commission on your sales. Do you?" She didn't bother to temper her tone.

Sadira jerked back, but quickly recovered with a strained laugh. "So you found out." She leaned forward and returned to a whisper. "Look, I don't like to brag about it, but when my uncle died, I received his life insurance policy. My parents were angry that I didn't dole it out to them like candy. But they're terrible with money. My dad would have pissed it away on booze." Sadira's head drooped and she fidgeted with the cuff of her jumpsuit. "I'm don't like to talk about it, because the money is the reason we no longer speak. Even my mom won't talk to me."

"Oh." The explanation was not the one Jillian expected. "That's . . . too bad. I—I'm sorry. I guess I can help with your delivery."

Sadira's head popped up, eyes wide, tears miraculously gone. "Thanks, you're my savior."

"Well, I don't know ab—"

Sadira cut off Jillian's demur, speaking rapidly in a low tone. "I'm supposed to pick up a package Wednesday night at seven o'clock. and deliver it to a house out in Great Falls. The information and pick up address is in the glovebox of my car. You still have the keys?"

"Yes. I can get it."

"You will have to take my car. It's the license plate connected with my courier account. Like Uber. When you arrive, you'll be given the exact location for the drop off. Got it?"

"O-kay. What happens when I don't match the face on the account?"

"That won't matter." Sadira dismissed the concern with a wave of her hand. "If he asks, just tell him I'm sick and can't make it. Also—tell him I'm going on vacation . . . and won't be able to make drops, I mean deliveries, for a few weeks. Tell him I'll contact him when I return." She leaned closer and continued, "At the delivery stop, they'll give you an envelope. Just lock it in the glovebox—but *don't* open it."

"Time's up," the police officer said, taking Sadira's elbow to help her out of the seat.

"Can you do that for me, Jillian?" Sadira asked as the officer led her to the door.

"Yes, yes. I'll get your passport too. So you'll be out by the end of the day. Don't worry!" Jillian called as the pair exited.

****

"What about in her lingerie drawer?" Bernard called from the kitchen, where he searched Sadira's cabinets.

"Nope."

"Are you sure?"

"Yes."

"That was the first place she told you to look."

"I'm telling you, it's not in here," Jillian answered, shuffling through Sadira's lacy unmentionables one more time before shutting the drawer with a frustrated thump. "Would you like to check yourself?" She and Bernard had been rifling through Sadira's apartment for almost an hour, to no avail.

"Uh . . . no."

"It's not in the jewelry box, nor any of the drawers in her bathroom." Jillian turned in a circle.

"Does she have a safe deposit box?" the lawyer asked.

"I have no idea. Not one she told me about." Jillian came out of the master bedroom. "Did she say something to you?"

"No." Bernard ran a hand through his hair, ruffling the stiff, moussed style out of place. He'd taken off his coat and tie and unbuttoned the top button of his dress shirt.

Jillian thought the tie and perfectly coiffed hair better suited the stuffy *Ber-nerd*. With the disdainful guise removed, this relaxed fellow looked more like— "Hey, do any of your friends call you Bernie?"

An appalled expression twisted his face. "God, no. Well—" He considered. "Once in college—" He looked up at Jillian as though realizing he was talking to a practical stranger and muttered, "Never mind."

She tilted her head. "Well, when you're not all buttoned up tight, *I* think you look like a Bernie."

He had no response to that and returned to the matter at hand. "Do you have any other ideas where we should look?"

"Check the medicine cabinet in the other bathroom. I'll look through the living room." Jillian continued her search, opening and closing drawers she'd been sure the police had already combed through, to no avail. They'd also put the apartment back to together as they searched. After another half an hour, the pair gave up.

Jillian locked the apartment and Bernard escorted her back to her car. "What happens now?"

He shook his head. "I doubt the judge will release her without the passport. I'll speak to her again, see if she can give us other places to search."

Jillian pulled her car door closed and rolled down the

windows to release the trapped heat. "It's odd, don't you think?"

"What's odd?" he asked, distracted by his phone.

"Where is your passport?"

"Mine?" Bernard looked up and adjusted his glasses. "Desk drawer at home."

"Mine's in a fire safe in my closet. It's just something that you *know*," Jillian mused. "I would think, if you were planning an international trip, you'd pull it out to check the expiration dates, or put it with your ticket confirmation."

Bernard's face betrayed nothing. "Maybe she misplaced it."

"Yeah, I suppose you're right. It was nice meeting you, Bernard. Here's my card if you need to reach me." She passed the small placard through the window. "That's my cell number. I can't answer during school hours. Send a text if you need something."

"Here, let me give you mine." He reached into the inside pocket of his suit coat and passed his card through the window before turning away.

Jillian glanced at the card. It read, Bernard T. Evans III, Esquire. *I guess when you're saddled with a name like that, you can't help being pompous.* "Bye, Bernie!" She couldn't help herself.

His shoulders stiffened, but he continued walking.

Chapter Eight

The soft spring breeze ruffled my hair as I trotted up 14th Street in downtown D.C. My stomach grumbled and I checked my watch—1:20 p.m. I hadn't eaten lunch and was riding on the fumes of a coffee I drank around ten. My choices were either fast food in the basement of the Ronald Reagan building a block from where I currently stood, or the deli across the street. A tall figure I thought I recognized ducked into the deli, making my decision for me. The pedestrian walk signal counted down from four, and I hurried across the six lanes, landing on the opposite sidewalk as the flashing red *DON'T WALK* sign turned to a hard red, and the rev of engines roared behind me. Pulling the door open, I identified my target.

"Jessica, it's good to see you," I greeted.

Jessica Williams turned from her menu perusal. The smile she delivered only enhanced her beauty, her white teeth bright against mocha skin tones. "Hello, Karina. What brings you to my neck of the woods?"

Even though I'm five feet nine and was wearing a pair of two-inch heels, I still had to look up to Jessica. She towered over most men, but where I'd noticed other tall women sometimes slouched to make themselves seem smaller, Jessica owned her height. I surmised she used it to her advantage in court and negotiations. "Meetings with one of our members, reviewing their legislative agenda for the fall. They ran long, and now I'm starving. Do you have to get back to the office, or can you join me for a quick bite?"

She checked her phone. "I'm free."

We received our drinks and sandwiches—tuna for me and a club for Jessica—and found a table for two in a front window. After some general small talk about her visit to the Hamptons, I dived into the reason for following her into the deli.

"How did Sadira's arraignment go?"

She gave me a confused look. "Didn't your sister tell you?"

"Jilly? No, we haven't spoken since yesterday. She told me she was headed to the courthouse to check on things, but I never heard back from her."

"Well, I can tell you, since it's all public record, the judge set bail at $200,000, she's got to surrender her passport and wear a tracking anklet."

My mouth dropped. "Is that usual for this type of case? I think you said you expected fifty or hundred for bail . . . and the passport?"

"The search warrant didn't turn up the diamonds, so surrendering the passport isn't unusual if they think she's a flight risk, which they do . . . because she bought tickets to Argentina—"

I drew in a deep breath and sat back in my chair.

"—two days before the diamonds were stolen," Jessica finished.

"When was she scheduled to leave?"

"Not until after school got out. I'm assuming you didn't know about the tickets?"

"Of course not. Wow . . . wow. Did she explain the tickets?"

"She's never visited before. She says she's on a bunch of travel discount email lists. This one came across her desk."

"Convenient timing. And the high bail?" I bit into my tuna sandwich.

Jessica finished chewing before replying, "It was a

compromise. The DA didn't want to set bail at all, her ties to the community are a bit tenuous and she's estranged from her family, but my associate Evans was able to talk him into setting one. He said the judge was in a cranky mood and wanted to make an example out of Sadira."

"Hm. I suppose it's good your associate got him to set some sort of bail."

"He is very good."

"Was she able to pay the bond?" I crunched into the dill pickle.

"I don't know. We can't find her passport."

"What do you mean?"

"Sadira's 'misplaced' it." She used finger quotes. "Your sister and Evans spent an hour searching her apartment yesterday. The cops didn't find it in their search."

"So where is it?"

Her brows rose and she shrugged. "You got me."

"She won't get out of jail without surrendering the passport?"

Jessica's cherry-colored nails reached in and pulled a salt and vinegar chip out of the yellow bag. "Nope." She crunched down on the crisp.

"Can't we look again? Maybe I can help search for it."

She sipped her water. "Evans said they turned the apartment upside down."

"What's that look?"

"I don't know." She shuffled around in the chip bag looking for the perfect specimen. "Something about this girl isn't adding up. Evans told me he felt Sadira was lying to him."

"About the passport?"

"No-o . . ." She put the bag down and contemplated her half-eaten sandwich. "Something else. He said he couldn't put a finger on it."

I thought about the lie Sadira had told my sister about making commissions. I'd already notified Jessica of the miscommunication and didn't feel rehashing it was valuable to the current conversation. Instead, I changed the subject. "Did you put an investigator on Tazim, or do you think it's a waste of time?"

"Actually, I did. My regular investigator was tied up with another case, so I reached out to someone you know."

"*Me?*" I pointed to my chest. "I don't know any PIs."

"Silverthorne?"

"Oh, right. I guess they do investigative work too."

"Apparently, they do everything."

"Yeah, they give Mike heartburn."

"I can see why." Jessica picked up the chips again and offered me one.

"No, thanks. Are you going to have them look into Sadira, also?"

She shrugged with a noncommittal look and bit into another chip.

Her non-answer spoke volumes, and we ate silently for a time, both of us ruminating on our own thoughts. There was no denying Jessica was smart. However this case shook out, the more information she knew about her client, the better her firm could prepare a defense. The dangers of investigating your own client could bring a lawyer to the realization that their supposedly innocent client was indeed guilty of the crime. Then the attorney is put in the position of defending a client, claiming they are innocent, even when they know the opposite. Some lawyers do this all the time. Others limit their questions, so they don't *have* to know the truth, and can put together a strong defense on the assumption of innocence. One of my

Constitutional Law professors, a retired criminal justice lawyer, explained this phenomenon. He also stated, "It helps lawyers sleep at night." It's one of the reasons I didn't end up working for a law firm. I also had a passion for politics, and even though some of my wide-eyed-just-out-of-college passions had the shine rubbed off, I wasn't yet completely jaded.

"Is there anything I can do?"

Jessica shook her head. "No, but I may need to get Sadira's keys from your sister."

"I think school lets out around two thirty. Do you need her number?"

"Evans has it."

"You're sure there's nothing I can do...?"

"I'll let you know."

"I feel bad. I thought I was giving you an open and shut case. Now it kind of looks like a stinker."

"That's the way the cookie crumbles sometimes. We all know it." Her phone rattled on the table.

I thought I recognized the phone number across display. "Isn't that Silverthorne?"

Her finger hesitated over the accept and dismiss icons.

"You can take it outside if you need to. Don't hold off on my account."

Jessica picked up and headed out the glass door. I watched her pace in front of the window where I sat. The conversation didn't take long and soon she returned to her seat, slipping the phone in her handbag.

"Anything of interest?"

She studied me for a moment, tapping a finger on the table.

"I understand if you can't—"

"Sadira never substituted counsel, she simply added my firm. Technically, you're still her lawyer and bound by privilege.

Did you know that?"

My eyes widened in surprise. "I figured I was bound by privilege, but I wasn't aware she left me on the paperwork."

"Against my associate's advice. That's the other thing that worries me about this girl. She's stubborn."

"Technically, you could share your information." I eyed my friend's pinched mouth and drawn features. "And . . . you're trying to figure out if you should."

"Not because I don't trust you to keep it confidential, and not that it really matters."

"Then what?"

"I worry your impulses might get you in trouble."

I couldn't help the chortle that escaped. "Seriously, I think you're overestimating my loyalties to this woman. She's a friend of my sister's." I made a dismissive motion with my hand. "No friend of mine. Right now, she's a client I was unaware I had. Do you need me to recuse myself and get off the roster?"

"Would you, if I asked?"

"Of course."

"I may do so. That call was from your friend, Rick. They've found a good bit of dirt on Tazim. Misty was correct, he's got a gambling habit. And Vijay *was* brought in to save the jewelry store. Apparently, he's an old family friend. From what Rick could find, a few weeks ago, Tazim was invited to a private poker game at National Harbor with a handful of high rollers. They think he was brought in as a pigeon to be plucked. Apparently, he's a bit reckless at play and a poor bluffer."

"How much did he lose?"

"Seventy."

I whistled. "Looks like a hundred grand in diamonds would help pay that off. Did you find his banker?"

"They're still looking into it, but a Russian mob-affiliated loan shark was mentioned."

"What about his broken arm?"

Jessica leaned closer and lowered her voice. "He told the ER doc he slipped and fell in the bathroom. Security cameras show that a black SUV, no plates, dropped him off around 1:00 a.m., less than a block from the hospital. It looks like he might have been shoved out."

"Could he have broken the arm when he fell out of the car?"

"Silverthorne doesn't seem to think so. Not with the type of fracture he obtained."

"In other words, the broken arm was a warning to pay up."

"Looks like it."

I wiped my mouth with a napkin and pushed the empty plate aside. "What's your next move?"

"Review the video from the store," she replied, sipping her iced tea.

"Jillian said there isn't any footage within the safe. So, he could have easily pocketed the diamonds and walked out without anyone seeing, just as he's accused Sadira of doing."

"We're looking to make sure it hasn't been tampered with. Silverthorne also wants to see if any interesting characters visited Tazim at the store within the past month few months."

"Ah—" the lightbulb in my brain lit up "—I see. Maybe the bookie came to him." I pinched my chin. "Do you think he paid the debt directly with the diamonds, or does he have to liquidate them?"

"Don't know, but you're right. It's something to check into." She took a moment to text Rick, her thumbnails tapped rhythmically on the screen. "Maybe he can find a batch of loose diamonds on the black market that match our missing ones."

"Can you subpoena the GIA certifications for those

diamonds?"

"We don't have to." She shook her head while continuing to type and talk at the same time. "The detectives took them. Evans has already requested it for discovery."

"If Rick finds something on the black market, a specialist could compare it to the paperwork to identify the diamonds. Yes?"

"That's what I'm hoping." Jessica tossed the phone back on the table, finished the last bite of her sandwich and washed it down. "You know, if you ever decide you want a job with a law firm, give me a call."

I laughed.

Jessica didn't.

I sobered. "You're kidding. Right?"

"Not at all. You're smart, loyal, trustworthy, and you think differently than a lot of my other attorneys. I believe you'd be a benefit to the firm."

"Well . . . thank you, Jessica. I'm . . . honored you think so." Her company—Geiger, Williams, and Portia, LLC—was repeatedly ranked in *US News and World Report*, Best Law Firms edition. "However, criminal law isn't my specialty."

"We'd find a place for you, and you'd bring contacts my other lawyers don't have. You're also a woman."

My brows went up at her last statement.

She shrugged. "We could use some more estrogen in the firm. If you ever want to sit down and talk about it, let me know."

The offer was tempting because I knew I could make a ton of money; even so, it wasn't my passion. However, I tucked the idea away in case things changed. "I will." We finished up and parted ways.

****

As I plowed through a backlog of emails, the theme song from the movie *Grease* sang out—my sister's ring tone. She'd played Frenchie her senior year in high school; it was still her favorite movie. "Hey, Jilly. What's happening?"

"Not much. You called me."

"Right." I closed my office door for privacy purposes. "I ran into Jessica Williams today and she told me about Sadira's arraignment."

"Yeah? Did she tell you we couldn't find the passport?"

"She mentioned it." I spun my chair around and stared out the window at the neighboring building, a red brick affair. "What's that weird tone in your voice?"

"I don't know what you're talking about."

"I'm your sister. Spill."

"It's nothing. Sadira asked me to do a favor for her."

I didn't like the sound of that. "What kind of favor?"

"Apparently, another one of her side jobs is as a courier. She asked me to make a delivery for her."

"What kind of delivery?"

"Some sort of package."

I didn't like this new development at all, but I knew if I flat out told my sister not to do it, she'd clam up. I had to tread lightly. "Did she say what was in the package?"

"No."

"And . . . you're thinking . . ."

"Whatifit'sthediamonds?" The sentence came out in a rush.

I replied with slow deliberation, "Do you think it's the diamonds?"

"I don't know what to think!" A huff blew across the line. "I mean, she's been a good friend at the school. She's always backed me up at staff meetings. She remembers my birthday. And I've never had cause to distrust her."

"I see." I spun back around to my desk. "Until now?"

"No. Maybe distrust is too harsh. Doubt or—or misgiving is a better word for it."

I picked up a pen and started doodling on a random envelope. "And you're not sure if you should do this favor for her?"

Silence.

"When are you supposed to make the delivery?"

"Tomorrow evening. Seven o'clock."

I did not like this at all. On the other hand, another kernel of an idea formed as my sister spoke. If I wanted Jillian's cooperation, I'd have to continue to be conciliatory rather than bossy, as she'd often accused me of being when we were kids. "I think . . . maybe . . . I should come with you."

"Oh, thank heavens. I thought you'd try to talk me out of it."

"Nope," I said firmly. "I think you *should* do it. It'll give us a better idea of what's going on with her."

"Okay. Swing by my apartment around six. That will give us enough time."

After Jillian hung up, I called Jessica. She didn't pick up, so I left a message. I debated making the next call for about ten seconds before dialing.

Rick answered on the second ring. "Karina Cardinal, what can I do for you?"

"Hey, remember our last conversation?"

"I do. Have you changed your mind?"

"No. I think I might need your services."

His cheerful voice—well, cheerful for Rick—turned serious. "What's wrong?"

"Nothing is wrong. My sister has agreed to make a pickup and delivery on someone else's behalf, and we're both a little leery. I want to make sure it's . . . safe."

"Is there some reason you believe it's not?"

I blew through my lower lip, stirring my bangs. "Okay, here's the deal, I know you're working with Jessica on Sadira's case. Officially, I'm also one of her lawyers, so I'm bound by privilege. We're unsure what this 'delivery' is all about, but I think Silverthorne should be there. You know, in case it helps with the investigation."

"Okay."

"That's it?"

"That's it," was his succinct reply.

I'd expected probing questions. It still rattled me how efficient Rick could be with his words. "Who will you assign? Josh?"

"Joshua is currently on another assignment. Jin is available."

I would have preferred Josh because of his lighter, more open personality. Jin's disposition could best be described as somber. He rarely cracked a smile; though I'd been successful in getting an occasional laugh out of him. However, from past adventures, I knew Jin's competence was top-notch, and there was the adage about beggars and choosers. "Jin is fine. I don't have his direct phone number."

"I'll have him text you."

"Thanks."

"And, Karina—"

"Yes?"

"Be careful."

"I'm always careful," I said offhandedly.

"No. You can be impulsive, headstrong, and stubborn."

I sputtered.

"I consider them some of your best qualities, but they have a tendency to get you in trouble."

"I'm sure I don't know what—"

He hung up before I could finish.

Two compliments today from people I respected. Must be a record. Although, Rick's praise was rather backhanded. I supposed I should take what I could get.

I realized Sadira's case had taken up so much of my free time, I'd completely forgotten my fight with Mike and how I'd left him swinging in the wind. Jillian had been correct about my lack of grudge-holding capabilities. It was time to let Mike off the hook. Though I didn't appreciate the invasion of my privacy, I knew it wasn't going to be a deal breaker between us. Riding my good mood high, I dialed his number; however, my pink nail hovered over the send icon as our parting words flashed through my head. Mike had warned me about staying out of trouble while he was gone. Not that *I* was in trouble, but he might see my interactions in this Sadira case as courting that fine line. Especially with the new escapade Jillian and I were set to embark upon tomorrow evening. I'll admit the last time he'd been out of town on a case, I'd left him a panicked voicemail as an assassin pursued Rodrigo and I up interstate 95. Was it better to simply wait and talk to him when he returned?

The other thing stopping me in my tracks—it hadn't occurred to me to contact Mike on Saturday when Jillian dragged me into this mess. Nor the past few days as the case developed. Granted, he *was* out of town and basically unreachable. The last time he went for training, I had to wait for *him* to contact *me*. And, technically, we were fighting. Still . . . I'd turned to Silverthorne.

Would I have reached out to Mike if he had been in town and accessible? Did I even want to tell him what was going on? Or would it be better to tell him ex post facto? After all, tomorrow's delivery could be absolutely nothing.

The screen turned black as my phone went to sleep while I dithered.

Was my fear of Mike's reaction the reason I hesitated to call him, or was it his job at the FBI that held me back?

"I'll call him after our courier job tomorrow," I said under my breath, tossing the phone back onto my desk.

Chapter Nine

"It's a hotel," Jillian said.

Sure enough, a large chain hotel about half a mile from Tyson's Corner rose high above us as Jillian pulled into the parking lot, and we rolled to a stop in Sadira's Audi. The luxurious leather hugged me in a cloying fashion, or perhaps it was simply the fact that, against my better judgement and over my objections, we were in a car we had no business driving. I wasn't aware we'd be taking Sadira's high end car until I'd arrived at Jillian's apartment and found the vehicle in her assigned parking space, my sister waiting inside, the air conditioning blowing at full speed. At first, I refused to get in and insisted my sister get out. However, after a hissing and immature back-and-forth with Jillian, I solved the situation with a quick text to Jessica. Her response reassured me; the police had found the vehicle in their parking lot and taken a crack at it. No diamonds. I still didn't like driving around in a possible felon's vehicle. However, my sister had made a good case for using the car as it was affiliated with Sadira's courier account.

"Where am I supposed to go?" Jillian asked. "Do I go inside?"

"Didn't you get directions?"

"Just the address and a name. Trevor."

"Well, we're driving Sadira's car. I suspect they'll recognize us. Pull on up to the front door. See if we get any action." Glancing in the side mirror, I was reassured by what I saw. Jin, driving a dark sedan, cruised into the parking lot and backed into a space where he could keep a visual on us. I had failed to notify my sister about our tail, hoping I'd never have to tell and she'd be none the wiser.

Jin had stopped by my office earlier in the day and offered to download an app to my phone so Silverthorne could track me. Having had such an app put on my phone, without my permission, in a former life, I wasn't too keen on doing it again, and politely declined the invitation. Accepting my refusal with equanimity, Jin then offered a small black device not much bigger than a man's thumb. It had a green light and a fat button.

"This is a GPS tracking device," Jin had informed me. "Put it in a pocket or your purse. Press the button for emergency." I accepted the compromise, tucking the doo-dad into a pocket in my purse.

"Jilly, I think that man is waving to us," I said, and pointed.

A young guy in ripped hipster jeans, a blue button-down, and unmarked navy ballcap indicated an open parking spot. He knocked on my darkened window, and it slid silently down when I pushed the button. His blue eyes were at half mast, but his facial expression clearly showed we weren't who he'd been expecting.

Frowning, he asked, "Where's Red?"

I sent a slanting glance at my sister.

"She's sick and sent me to take care of her job today," Jillian answered.

He took off his hat, and a thatch of bleached blond hair fell over his blue eyes. "I don't know about this," he mumbled, pinching his lower lip.

"Are you Trevor?" I asked.

"Yeah."

Jillian remained mute, so I took the lead. "I understand we're going someplace in Great Falls. You have the address, yes?"

Pushing the hair off his forehead, he planted the hat backward. "Yes."

"You've got a package for us to deliver, right?"

"Right."

"What's the problem?"

"You're not Red."

Jillian leaned forward. "I told you, she's sick."

"Red usually drives this car. It's her car." He scratched at the five o'clock shadow on his cheek.

My sister continued speaking with deliberation, "Yes. It's still Red's car. She's sick. She cannot drive today."

"And she sent you? She told you what to do?" He pinched his lip.

"Of course. It's not rocket science," Jillian snapped.

Pulling a cell phone out of his back pocket, he replied, "Maybe I should call J.T."

I rolled my eyes in irritation. Trevor couldn't have been more than nineteen or twenty, and he didn't seem to be the sharpest tool in the shed. "Look, you have a package. We're willing to drive it." I made a driving motion with my hands. "Either give it to us or move on. I haven't got time for calls to J.T. Quit monkeying around. Are we doing this or what?"

I didn't know if it was my irritation or reference to the illusive J.T., but whichever it was seemed to snap Trevor out of his indecision. I'd learned long ago, if you pretended you knew what you were doing, people tended to assume you did.

He replaced the phone and opened the back door of the car next to us. A short Latina wearing a royal blue, single-shoulder cocktail dress and black stiletto sandals climbed out. "You left your phone at home, right?" he asked her.

She nodded and opened her tiny clutch for him to check.

"Remember what I told you?"

She nodded again.

"Someone will bring you home after it's over," he assured her.

"Thanks, Trev. You don't know how much this means to me." She threw herself into his chest.

Trevor barely registered the hug. Peeling her off, he opened the back door and the girl—for that's what she was, behind the caked foundation, red lips, and heavily mascaraed eyes, she couldn't have been more than fifteen or sixteen—clambered inside. Jillian and I shared a shocked look, which I masked immediately when Trevor's face returned to my window with his phone in hand. "You ready for the address?"

"That's the . . . package?" I quirked my head.

"It is today. Is there a problem?"

"Nope. No problem," Jillian chirped. "Where are we headed?"

Trevor reeled off a street address and my sister typed it into the car's GPS on the dash. I rolled up the glass as Jillian backed out of the parking space and, following the GPS lady's directions, turned right onto Route 7.

We rode without speaking; the GPS voice was the only sound that broke the silence. I pulled down my visor and flicked open the mirror to observe our passenger. She stared out the window, watching the scenery of cars and buildings. Her profile held an excited half-smile, and her shoulders were tight with expectancy. The dress hugged her rather well-endowed teenage bosom, and her black hair hung straight over her bare shoulder. A small, inch-long white scar at her neck marred the toasted-almond skin tone.

Jin texted me. *Any problems?*

I considered this for a moment before responding. *I don't*

think so. It's not what we were expecting. Don't stop following.

Affirmative.

After ten minutes and half a dozen sidelong looks from my sister, I couldn't stand it anymore. "That's a pretty dress," I said.

She must have been in deeper contemplation than I thought, for she physically startled at my voice. Her eyes widened.

"I said, that's a pretty dress you're wearing."

"Th—" She cleared her throat. "Thanks. Trevor got it for me."

"That was awfully kind of him."

"I know, isn't he the sweetest?" She preened.

"The very sweetest," I replied with my own saccharine tones. She returned her gaze to the window, but I wasn't satisfied at all. "How did you meet Trevor?" I probed.

She stared at the back of my head, hesitant to answer, so I swung around in my seat and sent her a friendly smile. "Did you meet at school?"

"I thought we weren't supposed to talk. Isn't it one of the rules? No names, no talking," she replied sotto voce.

Jillian hit a pothole and we all bounced in our seats. We were thrown to the right, then left, as she swerved to miss a second pothole and over-corrected before getting the car under control. Luckily, there were no vehicles next to us in the neighboring lane.

I delivered her a withering glare.

"Sorry," she mumbled.

Replacing my friendly smile, I returned my attention to the girl. "Oh, don't mind Trevor's silly rules. It's just us girls. We won't tell if you don't."

"Well, I guess. . . ." She chewed her bottom lip.

"I'm Karina, and this is Jillian."

"Araceli, but everyone calls me Ara."

"Ara, you were saying about Trevor," Jillian prompted, keeping her eyes glued to the darkening road ahead as the day waned and the final rays of sunlight disappeared behind the buildings.

"We met at the mall. I was working at the Gap when he came in and asked me to help him pick out a shirt." She giggled.

"What's funny about that?" I asked.

"Well, I'm not . . . wasn't an associate, just a stock girl. I was folding some sweaters. He was so cute with that floppy hair, and kind of shy."

Shy was not the word that came to mind when I thought of Trevor. Barring his hesitancy putting the girl in our car, he'd been pretty forward in sticking his head in my window.

"You said you worked at the Gap," Jillian said. "You don't anymore?"

"No. My mom got real sick this winter, and I had to miss a few shifts to take care of her. They fired me. Can you believe it?" she said in an outraged tone.

"No. That's terrible," I agreed.

"Yeah. We needed that money—it's just her and me, you know."

I didn't, but nodded sympathetically. "And Trevor . . ."

"Trevor and I had kept in touch after our meeting at the Gap. I'd texted him about my mom being sick. She missed work, and when she don't work, she don't get paid. Just like me. You know."

More nodding.

"Anyway, we started getting together . . . after school and stuff." She dipped her head.

"Trevor is your . . . boyfriend?" I asked.

"Sure." Her head came up and she wore the infatuated grin

of a teenager in the throes of her first love. "He said he knew someone in the modeling business. I'd told him it was my dream to work in fashion."

"You want to be a model?" I tried my best to keep the skepticism out of my voice. She had the prettiness of youth on her side, but her teeth were crooked, she couldn't have been more than five foot three inches, and her plump cheeks were not those of the waifs strutting the New York catwalks.

"I know, I'm not tall. But Trevor says the Spanish magazines go for a different kind of look. It's true, I read *People en Español* and the girls in there *are* curvy. Latin men like ladies with some meat on their bones, Trevor says. That's why he bought this dress, it hugs my curves." Trevor was right about that. The poor girl looked as though she'd been sewn into it. "He said they'd probably start me with catalog work."

"And you're meeting these people . . . tonight?"

"Yeah, there's this swanky party tonight. Trevor got me an invite and a meeting with his connection."

I knew absolutely nothing about Latin magazine and catalog modeling, but I had my doubts. I sincerely hoped Trevor hadn't gotten this poor girl's hopes up. "Why isn't Trevor taking you to the party?"

"He had to work. But he gave me this 'letter of introduction,' he calls it." She pulled an envelope out of her clutch and waved it at me.

"Are you interested in other areas of fashion?" Jillian asked.

"Oh, yes. I'm in the fashion career track at my high school. I have an A in the design class. My teacher says I've got a real knack for it." Her eyes lit up as she spoke. "If I don't get a job with Trevor's friend, I'm going to try for *Project Runway*."

"That would certainly be exciting." Jillian slowed behind a line of traffic snaking its way through a four-way stop. "I love

Project Runway. Did you see last season's finale?"

The two chatted about the show, debating the best and worst winners and the idiosyncrasies of each judge. During their conversation, I texted Jin.

> *Everything still fine. We are headed to the following address. See what you can find out.* I forwarded him our destination.

As always, Jin was a man of few words. *Roger that.*

"The first season was still the best. Back when it was new and unpredictable," Jillian stated.

"I've never seen the first season. It was on after my bedtime," Ara replied faintly.

I frowned. "How old are you, Ara?"

There was a slight hesitation before she replied, "Eighteen."

I'd turned forward while texting Jin and regretted not seeing her face as she answered.

"So you're a senior?" Jillian asked, watching Ara in the rearview mirror.

I glanced back to see her response.

"Uh, yeah." Ara pulled at her skirt, then shifted to stare out the window.

"What high school?" my sister asked.

"What?" Ara's attention turned back to us.

"What high school are you graduating from?" I repeated.

"Oh, Woodsman," she mumbled.

"How does your mom feel about you attending this party?" Jillian asked.

"Oh, she doesn't know. I'm planning to surprise her with the good news. But . . . uh, you know . . . if I don't get the gig, I don't want to get her hopes up or anything."

I cleared my throat. "Where did you tell your mom you were going?"

"I didn't tell her anything," she said flippantly. "She works nights for a commercial cleaning company. I'll be home long before she knows I'm gone."

A thoughtless teenage plan that did nothing to set mine or, I'm sure, my sister's mind at ease. "Does that mean no one knows where you are?"

"Trevor does, of course. He told me to call when I get home."

"Don't you think you should tell your mom?" Jillian spoke gently.

"I'm a legal adult. I can do what I want," Ara replied in a sulky tone, crossing her arms. A mutinous pout altered her features. "I think Trevor was right, we shouldn't talk anymore."

Jillian and I shared a look, but her response effectively shut down conversation.

In a few more minutes we arrived at our destination—or the line of traffic leading to our destination, I should say. The cars crawled along the tree-lined, two-lane road. Red taillights lit up ahead of us, illuminating a six-foot wrought iron fence running along the roadside. The SUV ahead of us sped off down the street as the limousine ahead of him turned right through the open gate. GPS lady told us we'd arrived at our destination. Gravel crunched beneath our tires as we turned to roll through the six-foot iron gates.

A bald African-American man wearing a dark suit that stretched over his bulging muscles halted our progress, while a skinny Hispanic man in a white suit checked our license plate, marked something on his clipboard, and waved us forward to his location. I noticed a tattoo on his hand but couldn't discern its shape. Jillian rolled down her window as we approached.

White suit man leaned down to speak to her. "Do you have your letter of introduction?"

Ara passed the envelope to Jillian, and Jillian passed it out the window. The tattoo was a snake's head, from what I could tell, and the rest of the snake wound around his wrist and probably up his arm. We waited while the man in the white suit opened the letter.

He marked his clipboard again and returned the envelope to Jillian. "Give it to the major domo up at the house." Then he reached into the inside pocket of his suit, revealing a flash of black steel from a holstered gun. He removed a sealed blue envelope and passed it to Jillian. "This is for you. After you drop her off, proceed to exit out the west gate." He pointed to his left.

"Do we need to do anything else? Pick her up?" My sister blindly passed the blue envelope to me.

"No. Her return is taken care of. Proceed out the west gate when you're done." His words were delivered in the clipped manner I'd come to associate with my Silverthorne friends, and I noticed he spoke without accent.

"What's a major domo?" Ara whispered.

"Kind of like a butler, or head of the household. I'm sure we'll recognize him. He'll probably be carrying a clipboard and maybe a walkie talkie. Don't worry," I responded.

We continued our creeping pace up a driveway at least four football fields long. Oak trees with white fairy lights lined the gravel path. A few minutes later the trees parted, revealing a white manor house on par with the likes of Tara. At any moment, I expected to see Scarlett O'Hara tripping down the steps in a massive hoop skirt.

Men in suits and women in cocktail dresses exited their vehicles and meandered up an expansive set of marble steps onto the large verandah. The mansion was lit up like Christmas, every window illuminated, and more fairy lights wound around the huge Corinthian columns. Enormous flower arrangements lined the stairs and dotted the terrace. The double front doors were opened wide, revealing a curving staircase and hanging chandelier. Guests paused to pass their invitations to a dark-haired man at the top of the steps, wearing a tuxedo and carrying a clipboard.

I thought I heard Ara mumble, "Wow."

"That's your major domo. See at the doorway." I looked back at the starry-eyed teen.

Her stubborn bravado gone, she gulped and nodded.

"Are you going to be alright, Ara?" I wasn't thrilled to be leaving this young girl at this fancy party. Both Trevor and the front-gate guy had indicated that Ara had a ride home, but it didn't make me feel any better about leaving her. She seemed so young and inexperienced. "Here," I said, and dug into my purse, "this my card. Call me if—if you decide you want to leave early."

She took my card. "I don't have a phone. Trevor said they weren't allowed," she replied in a plaintive tone.

A woman on the steps hugged the gentleman she was with and snapped a selfie, giving lie to Trevor's assertions.

"Someone will have a phone you can borrow," I assured her.

The limousine in front of us came to a standstill. A uniformed valet opened the back door and half a dozen young girls in short skirts and stilettos piled out. They were closer to Ara's age than any of the other women I'd seen, and it made me feel nominally better.

Then it was our turn.

The valet opened Ara's door. "Parking or dropping off?"

"Dropping off," I replied.

"Don't worry about me. I'll be fine." Ara excitedly hopped

out. She gave us a cheery wave and bee-bopped up the front steps. Her enthusiasm stood out against the languor of the gray-haired man she bypassed on her way to the front doors, letter in hand.

The valet shut the door and waved us forward; Jillian followed the crowd heading out the west gate.

I looked down and realized I still held the blue envelope. "What's in the envelope?"

"I don't know. Sadira told me not to open it and leave it in the glovebox."

"It doesn't feel like diamonds." I flipped it over. "It looks like a greeting card."

"Can we open it?"

"It's sealed shut."

"Put it in the glovebox."

I did as I was told. A few vehicles ahead of us pulled off to a parking lot alongside the estate. The rest of us returned to our unhurried pace as we drove down a different winding gravel pathway, following signs that pointed to the West Gate.

"That girl's not eighteen," my sister said into the quiet. I didn't reply, and she continued, "Woodsman High graduated last Friday."

I phoned Jin.

He picked up on the second ring. "Any problems?"

"We are heading out the west gate of this plantation. Where are you?"

"Waiting at the west gate."

"Who are you calling?" my sister asked.

I ignored her. "Did you find out anything about the house?"

"A couple of things. When you get to the gate, turn left. There's a convenience store about three miles down the road. Pull in. We'll talk there." He hung up.

"Who is that?" Jillian repeated.

"Our back up." I pointed. "Turn left onto the road."

"Back up? What do you mean *our* back up?"

"You thought this had something to do with the diamonds. I made sure we had someone watching our back in case you were right and it went sideways."

My sister digested the information. "Well . . . I guess it had nothing to do with the diamonds."

"It seems so, but I want to know more about that house party. Pull into that convenience store up ahead."

Jillian turned into the brightly lit parking lot of a building that held the shape of a national convenience chain but had obviously changed hands; a big sign labeled it as High 7. Jin's black sedan pulled in next to me. He turned his face toward us, and I heard Jillian suck in a startled breath. I knew, from experience, the long scar that ran from Jin's brow to jaw could be jarring the first time.

"Stay here. I'll be right back." I exited Sadira's car and climbed into Jin's. It smelled of French fries, and a large fast-food soda rested in the cupholder. "What have you got?"

"It's nice to see you too."

"Oh, sorry. I wasn't aware we were observing the social niceties now," I replied with sarcasm. My interactions with most of the Silverthorne guys tended to be straightforward. Not much chit-chat.

He grinned at me. "You do it with Joshua."

"Josh looks upon me as an exasperating but loveable little sister."

"So?"

"So? So, I'm not even sure you like me."

"Of course, I like you." He said it so drily, I thought he might be pulling my leg. "Don't you remember? I told you,

'You're all right, Cardinal.'"

"Ah, and that's your stamp of approval? Thanks for enlightening me. I'll be sure to start all future conversations with such social niceties as, 'How are you doing, Jin? The sciatica still acting up?'" He guffawed, and I grinned back at him. "Is money changing hands back at the office?"

"No, the boys no longer take bets on *if* you'll make me laugh. They bow to your exceptional smart-ass-style sense of humor. Now their bets focus on which one of *them* can make me laugh. You want in?"

I crunched my face in contemplation. "That's a hard one because I don't know all the players. Is anyone a frontrunner?"

"That would be telling." He tapped his ear, where an invisible communication device must have rested.

It also let me know that our conversation was being heard by a random Silverthorne guy back at the control room. "Very well." I looked past his shoulder to find my sister leaning across the console, squinting at the two of us, as if trying to read our lips. Her inquiring actions returned me to the matter at hand. "Back to business. What have you got?"

"The manor is a privately-owned, historic estate. It can be rented out for parties, weddings, etcetera," he said, his voice returning to its normal, serious tones.

"Does anyone live there?"

"No. It's owned by Historic Land Estates, LLC."

"Who is hosting tonight's party?"

"A large IT company based in D.C. It's a junket for their clients."

A banging on the passenger side window startled me. Jillian's mutinous face stared back. I pressed the button and the window slid down.

"I'm getting some gum. You want anything?" she said in a

rather sharpish tone.

"Nope, I'm all set," I replied.

"What about him?" She indicated my seatmate with her chin.

I glanced over to Jin.

"No, thank you, ma'am." I swear if he'd been wearing a hat, he would have doffed it.

She waited for one of us to say something. Neither Jin nor I obliged her, and she gave up. With a *humph*, she stalked her way into the store.

I returned my attention to Jin. "Do you have a guest list? Is there a modeling agency on it?"

"No guest list but let me see if they have a client list on their website." Jin picked up the tablet he'd laid on the dash and began swiping and tapping. "Here's one, TCCM Modeling Agency. They're based in New York."

"Huh." I sat back in defeat. Trevor's contact was probably in town for the junket, and he'd been able to arrange for Ara to meet them at the party. "I see. Well, Jin, I'm sorry, I believe I've just wasted your time."

He flipped the tablet's cover closed and tossed it on the seat between us. "Don't do that."

"Do what?"

"Question your instincts. You have good ones. Eighty to ninety percent of the time they'll be spot on. This time it didn't pan out. If you start questioning them, you could put yourself needlessly in harm's way in the future."

"Thanks, Jin." I gave a sharp nod. "I appreciate that. You can clock out, I don't think you need to follow us anymore. Have a good night." I opened the car door.

"Good night, Cardinal. See? I can be nice." He flashed his teeth at me in a bad attempt at a smile.

Smirking, I closed the door.

He backed away as Jillian exited the store with a soda in one hand and a candy bar in the other. "You gonna tell me what that was all about?" she demanded.

I sighed. "Get in. I'll tell you on the way back to your place."

"Is he an FBI friend of Mike's?" she asked as we folded ourselves into the Audi.

"No. He's from a security company that I've worked with . . . in the past."

"That's a fairly nasty scar he's got. Ex-military?"

"Yes."

"Marines?"

I shrugged.

"You don't know?" She unwrapped her chocolate bar.

"Most of the Silverthorne guys are former spec ops. I don't ask a lot of questions."

"Why not?" she said with a mouthful of chocolate bar.

"Because they rarely get answered. I know he got the scar in Iraq, or maybe it was Afghanistan. I can't remember. He's *been there*. You know what I mean?"

She swallowed, nodding. "Too many have."

"He told me the party was legit. There's a modeling agency that's in attendance. If she's not eighteen, she'll probably have to get her mom's signature on the paperwork or something to work for the agency. Though I doubt Ara is modeling material, it sounds like this is a personal favor to Trevor. You know what I mean?" I laid my head against the rest, the leather smell surrounded me, and my shoulders relaxed.

"I agree, she doesn't seem to fit the mold."

Tension ebbed away, and I closed my eyes with a sudden onset of fatigue. "Who knows," I yawned, "maybe it'll work out." The car purred to life beneath us.

"Back to my place?" Jillian asked.

"Do you have any better idea?"

She pulled onto the road before answering. "You want to see a movie?"

"Not tonight." I yawned again.

"How about a glass of wine?"

"If I drink a glass of wine, I'll fall asleep on your couch."

"Coffee?"

I opened one eye. "What's up, Jillian? You have something you need to talk about?"

"No." She shrugged. "Just thought it would be nice to have company. We haven't had girl time in a while."

"What have we been doing the past few days?"

Jillian delivered an arch look my way. "That's not *quality* time."

"Tony is working tonight, isn't he?"

"He's on a twenty-four-hour shift."

I groaned. "Okay. Coffee. Decaf. Half an hour."

"Yay."

I ended up spending two hours at my sister's and was wide awake by the time I drove out of her parking lot past ten. Jillian had talked me into a game of gin rummy. While we played, we talked about Mom and Dad, her job, my job, her boyfriend, and mine. Both of us seemed to categorically avoid discussing Sadira and tonight's little adventure.

A few miles from home my mobile rang.

Chapter Ten

I heard a sniffle. "Hello?" I said.

"K-Karina?"

My heart jumped. "Ara? Is that you?"

"C-can you c-come g-get me?" The words were muddled by sniffs bordering on the edge of tears.

"Where are you? Are you hurt?"

"N-no. I'm not hurt."

I wheeled around the median, heading away from home. "Are you at the house?"

"No. There's th-this general st-store nearby. It says H-High S-Seven. I-I don't know the r-road. They had a p-pay phone."

"I know where it is. Go wait inside for me. It'll take me about thirty minutes to reach you and it'll be safer for you to wait inside. Okay? Tell the clerk you're waiting for your ride if he gives you any problems."

"Mm-hm. Okay."

The light ahead turned green, and the roadway, for once, was clear of traffic. I put my foot down, the little Honda's transmission downshifted, revved, and the car shot forward.

For once traffic karma favored me; it only took twenty minutes to reach Ara's location. I wheeled into the High 7 parking lot, slammed to a stop, and launched myself out of the car. Whipping open the glass door, I stumbled, slipping on the dirty tile floor, and barely caught hold of a shelf, which kept me from landing on my butt.

Ara stood in the corner near the lottery machine, a large

drink in one hand, her clutch on the counter, and her sandals dangling from a finger on her other hand. The graying Asian clerk leaned against the counter, chatting with her. The pair, startled by my entrance, stared. Another patron in the snack aisle popped his head up to see the commotion.

"Ara?"

Her eye makeup had been scrubbed off, all remnants of her crying gone. She looked even younger and more innocent without it. "Hi, Karina. Are you okay?"

"Yes." I straightened the handful of toiletries I'd knocked over. "Are you ready?"

Ara scooped up her little bag. "Thanks for the soda, Mr. Sing—and the advice. You're a wise man." Barefoot, she proceeded me out to the lot and paused, searching for Sadira's car.

"It's the Honda." I hit the button to remotely unlock my doors, and my car emitted a polite beep.

Ara got in the front seat, tossed her shoes and clutch to the floor, and buckled up.

We were five miles down the road before I spoke. "You want to tell me what happened?"

She shocked me by answering without further prompting. "They wanted me to take off my clothes."

"They—what?"

"The man, his name was DeShane. He had his assistant, Maria, take some pictures of me in my dress. Then he said I needed to strip down to my underwear."

"In the middle of the party?"

"No. They had one of the bedrooms set up. He said models must be comfortable in their bodies and he needed to see my lines. When I refused, he—he—"

I didn't pressure her, waiting for the story to unfold at her own pace.

"He offered me champagne. He said it would 'loosen me up.' Only, I think I saw him drop something in the glass, so I told him I didn't drink because my dad was an alcoholic, and he's in jail because he abused my mom."

The car's high beams raked along the winding road, lighting the sylvan woods on either side, throwing ominous shadows in its wake. I let out a breath through my mouth and said softly, "Is that true? About your dad?"

"Dad? I have no idea. He left my mom before I was born. She doesn't talk about him," the young girl delivered matter-of-factly. "But I didn't want to get roofied. I've got a final tomorrow in French. I can't afford to be messed up from Molly or Ex or whatever, you know. I mean, I'm not a square or nothing. I've done pot with Trevor and stuff, but for all I know, it could have been that date rape drug, GHB." Ara was a bundle of surprises.

"You're right. That's very smart."

"I don't know about that." She chewed on her soda straw as she spoke. "Because then he told Maria to explain it to me. Maria said that models are naked all the time at the fashion shows and shoots. They strip down behind a screen while two people throw clothes on them to send them back out."

Though I didn't like it, what Maria told Ara rang true. I used to perform in school musicals, and I remember one quick change the entire chorus had to make backstage—they didn't strip to their underwear but close to it, while half a dozen costumer moms threw the next outfit over their heads.

"They both tried to coax me to take off the dress. That Maria kind of creeped me out, because she got real close and . . . stroked my arm." Another car rounded the bend, lighting up our interior, and I glanced at my passenger. Ara's nose scrunched up. "I think she was trying to be motherly, but it just came off as weird. She was invading my space. You know, inappropriate touching. Then, you know, as they talked . . . I was thinking about doing it. But, you see, I have this big red birthmark on my tummy. I knew if they saw it, it would be all over. So I suggested a different outfit, maybe a robe. DeShane got mad, yelled, and threw his camera on the bed. He was a big guy. It kind of scared me. That's when Maria pulled him to a corner of the room and talked him down. Then he said forget the whole thing" —she sucked in a breath— "and he told me I was too short and too fat anyway, and that I'd need to lose at least thirty pounds before any man would want me. Then I ran out, crying." She exhaled noisily.

I couldn't imagine Ara losing *thirty* pounds off her petite frame. However, the modeling industry was known for its sticklike, bony figures and cutthroat competition. As much as I wanted to go back to that party and slap the shiznit out of this DeShane guy for being a jerk, he was probably right about Ara. She wasn't destined to be a NYC model, and, from what I gathered, Ara's heart wasn't really into the modeling side of fashion, but rather design. I said as much to her.

After chewing on her straw for a few minutes, she agreed. "Besides, I really hate wearing these super high-heels. They hurt my feet."

"Did you walk all the way to the store in those?"

"No. I took them off about halfway. It was too hard walking along the side of the road in them."

"I imagine so. Did you call Trevor?"

"Yes." She nodded. "Twice. But he never picked up. He probably didn't recognize the number. That's when I called you."

"I'm glad you did."

She sucked on her drink and we drove for a while, buried in our own thoughts. I felt bad for Ara's experience, but sometimes in life we must learn lessons the hard way. It was a good thing I gave her my number, or this night might have ended worse for her.

"Did you know" —she interrupted my thoughts— "that's the first time I've ever used a pay phone?"

"There aren't many left. I'm surprised that place still had one."

"Yeah. It's a good thing there were directions on it. Otherwise, I wouldn't have known what to do."

"You're a very industrious girl, Ara. I think if you put your mind to it, you'll make a splash in the design industry."

"You think so?" she replied in a hopeful voice.

"I really do." We were approaching the highway and I realized I didn't know where to take my young passenger. "Where do you live?"

She directed me to a low-income area in Arlington, but she wouldn't give me the exact address; instead, she had me stop on the corner of a major cross street. "Just let me off here. It's one way and a pain to get out of the neighborhood. I can walk from here."

"Are you sure? I don't mind." The sidewalk did not provide much lighting, and a dim yellow bulb marked the entryway to the apartment building Ara pointed to.

"It's fine." She gathered her possessions. "Thank you. You're a really nice person, Karina. Bye."

I waited until she disappeared into the apartment's vestibule before driving away. The red numbers on my digital clock glowed 11:21. Ara's apartment wasn't too far from my own home. With any luck, I'd be curled up in bed before midnight.

****

The elevator spat me out on the fifth floor, and I wearily dragged my tired body toward my condo. My ears perked up when I heard voices in the normally quiet hallway. The sounds grew as I rounded the corner and came upon a bizarre sight.

"Cripes. What now?" I muttered.

My elderly, eccentric neighbor Mrs. Thundermuffin stood in the middle of the hall, her hands on her hips, facing the scene that played out in front of us. A twenty-something girl with long brown hair who I ran into occasionally on the elevator was swaying her arms in the air like seaweed in water, eyes closed, humming to herself. Meanwhile, a paramedic and a police officer, seemingly oblivious to the girl's undulating, focused on something in front of my door.

I asked my neighbor, "What's going on?"

Mrs. Thundermuffin looked up from beneath a set of lavender bangs. She wore a salmon-pink silk kimono with an intricate black dragon embroidered on the back and a pair of Hollywood-style, fluffy mules. I'd seen her wear the mules before and had loved them so much I'd ordered myself a pair online. She sighed heavily and informed me, "Lysergic acid diethylamide."

"I beg your pardon?"

"These two apparently decided it would be fun to drop acid." She clicked her teeth in disapproval.

I eyed my judgmental neighbor, thinking her disapproval was rather hypocritical, being fairly certain Mrs. Thundermuffin had experimented with drugs in her heyday. However, Mrs. Thundermuffin's previous exploits were neither here nor there. What was of importance—the reason for the congregation in my hallway. "It's Wednesday. Who drops acid on a Wednesday night?"

"A pair of pikers, that's who."

I didn't know what a piker was and hadn't any interest in finding out. "Excuse me." I tapped the humming girl on the shoulder.

She opened her eyes, which were dilated and rolling in their sockets. "Oooo . . . bubbles." Her finger reached forward, as if popping invisible bubbles.

"Hello," I said as I waved a hand in front of her face, "do you know what's happening?"

Her eyes focused on me as much as they were able to in their current state. "He said he saw a dragon" —she continued popping her bubbles— "and it chased him down here. I don't know why. *I* didn't see the dragon." Her gaze returned to me. "Did *you* see it?"

"See what? The dragon?"

"Yeahhhhh. . . ." She breathed the word.

"Nope." I moved around her to speak to someone *not* high on drugs. "Hey, what's going on?"

The cop and the paramedic who were speaking in quiet tones looked up at me.

"Acid trip." The cop shifted, and I was able to see what they'd been hovering over.

A swarthy man with hair everywhere except his head was curled up on the welcome mat of my front door. The whitey-tighties he wore presented a distinct contrast against the dark Italian skin that muffin-topped over the elastic. He rocked back and forth in a fetal position, his eyes wide with fear, seeing a menace invisible to us. A mumbling spate of indistinguishable words poured from his lips.

"Is there anything you can do for him?" I asked the paramedic.

"Already done."

"Now what?"

He shrugged. "Now we wait."

"Are you going to arrest these two?" I directed my question at the officer.

"For what?"

I frowned. "Doing drugs, of course."

He raised a jaded brow. "They're just a couple of dumb kids. She" —he indicated bubble popper with a thumb— "told us she got it from a friend at work, and they thought it would be fun to try it out. They aren't hurting anyone."

"Well, maybe they could move their acid trip back to their own apartment. They don't even live on this floor," I complained.

"I know," the paramedic said, pointing at the pathetic figure at his feet, "we chased him up from the second floor."

"So what are you going to do about it?" I asked.

"Yeah, we can't have this going on in our building." Mrs. Thundermuffin stuck her nose into our little group. "I'll make sure the condo association hears about this."

"Oh, look, a UNICORN!" Bubble girl ran at the beige corridor wall, slammed face first into it, and then hit the deck.

I stared in shock. The officer behind me failed to hold back a snort.

Mrs. Thundermuffin hurried over to the prone girl. "Oh, my dearie, are you alright? Why, your nose is bleeding."

The paramedic sighed, picked up the orange and white box at his feet, and meandered over to the two women. A moment later, he had the poor girl upright with a wad of gauze held to her nose. She seemed none the worse for wear, as she promptly went back to her bubble popping. I doubted she'd feel the injury until morning.

Mrs. Thundermuffin was gabbling something at the paramedic.

"Ma'am, I think we've got it from here. You can't be of any further help. You should return to your apartment," he said in a sharp, abrupt tone.

Mrs. Thundermuffin rose to her full height of five feet one inch. "Well, I never—"

"The paramedic is right, ma'am." The officer cut off whatever tirade Mrs. Thundermuffin was about to rain over him. "Thank you for all your help. We can handle it from here."

Mrs. Thundermuffin glared at each of us in turn. I pressed a finger to my temple, just wanting it to all go away, but said nothing to contradict the two professionals.

"Well, then. I can tell when I'm not wanted." She stepped around the paramedic and swept down the hall, her kimono magnificently floating behind her in an exit worthy of the Broadway stage.

"Now what?" I asked the pair.

"Ma'am, you can return to your apartment too," the cop had the temerity to tell me, and the paramedic echoed his sentiments.

My lips thinned and I scowled at them, with eyes half-shut. "I would *love* to, Sherlock. Just as soon as you move Lard Lad out of my way." I pointed at the joker in front of my door.

They weren't expecting that. The paramedic looked down, shaking his head.

The cop rubbed his jaw. "I see."

"Um-hm. Just so," I said snidely, my patience wearing thin.

The cop leaned down toward the man and said in a cajoling manner, "C'mon, big guy, let's go back to your place."

"No, no, no. Dragon. Big green dragon." He stuck his thumb in his mouth.

"It's okay. I've slain the dragon. He's not there anymore." The cop crouched down and put a hand on the guy's shoulder.

He gave him a small shake.

"NO! NO! IT'S FIRE. I FEEL THE DRAGON'S FIRE. IT'S ON MY ARM." The mostly naked man slapped at the place where the officer touched him.

The cop shuffled backward. "When is that medication supposed to kick in?"

The paramedic shrugged. "Depends. Everyone's different. He's a big guy. It might not work at all."

"Can't you give him something else? Knock him out? Or put him on a stretcher and wheel him out?" the officer asked.

"Not if he's going to behave like that when you touch him. You're just going to have to wait."

"How long will *that* take?" I piped in.

"I can't give him anything more for another hour."

My jaw dropped "Another hour! You—you can't just leave him here at my doorstep."

The officer scrutinized the man, who was back to rocking in fetal position. "I'm sorry, ma'am, you'll have to be patient."

Frustrated, I snapped, "Are effing you kidding me?"

"If the medication I gave him kicks in, he may be ready to move sooner. Perhaps you can go to a neighbor's apartment to wait," the paramedic suggested as he helped the bubble girl to her feet. The bleeding had stopped, but her nose and mouth were a mess of dried blood.

I ground my teeth and glowered down at dragon boy. "None of you can do anything?"

No one bothered to answer my question.

I had no interest in commiserating with Mrs. Thundermuffin, though I'm sure she would have welcomed me. My neighbor at the end of the hall, Jasper—who I was surprised hadn't come out already—housed a small farm of reptiles in his condo. He was a nice enough guy, but I couldn't get past the snakes, so he was O-U-T, out. My neighbor across the way was a traveling salesman for a tech company and rarely home during the week. I had a spare key to his apartment, but it was inside my own, and frankly, I didn't *want* to go to a neighbor's. It was close to midnight, and I had work tomorrow. *Damnit!* I'd had it with this day. Between Sadira, Jillian, the Ara mess, and now this! All I wanted to do was get into my condo. I wanted to crawl into *my own* bed.

Is that too much to ask?

An impulse came over me. I'll admit, the following actions contained very little thought.

"DRAGON! RUN! DRAGON AT YOUR FEET! RUN!" I shouted at the acid-tripping mess, then grabbed a hairy foot with both hands. "DRAGON'S GOING TO EAT YOUR TOES! RUN FOR YOUR LIFE!"

He snatched his foot away, scrambled up, and proceeded to strip off his underwear, screaming, "HOT! IT'S TOO HOT!" Freeing his junk, he left his underwear in a white puddle at my doorstep and shoved the cop aside, then streaked down the hall, ricocheting off the walls as he scurried past his girlfriend and around the corner. "DRAGON! IT'S AFTER ME! DRAGON!"

I heard the door to the stairwell slam, and the last echoing calls of "DRAGON!" disappeared as he escaped from the imaginary fiery devil. The entire episode happened so quickly nobody had time to react. Except for the girlfriend, who was back to her seaweed impression, we all stood in stunned silence.

"Sonuvabitch," the officer mumbled.

"You better go get him," the paramedic advised.

The officer did not look keen on that suggestion.

"Whelp, problem solved." I dusted my hands together. "As you suggested, I'll return to my apartment now." Both men stared at me with equal parts hatred and admiration as I keyed into my home and stepped gingerly over the underwear. "Nighty-night, y'all." I slammed the door, flipped my deadbolt, and drove the slide bolt into the floor. Punching in the code, I silenced the beeping alarm system and staggered to my bedroom, shedding purse and shoes along the way.

I would probably regret my actions by morning, I thought, flopping face first onto my downy comforter. Then again, maybe not.

Chapter Eleven

Thursday morning dawned much too early, but I slapped at the alarm with a sense of relief and stared thoughtfully up at the ceiling. Sadira's little side job turned out to be a nothing-burger, and Ara made it home safely, a little wiser but none the worse for wear. It also meant I could call Mike with a clear conscience. Running half an hour late, a to-go cup of java in one hand, keys in the other, and computer bag slung over my shoulder, I opened the door.

"Oh, for crying out loud." I'd assumed the cop or paramedic would have disposed of the underwear in front of my door. They probably left it on purpose. Neither one of them had been impressed by my efforts to remove my neighbor. *This is my punishment.*

Leaving my work things in the foyer, I returned with a broom. Using the long handle, I scooped up the tighty-whities and trotted down the hall to the garbage chute. The underwear hung off the end of the stick like a white flag of surrender. To my relief, I met no one on the way that I might have to explain it to.

As I rode the elevator down, it stopped on the second floor, and guess who got on—dragon boy, dressed in a suit and tie, his eyes bloodshot, and his face drawn. He gave me a nod of acknowledgment, took the back corner, then faced the closing doors. I waited until we arrived on the ground floor, and as the elevator doors slid open, I turned and said, "Hey, seen any dragons lately?"

His eyes bugged, mouth dropped open, and his face turned a deep shade of scarlet. The elevator doors closed with him still on it, my peals of laughter still ringing in his ears.

I phoned Mike from the car. Unsurprisingly, the call went straight to voicemail. "Hey, it's me. I've thought about our last discussion, and I . . . may have overreacted. I know you always have my best interests at heart and understand why you did what you did. How about apologies all around, and . . . and give me a call, you know, whenever. And . . . um . . . well, I guess that's it. Talk soon." I'd practiced that little speech in the shower. It went better in my head, but I could live with it.

The morning was busy with internal meetings. A luncheon fundraiser in Crystal City took me out of the office for the afternoon. I left the office, wishing I'd roped one of my colleagues, like Rodrigo, into joining me. Fifteen minutes into the event, ennui and regret crept across my weary shoulders. None of the elected officials or staff members I'd expected to see had shown up, including the congressman who was the guest of honor. As a matter of fact, the entire event was thin of people. Our host made an announcement that a House vote had been delayed and the honorable representative would be arriving shortly. The little plump man in pinstripes and bowtie announced lunch would be served and invited us to check the seating chart to find our table.

Somehow, I got stuck next to a gentleman hereto unknown to me. About twenty minutes into the meal, I wished it would've remained that way. Normally, I enjoyed meeting new people. Not this time. On top of the fact that he hadn't stopped speaking since I sat down—talking with a full mouth, occasionally spitting food as he went—he also had the beastly habit of dropping names. You know the type—a person who throws around politician's and Hollywood names as if they were best buds and regularly vacationed on the Riviera together. Perhaps they were. I had my doubts. The four other people at the table were quietly talking amongst themselves. I envied them. A lady in a brown suit seated across the table shot me a pitying look. Clearly, everyone was on to this blowhard, but none willing to come to my rescue, lest they become the next victim of his jabbering.

I searched my mind, trying to hit upon a tactful escape that didn't make me look as boorish as my companion. He'd already ignored one of my dampening responses to his blathering. "And you know David, of course."

"David who?" I foolishly took the bait, giving myself a mental head slap as soon as the words left my mouth.

"David Geffen."

My brows rose. "The film producer?"

"Yes."

Of course, I didn't know David effing Geffen, but I saw my chance. "I'm afraid David and I had a falling out. We don't speak anymore," I said deprecatingly, and returned my attention to the salmon in front of me. I expected consternation, or at least a pause in the yammering.

Neither happened.

He chuckled. "Well, that's David for you. A man like that didn't get to his position without making some enemies."

I delivered him a withering glance through half-closed lids, which he seemed impervious to, because he carried on with his nonsensical story.

The tones of *Grease* chimed out of my handbag and I grabbed my phone like a lifeline. "I'm sorry, I must take this." Scooping up my purse, I exited the room. "Hey, Jilly. What's up?"

"Do you have time to meet me at Sadira's apartment?"

"What? Now?" My watch read half past one.

"Uh-huh."

I waffled. There was no way I'd return to the table to be yammered at, but I still held out hope the illusive congressman would show. "I'm at a fundraiser. Why?"

"I—I think there's something you should see."

"Are you there now?"

She hesitated. "Uh-huh."

"Shouldn't you be at school?"

"I . . . uh . . . called in sick today."

Little alarm bells clanged in my head. "Jillian, are you okay? If something is wrong, say the word coffee."

"Everything is fine. I'm here alone," she assured me.

"What's going on?"

"I'm . . . working on a hypothesis. Can you get away after the fundraiser?"

I checked my calendar. "I could get away by two."

"Okay."

"Text me Sadira's address again."

"Done. See you soon."

Chapter Twelve

JILLIAN

Jillian answered the imperious knocking at Sadira's door. "Good. You're here."

They hugged. Karina, dressed in a chic black pencil skirt and blouse, her long chestnut hair pulled back into a French twist, made Jillian feel a bit shabby in her jeans and green George Mason University T-shirt. However, in a moment clothing would be the least of her concerns. For the past half hour, Jillian had been having second thoughts about inviting her sister over. It was too late now, so with a tone of trepidation, Jillian said, "You'd better follow me."

Karina sucked wind as she entered the kitchen. "Jilly! What have you done?!"

A swath of credit card bills and bank statements lay across the long counter. Jillian blanched, wringing her hands. "I needed to pick up some more cat food. A-and I picked up Sadira's mail while I was here."

"Jillian Sarah Cardinal! What were you *thinking*! Opening another person's mail is a federal offense!" Karina exclaimed, flapping her hands in dismay.

"Relax. I didn't open her mail. It's over there." Jillian pointed to a small stack on the coffee table.

"If you didn't open it, where did this come from?"

"Uh . . . the desk drawer."

Karina's gaze speared her sister.

Jillian put up her palms. "Rina, just listen before you freak out on me."

Karina crossed her arms and her mouth settled into a grim frown. "Go on."

"Things aren't adding up." Jillian paced away, rubbing her hands together. "The diamonds. Sadira lying to me. Driving that young girl to the party last night." Karina opened her mouth to interrupt, but Jillian hurried on with her explanation. "Just listen, that courier job. And what happened earlier today. Everything is—I don't know—hinky."

"Wait. What happened today?"

Jillian rubbed her forehead. "I guess I should start from the beginning."

"That's usually the best place to start," Karina drawled. "You can begin by telling me why you skipped out on work this morning."

"It was Ara. I had this—this bad feeling about her. You did too." She pointed. "Oh, you can give me that blank lawyer stare, but I saw it."

Karina sighed. "Well, you can rest easy. I ended up taking Ara home last night." She went on to explain the unexpected rescue of Ara at the High 7.

When she finished, Jillian was momentarily stymied. Her mouth opened and closed a few times before she could form a response. "Huh. Well, I guess it's a good thing you gave Ara your number."

"You see, the courier job must be legitimate."

"Yes . . . well, that's . . . certainly a relief, but there are other things that don't add up."

"And those things led to this?" Karina indicated the paperwork.

"Hear me out."

Karina put her hands on her hips. "I'm listening."

Jillian's handwringing resumed. "First, Sadira lying to me just hasn't been sitting right."

"I can understand that."

"And . . . and . . . I began to think what *else* did she lie about. Maybe she *did* steal the diamonds. She had the means, but what's the motive?"

Karina's brows rose. "Did you find a motive among her bills?"

"Not what I was expecting to find. But I did find something strange."

"Go on."

"Look here, these are her credit card bills." Jillian picked up a sheaf of papers. "She's got a gas credit card, and a VISA. The gas one is normal. Regular fill-ups. Nothing unusual."

"And the VISA?" Karina didn't touch the papers Jillian held toward her.

"From what I can tell, she puts her groceries on here, drugstore purchases, and stuff—you know, average day-to-day stuff." Jillian put the bills down.

"Okay. . . ."

"And she pays it off every month. She's carrying no debt."

"I would imagine that's a good thing," Karina stated.

Jillian opened her mouth, then closed it and swallowed. "You know what, it's best if I show you, follow me." She led her sister through Sadira's bedroom into the large closet. "What do you see?"

Karina shrugged with palms up. "A bunch of clothes?"

"Exactly." Jillian turned in a circle with her arms out. "This closet is full of designer clothes."

"Yes, I remember."

"In the six months of credit card bills that I reviewed, there's not a single charge to a department or designer store, nor any online retailers that would sell this sort of clothing."

Karina fingered a silk dress. "Did you miss a credit card bill? Perhaps she's got a department store card, like Neiman Marcus or Bloomingdale's."

Jillian's cheeks burned. "I searched high and low but didn't find one. Everything is filed in an orderly fashion in her desk drawer."

"Maybe the police took them for the DA's case."

"Wouldn't they just gain access to the electronic files?"

Karina frowned thoughtfully before responding, "Maybe, yes. You're probably right. Maybe she has a PayPal or Venmo account."

"Which brings me to the bank statements," Jillian explained as she exited the closet, returning to the kitchen. "Look—" She picked up a statement at the end of the row. "—this is her regular deposit from the school. Mine has the same signifier. And these smaller ones I'm thinking are from the jewelry store. And here you see the outgoing bills, her credit card payments, cable, mortgage and HOA dues. I see no car payment. And there's no PayPal account. And you see here and here—random cash deposits of between $200 and $900."

"Yes. I see that. What I don't see is regular ATM withdrawals. Everyone needs cash occasionally. Or did Sadira strictly run on credit or debit cards?"

"Aha. You see it too. Anytime I went out with her for drinks or something, Sadira was always flush with cash. Yet, you can see right here, she deposited her jewelry store money." Jillian shook the paper in front of her sister's face.

Karina pushed the bank statement away from her nose. "Maybe she didn't deposit all of it. Maybe she'd keep out a few hundred for incidentals."

"Maybe, but what is also missing here?"

Karina took the statement and studied it. After a few moments her brows crunched together. "How does she receive money for her courier business? I don't see any deposits from an electronic account."

"I found nothing."

"Nothing?" Karina handed the bank statement back to Jillian. "It's probably an app on her phone. Maybe she does have PayPal or is paid in bitcoin or another electronic currency, and that's how she pays for her designer habit."

Jillian deflated a little, dropping the paper on top of the others. "I hadn't thought of that."

"See? I'm sure there is an explanation." Karina crossed her arms.

"I think there is one. But not the one you think." She reached into her back pocket and pulled out the blue envelope that Karina had put in Sadira's glovebox.

Karina arched a single brow. "What do you plan to do with that? It's sealed and neither one of us has X-ray vision."

"Well—officially, it wasn't mailed through the post office." Jillian gave Karina a look of wide-eyed innocence.

Karina's mouth flattened. "Jilly—"

Jillian held up a finger. "And it was handed to us. Sadira's name isn't even on it. Just this number in the corner, T-689."

"Are you ready to explain to Sadira why you opened an envelope she specifically told you not to?"

"She won't know."

"What do you mean, she won't know?"

Jillian pointed to the tea kettle. "I watched a few YouTube videos on how to steam open a letter."

"Cripes!" Karina threw up her hands. "What was it called, Spy School 101?"

Jillian's mouth twisted and she held back a grin.

Karina shook her head. "I guess you really can find anything on the internet."

Jillian fluttered the blue envelope, her gaze silently begging for her sister's permission—or maybe it was her blessing. Karina's jaw flexed. "Fine," she said through gritted teeth. "But you better be sure you can seal it back up."

A few minutes later, Jillian skillfully steamed the flap until the glue released, and pulled out a blank white card. Laying it on the counter, she opened it. Benjamin Franklin stared up at the sisters. Jillian counted ten crisp, unused bills.

Karina whistled. "A thousand bucks for driving a girl to a party?" Her sister carefully replaced the bills in the card and resealed the envelope. "You don't look surprised. Jilly, did you already open it?"

She shook her head. "I have something else to show you." The pair returned to the closet. Jillian walked to the back wall of shoes, which had been organized since the last time Karina saw it. She grabbed a hook at the top and pulled. The shoe rack swung away to reveal an in-wall two-by-two-foot safe with a digital keypad.

Karina didn't speak.

"Sadira didn't tell me about this. I found it—by accident," Jillian said.

"And you think it's got cash in there?"

"Yes. I also think it's where her passport is." She tapped the gray metal with a hot-pink polished nail.

Karina's mouth twisted. "Why didn't she tell you?"

"My thoughts exactly. Why not tell me where the safe was and give me the combination?"

"Because she's got something to hide."

"Like a bagful of diamonds and a pile of cash." Jillian wiggled her brows with the revelation.

Karina's jaw flexed and she pursed her lips.

"Should we tell the police? Can she be compelled to open the safe under court order?"

"I'm not sure, but *I* can't tell the police anything. She still has me listed as one of her attorneys on record. Everything you've just shown me is privileged."

"But—"

"But nothing. Legally, I'm required to provide Sadira the best defense. Contacting the police about a safe when I have no knowledge of what it holds and telling them my client *might* be hiding the diamonds the DA is searching for is paramount to malpractice. Worse, because Sadira didn't tell you or me about this stuff, *you* discovered it from snooping. *She* could bring us both up on charges. Damnit." Karina turned on her heel and stalked out of the closet.

Jillian found her pacing in front of the fireplace.

"I *knew*, the moment I saw all that damn paperwork on the counters, I should have turned around and walked out. But— you're my sister and I've got to support you." Jillian tsked and Karina continued, throwing her hands in the air, "Oh, all right, I suppose my own curiosity got the better of me. Damn, damn, damn. What a fool I am." She rubbed her temple as she marched back and forth.

Jillian twisted the ring on her middle finger. "Then—you may not want to hear about the other thing that happened to me this morning."

Karina's flashing green gaze speared Jillian. "Geez! There's more? *What else happened?*"

Jillian cleared her throat. "Well—I began to wonder what other courier trips Sadira had made in the past. And since I still have her car keys . . . well, I checked her GPS history." Jillian gulped at the glare Karina sent her. "I . . . uh . . . followed her last one to a rough neighborhood in Arlington."

"Mm-hm."

"As I . . . uh . . . was sitting at a stop sign, suddenly this teenaged girl threw a milkshake at the windshield. *Splat!* Chocolate shake everywhere. I hopped out and yelled 'What the hell,' at her. She seemed startled to see me, and she said, 'That's not your car.' I'd no idea how she knew the car wasn't mine, but I replied, 'You're right, it's a friend's car. What's your problem with it?' She said, 'I got no problem with the car. But your friend is a piece of shit.'" Jillian barreled on with her story, picking up speed as she related it. "Whoa! I figured, maybe, Sadira had given this girl a bad grade or something, and I said as much. The girl just laughed, flipped me the bird, and said, 'Tell that red-headed bitch I'll see her in hell.'"

During Jillian's story, Karina's frown turned into open-mouthed shock. "Then what happened?"

"I told her to wait, but she ran off. The car was a mess. I had to take it to the carwash."

"Where in Arlington were you?"

Jillian named the street.

"That's not too far from where I dropped off Ara. Hm." Karina chewed her lip. "Was this girl sober? You know, in her right mind?"

"I'm not sure." Jillian stared at her shoe, replaying the episode in her mind. "The entire incident was disturbing, but now that I think about it—she seemed a little whacked. Her hands were shaky, hair lanky and unkempt."

"Drugs?"

"I suppose she could have been high on something."

"Sadly, it's probably the explanation."

"*No.* High or not, she *knew* that car. And she *knew* I wasn't Sadira." Jillian stabbed the air with her pointer finger for emphasis.

Karina sighed. "Okay, run me through your timeline. *When* did you go for this little ride? Before or after searching Sadira's files?"

"After."

"When did you find the safe?"

"I found the safe when I returned. After the milkshake incident. That's also when I took the blue envelope out of the glovebox."

"How did you locate the safe?"

"Uh . . . by accident." It was Jillian's turn to pace away. "I . . . uh . . . kind of had a fit."

"A fit?" Karina asked.

Jillian turned back to her sister, nervously playing with her earring. "Okay, okay, I grabbed a bunch of Sadira's shoes and threw them to the floor because nothing was making sense. And . . . one of the stilettos got caught, so I jerked it hard enough to break the heel . . . and it shifted the rack."

"Maybe you should consider changing professions and becoming a private investigator, Jilly," Karina said drily.

Jillian crossed her arms defensively and shot back, "Oh, you're one to talk."

"Why I—"

"Painting. Dead senator."

Karina snapped her mouth shut.

"Don't forget the role I played in the painting incident. You didn't even have the decency to warn me what you were dragging me into." This time the hot pink nail pointed directly at her sister.

The two stared angrily at each other, waiting to see who would blink first.

Karina sighed, rubbing her temple. "Okay, this is a lot to

think about. I've got to decide who I'm going to speak to first. There's really nothing concrete here. Just a lot of supposition. And neither of us knows what that girl on the street was going on about. Who's to say she wasn't a disgruntled former student? What I can do is contact my Silverthorne friends and find out what they know. If there is anything to back up your—your suppositions, I'll have to tell Jessica. I won't allow her to be sideswiped by Sadira. In the meantime, I want you to—very carefully—put away everything you took out of Sadira's files, exactly how you found it. When you're done, put that blue envelope back in Sadira's glovebox. I'm going outside to make some phone calls."

Chapter Thirteen

Back in my car, I rolled down the windows to allow the warm breeze to clear my head. Too many thoughts bing-banged around in there, not the least of which—what had I gotten Jessica's law firm into? What if those diamonds were in the safe, and Sadira guilty? Moreover, how would I explain it all to Jessica? She would *not* be happy with my sister's "investigation." I puffed out a breath and decided to start in a different location. Scrolling through my contacts, I found the number I needed and pressed the dial button.

"Karina Cardinal, I presume."

"Batman, how's it going?"

"What can I do for you?" Not one for chit-chat, Rick got straight to the point.

"Have you finished your background search on Sadira?"

"It's not complete, but we've got a fair amount."

"What can you tell me?"

"Hold on." The tip-tap of computer keys came across the lines. "Her bank accounts look normal, and she's got a credit card which she seems to pay off every month."

Same thing Jillian found.

Rick continued, "She's got a hundred thousand loan on the condo."

"What about her car?"

"Hm, I don't see a car loan." Rick paused as he read the dossier. "Ah, here it is, she bought the Audi almost two years ago. She had a fifty-thousand-dollar loan on it, but two months later, she paid the entire thing off. It seems above board."

I chewed a fingernail. "Did you find out anything about her family life growing up?"

"That's . . . where it seems to get interesting. Six years ago, Willadeene Carson legally changed her name to Sadira Manon."

I frowned. "She changed her name?"

"Yes. She grew up in Oklahoma, went to Tackleberry High School. After high school she went to the University of Oklahoma, where she graduated with a degree in Education."

"What about her parents?"

"Mom and Pop Carson are still alive and living in Oklahoma where Willadeene grew up. It looks like they divorced four years ago. Kordetta Carson works as a secretary for an accountant, and Jacob Carson . . . he seems to have bounced around jobs."

"What kind of jobs?" I asked.

"Let's see—worked for a plumber, insurance sales, sold tires, construction, pizza place, about a dozen other jobs. Lately, he works for a fertilizer plant. What's with all the jobs?" he mumbled to himself. There was another brief pause. "Ah, this explains it. He's been arrested multiple times for drunk and disorderly and one DUI. Willadeene worked at a local restaurant from the age of fifteen. She doesn't seem to have much contact with her parents. No visits or phone calls from what we can see."

"Were there any abuse charges against the father?"

"No domestic violence charges. I only see one hospital visit by Kordetta; she had her appendix out. One for Willadeene when she was seven, sprained ankle. It says here that he's a member of AA. Sober four years," Rick said.

"Sounds like he was a drunken loser." The breeze blew a stray lock of hair into my eyes and I pushed it behind my ear. I thought about the uncle that left Sadira some money, and how it supposedly caused the rift between her and her parents. "What can you tell me about an uncle who died and left Sadira some money?"

"Just a sec." More rapid tapping commenced. "Nope. I don't see anything about a dead uncle. Kordetta has two sisters, both of whom are alive and living in Texas."

"What about the father?"

"Only child."

I let that sink in for a moment before responding. "So you didn't find any sort of insurance payout to Sadira or Willadeene?"

"Not that I see here. But, like I said, the background check isn't complete. Is there something I should be looking for?"

"I'm not sure." I drummed my fingers on the steering wheel. Jillian had told me Sadira mentioned getting a scholarship. "How did Sadira pay for college?"

"Scholarship," Rick affirmed.

Well, that rings true, at least.

He continued, "Although . . . it looks like she had to take out loans for living expenses. However, she paid them off in a lump sum last year."

"How much?"

"About twenty grand."

"That and the car seem like a lot of money." A gray-haired couple exited Sadira's building and I watched them get into their BMW. "Any indication where it came from?"

"None. She paid them both off in person. Cash."

"Any idea why she changed her name?"

"None. But might have something to do with her juvenile record."

I sat forward. "She's got a record. What's on it?"

"Don't know. Juvie records are sealed on the eighteenth

birthday."

"You can't get into it?"

"No-o." There was hesitation in his voice, and I waited to see if it would be accompanied by an explanation. The slightest sigh whispered across the line. "Let's say, not without calling in some favors. And even then . . ."

I remained silent.

"How important is the juvie record?" Rick asked.

I could supply no good answer. Not knowing what was on the juvie record, I had no idea of its importance. Maybe kids bullied her and she got into fights because her dad was the town drunk. Or she smoked weed, like so many teens. What would that information supply me? Or maybe she shoplifted because her dad took all the money to buy booze. That might be important to know. "I assume there is a high price to pay for sealed documents?"

"Something like that."

"So, let's assume, small town, the father's the town drunk. She's got in trouble at some point and ended up in juvie court. People talk. Makes a good reason to change your name." I bounced the theory off Rick.

"I generally assume nothing, but your conjecture makes good sense."

I played with my earring. "Do you see anything on her record as an adult?"

"It's clean. Sadira Manon has nothing more than a couple of traffic violations."

On par with what she'd told me in jail. She'd told me the truth about that, at least, so Sadira wasn't a complete liar. "Well—thanks for the update." I shifted and lowered the visor to block out the sinking sun. "So, who's up in the ring with me tomorrow for my lesson?"

"Me."

"Ha. You lost the rock, paper, scissors throw down?"

"I haven't worked with you in a while. I want to make sure the guys are teaching you what you need to know. Trouble tends to follow you, and you need to be prepared."

Startled and a bit taken aback by his sincere answer, I stuttered, "Well, I . . . th-thanks. That's very thoughtful of you."

"I take my responsibility toward you . . . all my clients very seriously," he said gravely.

"Yes, yes, I know you do. I never thought any different. And . . . you have *no* idea how much I appreciate it. You saved my life, and I can't ever repay you for that. . . ." I trailed, off unsure how to put into words how much Rick and his team meant to me.

"Also, your J-squared team is unavailable. Josh is still on assignment, and Jin's got the night off," he said with a hint of laughter in his voice, and I realized Rick had been yanking my chain.

"Smartass," I muttered under my breath. "If there's nothing else, then I guess I'll see you tomorrow."

"Did Jessica tell you about Tazim?" he inserted before I could hang up.

"Tazim? N-no. Is there a new development?"

"Tazim approached the Bulgarian."

I blinked and threw up a hand. "I'm lost. Who's 'the Bulgarian?'"

"He owns a liquor store in D.C. Lots of items come and go out the back of that liquor store. He's a known fence. From the intelligence we gathered, Tazim is getting desperate to sell a handful of diamonds."

I drew a breath. "And did the Bulgarian make the deal?"

"Not after he found out Tazim owes money to the

Russians."

"Why should that matter?"

"Protocol."

Totally lost, I threw up my hand again. "Protocol? Whose protocol? Gangster protocol?"

"Something like that. The Bulgarian wouldn't touch the diamonds. Sent Tazim to Yuri. Things like that are kept in the family." He spoke as if I should know these people.

"And Yuri is . . . ?"

"Russian fence. He owns a string of dry cleaners."

When he didn't elaborate, I prompted, "Did Tazim go to this Russian fence?"

"Last night, but the office was closed."

Again, he didn't elaborate further. I swear, sometimes getting information out of Rick was like getting a cat to poop on command. "I assume there's more."

"I've got Hernandez following him."

"Uh-huh. And Hernandez fouuunnd . . . ?" I drawled.

"Tazim's been on the phone most of the morning. We expect him to make the exchange soon. He has until midnight Friday to pay off the loan."

"Wait, Friday?" I frowned in confusion. "How do you know all of this?"

"We're good at our job."

"Yeah, yeah, but how do you know about his phone calls and stuff?"

"We have our ways," he replied in clipped tones.

"And what are those?"

Silence.

"You're not going to tell me, are you?" It wouldn't be the first time Rick didn't bother to explain. Our conversation about Sadira had gone so well, I'd assumed we'd crossed into that realm where he felt comfortable confiding in me. Silly me.

"We have our ways," he repeated.

Realizing it was likely they'd illegally tapped Tazim's phone, I blew out an audible sigh.

"Relax. We're the good guys. Remember?" he cajoled.

"You know what—forget it. I don't want to know. Tell me, are the police involved?"

"I've been talking with a detective I know at D.C.P.D. who works for the Intelligence Unit. They've been trying to shut this Russian family down, but nothing sticks. Tazim may be the catalyst. They're surveilling the fence."

"I see." I fidgeted with my earring again.

"Hey. This is good news. If all goes well, Sadira will be out by the weekend."

"Right, right. Great."

"That doesn't sound great. What's going on?"

"It's—" I struggled to put into words my confusion over Sadira. Rick's new revelations about Tazim toppled all of Jillian's conjectures, and my own, on their head. "It's nothing. I believe I've allowed my sister to spin me up and go against my better judgement."

"You were thinking Sadira had *actually* stolen the gems," he stated matter-of-factly.

"Maybe. Yes," I confessed, "we thought there might be a possibility."

"Because?" he drawled.

I squirmed in my seat, a bit embarrassed to confess, "We found a hidden safe in her apartment."

"Lots of people have safes in their homes."

"True."

"People keep money, jewelry, personal property titles, birth certificates—"

I interrupted his list. "Court documents."

"Correct. We didn't find a safety deposit box for Sadira at her bank. She probably keeps her documents at home. It's smarter than leaving them in a desk drawer." His arguments, delivered in a no-nonsense style, made me realize I'd gone against commonsense and followed my sister down a rabbit hole.

"Yes. You're right. Of course." If Sadira had her birth certificate and court documents from her name change in that safe, it could be the very reason she didn't want Jillian to open it. She'd changed her name for a reason and seemed very protective of her old life. Even if she had a juvie record, as far as I could tell, she was on the straight and narrow path now. Still, hanging out in jail seemed a bit extreme to hide your childhood identity from a person who's shown you nothing but friendship. On the other hand, if she did a stint in juvie, maybe jail wasn't too difficult for her to handle. "Thanks, Rick."

"No problem. See you tomorrow."

"Tomorrow."

"And, Cardinal, bring your stun gun. I want to make sure you know what you're doing with that thing." He hung up before I could answer.

I stared blankly out of the windshield, trying to put all the pieces together. Were Jillian and I a pair of fools searching for conspiracies around every corner? Did my past dealings with nefarious characters cloud my judgement? Was Jillian creating schemes because she was bored, or was she simply angry at her friend who'd broken her trust? I loved my sister, but growing up, she always had a tendency toward drama. She'd been a terrible gossip in high school—a trait she'd forsaken after rumors turned back on her in the summer between her junior and senior years.

Jillian trotted into my line of sight, carrying a case of cat food and a bag of kitty litter. She tossed it into the back of her car, then got into the passenger seat of my car.

"Did you get everything put away?" I asked.

"She'll never know." She wiggled her fingers at me.

"What about the cash?"

"Blue envelope is back in the glovebox. What did you find out from your friends?"

"Well, it looks like we're barking up the wrong tree. Tazim reached out to a fence with a bunch of diamonds to sell."

"No," she breathed.

"Yup. The exchange will happen soon. The police will be involved. If all goes as expected. Sadira will be out this weekend," I said succinctly with little inflection.

"Well, hm."

"Just so."

"I still think the envelope full of cash is suspicious."

I pursed my lips. "It does seem odd, but Sadira did perform a service. Maybe part of what those people are purchasing is Sadira's discretion. It did seem to be a pretty fancy party."

Jillian shifted to face me. "You know, she could be couriering other things—like drugs."

My brows rose. "Perhaps. But we have absolutely no proof she's ever done anything like that." I raised a finger, cutting off my sister's rebuttal. "Or that she's involved with drugs or anything else illegal for that matter."

Jillian harrumphed and crossed her arms.

"By the way, did she ever tell you that Sadira was not the name she grew up with?" I asked the question simply, keeping all manner of accusation out of my tone.

"As a matter of fact, she did. Said her childhood sucked and that she wanted to get rid of all memories of it."

I tilted my head in surprise. "She told you that?"

"Well, something like it. When I asked her what her real name was, she basically shut me down." Jillian shrugged. "And then the fashion show started, and nothing more was said about it. Why?"

"No reason."

"Was she a bank robber or did she murder her parents in their sleep and then change her name?" Jillian leaned forward, her eyes wild. "And she's on the run? And now we know who and where she is, we can tell the police, and you'll be protected because she misrepresented herself to you?"

I pulled back and choked out, "Lord, no! Jilly, you should write thrillers with that imagination."

"Maybe I will. I'll call it *Murder in the Night*. Mwahaha!" She laughed like a character in an old B-movie horror flick, tapping her two forefingers together.

"Her parents are alive and well and living in Oklahoma, as far as I'm aware," I said archly.

She dropped her nefarious character act. "Bummer. Thought we were on to something exciting for a moment."

"No, it looks like we've simply allowed our imagination and prejudices to jump to conclusions." I leaned back against the headrest and closed my eyes.

"Oh, come *on*." Her hand whacked my shoulder and my eyes popped open. "Admit it, there were some weird things going on. We just followed the trail."

"No. *You* pried into your friend's private files. A person who trusted you."

Jillian folded her arms in front of her chest. "She still lied to me."

"And apologized for that lie," I pointed out.

"Well, if Tazim really did steal those jewels, then I do feel bad. But what about the girl who threw the milkshake at the car? She's got *something* against Sadira."

"Like you said—disgruntled student. Whatever the case, I suggest you let Sadira know what happened when she gets out of the clink. If that girl is on drugs, she might be a danger to Sadira."

"Yeah, I guess you're right. So—want to grab some chow?"

"No. As fun as this adventure has been today, I now have to catch up on work. There's a swath of emails in my inbox that need answering," I replied tersely.

A crestfallen look crossed her features and her mouth drew in. "Fine." She opened the door to step out.

Feeling guilty for my irritation, I grabbed her arm. "Jilly, wait. I've been . . . meaning to talk to you about . . . taking some self-defense classes. I've been taking them for a while now and was wondering if you wanted to join me. I think it would be good for you to have some skills."

Her pinched demeanor changed to hesitant interest. "Sure, okay. How much do they cost?"

"I'll take care of your first lesson. If you like it, we'll figure something out. Meet at my place tomorrow evening at six. I'll drive."

"Okay, great. Uh, thanks for inviting me."

"Don't be bummed about the Sadira stuff. We just got carried away. These self-defense classes will cheer you up and take your mind off everything. I know the teachers. They're really good at their job and will prepare you to . . . well . . . to defend yourself, should the need ever arise."

Confusion crossed her pretty features. "Is there something you're not telling me?"

"No. It's simply smart for single women like us to be prepared for anything. You watch the news, violence can happen anywhere."

"Like today? With that girl?"

"Sure." I nodded in agreement. "Would you have been prepared for her to physically attack you?"

"Well, no. But the car was between us. I would have had time to evade her," Jillian replied in a sulky manner.

"But what if it wasn't?"

She chewed her lip. "Yeah, you're right. I should get some moves under my belt. See you." The door slammed shut.

"Tomorrow. Six. Sharp." I called through the open window.

She gave an absent-minded wave and climbed into her car.

I waited until she was gone, despising myself for the misgivings about Sadira that were still hanging about in my head, tapping my shoulder like an invisible ghost.

Chapter Fourteen

The *X-Files* theme song drew me out of the report on the new teen vaping statistics I'd been reading. The clock read half past nine and my living room had grown dark, lit only by my computer screen and my now glowing phone. The eerie song reverberated through the gloom. Months ago, I'd sworn to change it, but sentiment kept me from acting. I switched on a light, took a deep breath, and answered the call.

"Hello, Mike," I said neutrally.

"K.C., I got your message." His voice sounded wary but positive.

So much had happened today. It seemed a long time ago that I'd left that stammered message for Mike. "Right. So . . . how's it going?"

"Fine. It's fine. . . ." he trailed off, as unsure as I.

"I should tell—"

"Listen, I'm really—" We both spoke at once and then stopped.

"You go first," he said.

"No, I think I'll cede the floor to you."

Mike sighed, and I envisioned him running a hand through his dark hair the way he did sometimes. "I'm sorry. There's not much more I can say. I wasn't doing it to hurt you. I wanted to help."

"Our relationship put you in a difficult situation."

"Yes."

"You're forgiven," I said plainly. "And I need to apologize. I should have called you earlier."

"Why didn't you?"

It was my turn to sigh and stare up at the ceiling.

"K.C., are you in trouble?" His tone was curious with concern but without the censure I'd come to expect.

"No, *I'm* not in trouble. However, my sister has a friend who *is* in trouble, and I offered to—well, maybe a better way to put it—Jilly forced me into helping."

"How can you be *forced* into helping?"

"My sister is better than a Jewish grandmother at delivering a guilt trip."

He laughed. "What's the story? I'm all ears."

"How much time have you got?"

"Until six a.m. tomorrow."

I launched into a truncated version of Sadira's story, leaving out the courier services we'd provided and my sister's snoop-fest through Sadira's house. Although, I did tell him about the hidden safe she'd stumbled across. Mike, like Rick, felt the clue insignificant, and after hearing more about Tazim, dismissed the hidden safe all together.

"Tons of people have safes in their homes."

"Hidden behind a shoe rack?"

"You wouldn't *believe* the places we've found contraband and hidden safes."

I hear a distinct rustling and crunching, a sound I recalled from our college days. "Wait a minute, I know that sound. Are you eating those nasty pork rinds?"

He paused mid-crunch. "Um."

I rolled my eyes. "For the life of me I can't understand how you can eat those things. Your arteries are clogging as we speak."

"Yes, I'm aware of your feelings about the pork rinds. I

remember being in your dorm room one night watching a football game, having my snacks unceremoniously snatched from my hands and a tirade of their nutrition-less value rain down upon my head. Then I believe you flushed them down the toilet."

I blushed at his recall of the memory. "I think that's an exaggeration of what happened."

"It's exactly what happened."

"Well . . . I . . . thought you'd taken my lecture to heart and stopped eating them."

"Only in your presence."

"Oh."

"And now only on rare occasions. You're right, they are not good for anyone."

"Ha!" I said triumphantly.

He didn't respond, but I could hear, clear as if he was sitting next to me, the snapping crunch of those fried rinds, and it suddenly occurred to me that there might be a reason he chose to indulge today. "How has your week gone?" I asked.

"Fine."

"Just fine?"

"Not much I can talk about."

"Buuutt . . . you're okay?"

"I'm okay. There's nothing wrong."

My stomach grumbled. Mike's late-night snacking set off my own appetite. Dinner had consisted of a cup of yogurt and a pickle a few hours ago. I headed to the pantry to see what I could dig up. "Well, then, where were we? Oh, right, the safes. Tell me some of the nuttiest places you've found them."

"In the dishwasher. He'd pulled out all racks and stuck a big one in there."

I pushed some canned goods out of the way and rummaged

in the back, pulling out a box of cereal. "What was in the safe?"

"Ten keys of heroin, a hundred thousand in cash, and some jewelry."

The bowl I'd just laid hands on landed with a clank on the counter. "Holy crap. Is this something you should be telling me?"

"The case is closed."

"In comparison, behind a shoe rack seems relatively tame."

"Actually, many people hide safes in their closets. Sounds like your friend is a bit fancy with the shoe rack, but to each his own," he said with indifference.

I knew Mike had a safe for his gun in his bedside table, but our discussion suddenly made me wonder if there wasn't another one. "Do you have a hidden safe?"

He hesitated. "Yes."

"You do?"

"Yes."

"Where?" I froze with cereal poised above the bowl.

"That would be telling. I can't give all my secrets away."

"Is it like an FBI secret?"

"No. One day I'll show you," he hedged.

"Huh, one day? Like when I make it into the inner circle?"

He grunted. "I think you're already in my 'inner circle.' If you really want to know, I'll show it to you when I get back."

Okay, I'll admit, that made my heart do a little pitty-pat. Reanimated, I tilted the box and the cereal rattled into the bowl. "Now you're making me think *I* should get a hidden safe."

"Do you have a safety deposit box?"

"Yes, I got it years ago."

"Then you probably don't need a hidden safe."

"Why? My stuff isn't important enough for a hidden safe?" I teased, pouring the milk.

"I didn't say that. A home safe is good for things you want to be able to access easily. For you, something like any high end or sentimental jewelry would be a good reason to get a safe."

"Hm." I spooned in a mouthful of the fruity cereal as I contemplated. "I do have my grandmother's sapphire ring sitting in that safety deposit box. I don't wear it because it never occurs to me to go fetch it before fancy affairs, and I don't want it hanging around the apartment."

"Have you had it assessed?"

"Yeah. It's worth about twenty-eight grand."

He whistled.

"Yeah, Gramps must have had a good day at the stock market. It is a pretty piece and fits perfectly on my ring finger. I really should make an effort to take it out more often." I slurped up another mouthful.

"Tell you what, when I return, I can help you find a small safe to install, and you'll have a place to put Grandma's rings and pearls and whatnot. Sound good? And what are you eating?"

I swallowed, wiping milk from my chin. "Sounds good. Cereal. Your pork rind binge made me hungry. I only had some yogurt and a pickle for dinner."

"Don't tell me you're eating that sugary, fruity cereal with zero nutritional value? The box you keep hidden in the back of the pantry?"

Caught. "Uh."

"We all have our vices." I could visualize the triumphant grin on his face as he delivered the jab.

"Hoisted with my own petard," I conceded good naturedly. "Can we hide it behind my shoe rack?"

"Hide what? The cereal?"

"No, silly. Can I hide the new safe?"

"Darling, you can hide it wherever your heart desires."

I grinned.

We both chewed our fatty, sugary foods for a moment before Mike asked, "What's on the calendar for tomorrow?"

"Normal work stuff. No fundraisers or anything. I don't think I have any meetings on the Hill. So probably a quiet day, overall. You?"

"Last day of training, then dinner out."

We hung up a few minutes later. That little cloud of discontent that I'd been dragging around since my fight with Mike disappeared, tilting my world back on its axis. I finished the cereal and, still hungry, rummaged in my fridge for something nutritious, and barring nutrition, I searched for something edible that hadn't surpassed its expiration date.

Chapter Fifteen

Friday, a day a restaurant chain was established to celebrate, a day working slobs like me rejoiced in achieving by either dancing or, depending upon the week, crawling across that finish line at five o'clock. Today, I planned to meander across it in a stately manner; however, it was only morning, still hours away from the goal. I arrived at work on time with a cup of coffee in one hand and a stupid grin plastered across my face. I'd slept well, awoken refreshed and ready to tackle the day. Moreover, it was casual Friday, and since this was the first time in months when I didn't have a meeting outside the office, I was able to participate. I'd chosen a pair of dark skinny jeans, ballet flats, and a flowy blouse.

"What are you grinning about, Karina?" My coworker Rodrigo asked as I passed him in the hallway.

"It's Friday, of course," I threw over my shoulder. "And that checkered vest looks very snazzy on you."

He looked down at his bold black and white checkered vest and black jeans. "Too much?"

"Not at all." I paused at the door to my office.

"We're hitting happy hour at five over at Ramparts. Coming?"

"Count me in. But only for half an hour."

"Hot date tonight with your adorable fed?"

I laughed. "Self-defense class with my sister." My office phone shrilled, and I scooped it up. "Karina Cardinal, how can I help you?"

"Karina, it's Jessica."

"Hi, Jessica. I heard through the grapevine that your case may be dismissed soon."

"We're not counting on anything yet." Her voice sounded harried.

I sat down in my chair. "What's wrong? Something up?"

"Not exactly. The way this day is going, I just have a bad feeling."

"I'm sure it's going to be fine. Silverthorne is the best. They'll get everything nailed down for you to take to the DA." I couldn't keep the cheerfulness out of my voice.

"That's not why I'm calling."

"Okay, what's up?"

"Sadira's asked to see you."

"Me?" I said, surprised. "Are you sure?"

"Bernard passed the message along to me. It seems there is some urgency."

"What's this all about?"

"I have no idea, she wouldn't tell Bernard. And he said she seemed very agitated when she called. What?" A person in Jessica's office must have been speaking to her. "What do you mean, it's too late? Hang on, Karina." The lulling strains of Beethoven wavered across the phonelines.

Well, at least they have nice hold music.

The symphonic concert ended abruptly. "Do you think you can get over there today to see her?"

"Let me check my schedule." I tapped my cell phone, bringing up the calendar app. "I have time at ten thirty. Is that early enough?"

"It'll have to be," Jessica snapped.

Taken aback by her attitude, I wondered if she'd somehow found out about my sister's stroll through Sadira's files. I sent out a tentative feeler. "Is something wrong, Jessica?"

"I'm sorry. We just got screwed by one of our clients. I'm working on an injunction. Half my associates are ass-deep in a case of corporate espionage, the other half has now been reassigned to the newest debacle. I don't have time for this girl's hysterics right now. You'd be doing me a huge favor if you can go down, hold her hand, pat her on the head, and tell her everything is going to be fine."

"No problem. I'm sure it's nothing. She's probably in a froth over her cat or something. Don't worry. I can deal with it."

"Thanks, Karina. Sorry to cut this short, but—"

"No worries. Go get 'em." I shook my fist in the air.

The phone went dead, and I dove into my morning routine.

It was after eleven when Sadira walked into the olive-green, square room provided for lawyers and their incarcerated clients. Reinforced glass swathed one side of the wall for guards to keep an eye on things. Her pale face, less exotic without makeup and hair pulled back in a messy ponytail, remained neutral as the rotund female guard removed her handcuffs upon my request.

As soon as the guard exited, Sadira, still standing, slapped her palms against the metal table, leaned forward, and hissed, "What the hell does your sister think she's playing at?"

Needless to say, this was not the greeting I'd been expecting. Rising so Sadira wouldn't have the height advantage in this attack, I replied coolly, "I beg your pardon?"

"You need to tell your sister" —she bit off each word— "that she needs to stop driving *my* car around and asking questions that are none of her business."

"I haven't the foggiest idea what you're speaking of. What questions?" I'd never give my sister away. More precisely, I needed to know what Sadira knew—who'd been talking to her, and why she wanted me to deliver such a message.

"You don't need to know the specifics." She pushed off the table and pivoted away. "Just deliver the message."

Au contraire, my dear. Though I remained quiet, I stated in no-nonsense terms, "If you think for an instant I'm going to deliver a threatening message to my sister, you have another thing coming, *Sadira*." She crossed her arms. Before she could speak, I shifted my stance and changed my tone to a more placating one. "Now, if you'd like to have a seat and talk about it, I'm sure I can help clear up any concerns you might have. Come on now. Sit." I indicated the chair.

Sadira, her arms crossed defensively and with narrowed eyes, scrutinized me for a few moments before yanking out the chair and plopping herself down.

I returned to my seat. "Now, why don't you start from the beginning."

"Your sister has been driving my car around town. She needs to stop." She slammed down her hand, making the metal table reverberate. "End of story."

"I see. I will convey the message." Sadira seemed satisfied, but I wasn't about to let her off so easily. "How do you know she's been driving your car around town?"

"I just know." Her mouth flattened. "I asked her to do me one favor, and now she's joyriding around like she owns it."

"Um-hm. Well, I can see why that would be upsetting. As I said, I'll speak with her. Now, you mentioned she'd been asking questions. What kinds of questions?"

Sadira stiffened. "Questions."

"Who has she been talking to that concerns you?"

"People."

I waited, tapping a finger against my thigh. "Can you elaborate on that?"

"No." She picked at her chipping nail polish. "Suffice it to say, she's been asking questions that could get people hurt."

As soon as Sadira said the word 'hurt,' my cool cucumber act disappeared. My brows slammed together, and I hammered questions at her. "People? What people? Who's getting hurt? Is it my sister? You? Has someone been threatening you? What are you involved in? Drugs? Something is going on! What is it?"

She glared mutinously at me.

I drew in a breath and made a distinct effort to channel my tranquil Buddhist Monk imitation. "Sadira, I think it would behoove you to tell me what the problem is. If someone is threatening you, I can help."

"Ha! You have no idea what you're talking about. No one can help me on the inside. We're done here." She jumped up, banged on the door, and hollered, "I'm ready to go back to my cell."

I quickly stood, but the scraping of the chair against the concrete covered my exclamation, "Sadira, wait!"

The guard opened the door before I could say anything more. She replaced Sadira's cuffs and led her away.

I dialed my sister's number on the way to the car. It went to voicemail. "Call me as soon as you get this." I sent the same message in a text and waited.

After thirteen minutes, I gave up, started my car, and rolled toward the exit. At the red stop sign that led out to the street, I paused. Glancing left and right, I debated my options—return to work? Go to my sister's school to check on her and confirm she'd gone in today? Maybe stop by Sadira's apartment complex, make sure her car was still there?

Checking the clock on my dash, I realized I only had twenty minutes to make it back to work for an internal meeting. Sadira's apartment was the closest to my current location and the highway. A few minutes later, I cruised into her condo's parking lot. With relief, I found the Audi parked in the same spot my sister left it yesterday. On my way up the highway, I phoned Jillian again, with no luck. Figuring it meant she was in class, I didn't leave a second message.

My next dilemma for the day was deciding what to tell Jessica the next time we spoke. The drive back to work allowed me time to process the full ramifications of Sadira's warning. Jillian had been asking questions. Questions about what, and to whom, was first up on the roster. All the concerns we'd dismissed yesterday after my discussion with Silverthorne came flooding back. At the heart lay a thousand dollars in a blue envelope. Something else came back to me—Jin's warning not to dismiss my intuition. Clearly Sadira was into something dirty, but was it the diamonds?

I walked into the office meeting a few minutes late, sliding into the seat Rodrigo had saved for me.

"Where were you?" he whispered.

I shook my head.

Luckily, Hasina, my boss, arrived later than I, which gave me the few minutes I needed to gather my thoughts and organize my notes.

Hasina folded herself into a chair at the head of the table. She wore an elegant eggplant pants suit, which enhanced her olive skin tones, and her shiny dark hair was pulled into a low ponytail that hung down her back. Though she supported casual Fridays, I'd never seen our middle-aged CEO don a pair of jeans. I wondered if she owned any. I had difficulty picturing her in something as pedestrian as jeans. "Everyone, please turn your phones off," she said, taking the lead by laying her darkened phone on the table in the center.

Meetings with Hasina always began this way. Though I

appreciated her reasons for going phone-free, I'd been hoping to hear back from Jillian before now. With concealed reluctance, I shut down my cell and laid it in the growing pile.

"Karina, can you start us off? Bring me up to speed on your regulations committee meeting last week."

Hasina must not have had any afternoon appointments; our normally efficient boss allowed the meeting to drag on for over two hours. When it finally ended, I snatched my phone from the pile and drummed my fingers against my thigh as it booted up. The rest of the staff gathered their things and exited the room. A text notification from Jillian popped up on the home screen. Before I could bring it up, Hasina sat in the chair vacated by Rodrigo. "Karina."

I put the phone face down in my lap and gave her my attention. "Yes?"

"I wanted to congratulate you on your efforts getting the Harper-Finley Prescription Drug bill passed." She swiveled the chair to face me.

"Thank you, but I hardly did it alone. Rodrigo was my righthand man, and I never could have done it without the public outcry and change in political climate," I said with a wry smile.

"Be that as it may, it is a feather in the Health Alliance's cap, and in your own." Crossing her legs, she leaned back against the cushioned leather, laying a casual hand on the glass tabletop. "Rodrigo's too, of course. With your success, we've seen a bump in donations."

"That's nice to hear." Antsy to get to the text message, I felt my leg started to bounce. I had to make a purposeful effort to stop it.

"I'll be candid. Initially, I was worried I'd made a mistake in hiring you," she mused.

The statement didn't surprise me. It's never good for a member of your staff to be caught up in the middle of an FBI investigation, even worse immediately after a failed legislative initiative. If I'd been in her position, I would have considered firing me too.

She continued, "Your contacts and passion for the work kept me from replacing you. I'm glad to see my instincts paid off."

"Uh, thank you."

"Now that you've proven yourself, I look forward to seeing what the coming year brings."

"I do too."

She didn't make an effort to leave.

"Was there anything else you wanted to discuss?" I asked.

"Will you be joining the staff at happy hour tonight?"

"For a little while. I have plans tonight. Why? Is there something you want me to work on this weekend?"

"Not at all."

"Are you coming tonight?" I asked in return. The staff did the happy hour thing once or twice a month. The few times I'd gone, Hasina had not been there.

"I don't think so." She gave a wan half-smile. I noticed her lipstick matched her suit.

"No? Other plans?"

"My days of happy hours with the staff were over when I took this position," she sighed, and I wondered if that was a tinge of regret I heard in her voice.

"I don't think anyone would mind."

"Perhaps not. I used to go all the time. But my predecessor warned me about becoming too friendly with the staff." Hasina had been hired from within and made CEO less than a year before she hired me. Her youthful looks belied her age, somewhere in early forties, but I knew the establishment considered her young for the position. The last CEO had been in the position for over a dozen years—another woman, who retired at the age of sixty-one. D.C., though filled with high-powered, intelligent women, still had pockets of "good ol' boy" mentality. Undoubtedly, her predecessor had to fight to get the position and prove her worth on a regular basis.

Understandingly, I nodded. "I get it. No longer your colleagues, we're your subordinates." She glanced away. "Can I give you a piece of advice?" I continued.

"I suppose," she replied faintly.

"We all know you're the boss. The staff respects you. Coming out for a single drink for half an hour, maybe buying a round, wouldn't hurt your reputation, and it might go a long way toward increasing morale."

Looking surprised, she said, "I wasn't aware morale was low."

"It's not. You'd be banking it for the future. I think there are staff members who feel you've become—" I searched for a word that wouldn't be offensive. "—stand-offish."

"You mean an ice princess."

My lip curved, for that's exactly how I'd heard her described within a week of being hired. "As an outsider who's come in since you became CEO, I can tell you, no one doubts your ability to perform the job. I think people miss Hasina, the colleague. Showing a little bit more of that side wouldn't jeopardize your position and might make things a little less lonely for you."

Her deep-set gaze studied me, and I wondered if I'd taken my confidences too far. "Thank you, Karina, I'll consider it." To my relief, she rose, and I stood with her. "Perhaps I'll see you this evening."

I gathered my things and followed her out the door, where we parted ways. Hot-footing it to my office where I could check my messages in peace, I was intercepted by Rodrigo.

"Hey," he hissed, "what did Hasina want?"

"She just congratulated me—I mean, us, on the Harper-Finley bill." I didn't stop to chat. To my chagrin, Rodrigo trooped after me, parking himself in my guest chair.

"You were in there a while."

"I invited her to happy hour tonight."

Rodrigo's eyes widened in astonishment. "Is she coming?"

I shrugged. "We'll see."

"I'd be surprised. She hasn't deigned to join us since becoming CEO."

"It's a big job. She's busy."

"Or she doesn't want to play with the peons anymore."

"Or she's busy," I repeated, defending her.

Rodrigo lifted a shoulder.

I gave up with a sigh. "Is there some business you'd like to discuss, because if not, I've got emails to catch up on. That meeting ran longer than expected."

"I know. It went on for-ev-er." He rolled his eyes.

I waited in silence.

"I guess I'll see you tonight." He got up.

"Close the door on your way out, please." Finally, alone in my office, I checked my text from Jillian.

What's up?

That's it? I pressed the little phone icon. It rang and rang until it went to voicemail. I checked the time—2:38 p.m. She should be out of school. I rang again. The third time I phoned, she answered.

"What? What is it?" she answered testily.

"Why weren't you picking up?"

"I'm busy."

"Busy doing what?"

"Stuff."

I squinted at the evasive answer. "What kind of stuff?"

"None of your business stuff."

"Are you with Tony? Did I interrupt?"

"No. Why do you keep calling?"

Blowing at my bangs, I decided my sister wasn't going to illuminate my curiosity with the truth, so I tried a different tack. "Jillian, I had an interesting meeting with Sadira this morning. Someone has threatened her."

"Oh? Hold on a sec." In the background I heard her say, "Hi, do you know this girl? Are you sure? I think she lives around here. No? Okay." Her voice came back full volume. "Now, what's going on with Sadira? What did she do?"

"It's apparently something you've done. She told me to tell you to, and I quote, 'stop asking questions.'"

No response.

A prickle of unease skittered across my shoulders. "Jillian, where are you?" I asked with slow deliberation.

"Around."

Alarm bells went off in my head. "Did you go back to that neighborhood where the girl threw the milkshake at you?"

"What if I did?"

"Have you been there all day?"

"No, I went to work today."

"What about last night?"

Silence.

"Jillian!" I exclaimed with frustration.

"What?!"

"Were you there asking people about that girl last night? Don't lie to me, this is important."

"So what if I was? I snapped a photo of her. I'm worried about her. I think she might be caught up in something bad. Maybe I can help."

Oh, my bleeding-heart sister. "Jillian, whatever you're doing is putting Sadira, and probably you, in danger."

"I don't see how," she said defensively.

"Don't play dumb. That neighborhood is sketchy. You—one of the whitest girls on the planet—will stick out like a sore thumb. On top of that, you're asking questions about one of their own. You're never going to get anything out of anyone. Now listen to me—"

"Wait a minute. Yoo-hoo, excuse me, ma'am—Call you back, Rina." She hung up.

It took all of twenty seconds for me to debate my next actions. Snatching my purse, I trucked out of the office, pausing for a moment at Rodrigo's cube. "I have an emergency. Can you cover for me?"

Surprise etched across his features. "Sure. Is there anything I can do to help?"

"I'll let you know. Thanks!" Not bothering to wait for the elevators, I descended the stairs two at a time all the way to the garage and tore out of my parking space, thanking Karma that nobody got in my way.

Chapter Sixteen

The traffic—more congested than the middle of the night when I came back from picking up Araceli—had me gritting my teeth and reluctantly applying the brakes. I had to make a concerted effort to slow down, because getting into an accident would not help the situation. Twice, I hit the redial button. Jillian sent me straight to voicemail both times. I screamed in frustration. Sadira's agitation from this morning's interview and my own intuition jacked up my fear levels.

Finally, I reached the neighborhood where I had dropped Ara off. Not having a clue where Jillian could be, I began a grid search, circling one block and then the next. Slowing, I turned onto a one-way street; the driver behind me honked, and I waved him around. He sped past, blaring his horn, but I didn't care, because I'd spotted Jillian's sedan ahead. Karma continued to work in my favor because an empty space opened two cars ahead of where she'd parked.

Standing on the sidewalk, I realized I didn't know which way to go. On the side of the street where I'd parked, brick rowhouses that had seen better days lined the boulevard. The ugly brown brick had darkened to black in places from pollution, and chipped paint flecked off the row's white and green metal awnings that were popular in the sixties. Ratty air conditioners hung out of upper windows, the one above my head listed crookedly, defying gravity. I skittered sideways, fearful it might drop to the sidewalk at any moment.

Across the street, a grizzled man in a lawn chair sat in the shade of an apartment complex's roof overhang. The complex, too, had seen better days—graffitied walls, a broken street lamp, and general rundown condition revealed how little the landlord cared. The tenant rocked gently back and forth, humming to himself, and I considered asking him if he'd seen my sister, when she popped out of the alleyway between the two complexes.

"Jillian!" I hollered, and dodged my way across the two lanes of one-way traffic. The onlooker in the lawn chair yelled something at me, but I ignored his gap-toothed warning. Tires squealed and a horn blared at my thoughtless move.

"Rina, what are you doing here? Jiminy Crickets! You almost got mowed down!" Jillian snapped.

Stressed from my traffic-filled drive over and near miss crossing the street, I grabbed my sister's hand and hissed, "It's time to go."

"Wait!" She tried to pull away. "I've got her name: Trudea. That's the girl with the milkshake."

"Fantastic. Let's roll." I tugged harder.

"Rina, no," she retorted, standing firm. "*Listen to me.*"

Lawn chair guy had gone back to his humming and rocking, but those sharp eyes remained fixated on us. I took a beat and released my sister. "Okay, Jillian, why don't you tell me what this is all about. Why this girl? What does she matter to you?"

"Rina," she implored, her brows furrowed, "she's in trouble."

"How can you be sure?"

"A little boy told me. And before you open your mouth, you need to realize he's a smart kid. Just because he's young doesn't mean he doesn't know what's going on around here."

She was right. Kids often know exactly what's going on and are usually more honest than grownups.

"She's got a boyfriend who is bad news. She used to go to school regularly and get good grades, but this year she started staying out late, skipping class. The boy said she used to play with him in the afternoons before his mom got home, but now she tells him she is too tired, and to quit bothering her. He said he tried to help, but she told him to leave her alone. Rina—he described needle tracks on her arm."

My face drew down the more my sister revealed. "Sounds like she got involved with a bad dude. Maybe a gang member?"

"Yes, I think so too."

I glanced around at the low-income apartment buildings, then pointed. "You see that tag on the side of that building? It's MS-13. We are standing in the middle of gangland. It's not safe for either one of us to be here. Why are you taking this on?"

Jillian threw back her shoulders and put her hands on her hips. Her neon pink nails stood out against the dark slacks she wore. "I'm a teacher. It's my job."

"You're not *her* teacher."

"We're trained to look for this type of thing and report it," she said, justifying her position.

"So, report it!" My hand slashed through the air. "You have a name and a photo."

"I—I want to talk to her first."

I rubbed the beating pulse at my temple. "Okay, Jillian, what do you plan to do about it? Hm? She's not going to give up drugs just because some stranger tells her to. You and I both know she needs to take that step herself. She has to want to take it. If she really is the girlfriend of a gang member, she's certainly been threatened not to leave him. What's your plan?"

"Well," Jillian mused while she chewed her lip, "maybe I'll be that catalyst to help her. Maybe she just needs someone to give her a hand."

I shook my head. "I think your best bet would be to go to the authorities or the school system and tell them what you know."

"I plan to, but—" Concern and confusion washed over Jillian's face. She didn't speak, but through our sister connection, she might as well have.

"You're thinking about Sadira?"

"That's right. I want to ask her about Sadira. I've got to know what her connection is to this."

"You think Sadira's involved with this girl and her boyfriend? How? Drugs?"

"Maybe. No. I don't know." My sister waffled, chewing a neon nail.

My brows rose in disbelief. "You can't tell me Sadira is an MS-13 gang member. That's a stretch."

She looked away. "She's into something. You've got to admit, Sadira being threatened—after I started asking questions—is just a little too coincidental."

My sister wasn't wrong. Something was going on here. How Sadira played a role, I couldn't quite put my finger on it. "I get it. I understand why you want to help this girl. I just think you're going about it in an unsafe manner. There's got to be a better way."

"Let me tell you a little story. Two years ago" —Jillian held up a pair of fingers— "a *Washington Post* journalist came to our school for career day. She spoke to a couple of my classes. Afterward, we struck up a conversation. Something she said has stuck with me ever since: 'If you're not receiving death threats, you're not doing your job.'"

I rolled my eyes so hard, I believe I saw my frontal cortex. "You're hardly an investigative journalist, Jilly."

She crossed her arms and shot me a mutinous glare.

My phone rang, startling the both of us. "It's Jessica. I never called her back after seeing Sadira this morning. She's going to want an update."

"You should tell her."

"It's not that easy. I don't know what to tell her about my meeting with Sadira without revealing all the crap you did yesterday. Moreover, today's exploit can't be explained without yesterday's."

Struck by the reality of my statement, my sister pinched her lower lip in thought. "You might be right."

The ringing stopped and Jessica's call went to voicemail. I breathed a sigh of relief and assessed my sister. She seemed dug in like a tick, trying to find this Trudea girl. I figured I'd humor her and give her fifteen more minutes before pulling the plug on this research project. "Have you figured out where milkshake girl lives?"

"In that apartment complex." She indicated the big building to our right.

Music blared from one of the homes across the street, and an argument, whether on TV or real life I wasn't sure, raged somewhere above us. Three elementary-aged schoolkids ran out of a rowhouse with green shutters. A woman's voice hollered something in Spanish, and the tallest of the three turned back to close the front door, before catching up to his younger siblings. The three of them went as far as the corner where the older two began a game of keep-away with a basketball. Occasionally, pedestrians ambled along the sidewalks. Traffic ebbed and flowed down the street in spurts dependent on the light two blocks down. Lawn chair man had lost interest in our conversation and returned his attention to the street activity.

"Have you talked to neighborhood watch over there?" I asked softly, tilting my head toward lawn chair man.

Jillian frowned. "That guy might as well be 'hear no evil, see no evil, speak no evil.' I'm sure he knew exactly who I was talking about. He didn't even glance at my phone, just shook his head, hummed louder, and swatted at an invisibly fly."

His attention shifted back to us and his withered gaze met mine. I smiled disarmingly and his eyes narrowed. "Maybe we could try again. Excuse me!" I waved at him.

I couldn't have taken two steps before he rose and said clearly, "Time for *Hot Bench*." Quicker than a frog snapping up a meal, with agility that belied his age, the man folded his chair and entered the apartment complex's vestibule.

"See what I mean?" Jillian stated.

"Yes. Exactly what I told you would happen. These folks see us as outsiders." The blaring music ceased, and my last words were spoken too loudly in the sudden quiet. I glanced around. The boys on the corner with the basketball had disappeared, and the sidewalks were devoid of pedestrians. My Spidey senses went on alert.

The unsettling stillness was broken when a middle-aged black woman wearing blue scrubs exited a rowhouse directly across the street from where we stood; the screen door slapped shut behind her. Spotting us, she leveled a hard stare our way, then glanced up and down the street. "You'd best be moving on," she called to us before getting into a beat-up green Toyota, circa the '90s; the engine sputtered to life and the muffler rattled noisily as she pulled away from the curb.

I turned back to Jillian, who looked disconcerted by the woman's warning, and whispered urgently, "She's right. They probably think we're cops, or narcs. We don't belong and it's as obvious as the nose on your face. I've got a bad feeling."

Jillian, perhaps finally realizing there might be danger, nodded. "Yeah, okay. It's time to go."

She tucked her phone into her back pocket, and we approached the street. The rumble of an accelerating high-end SUV skidding around the opposite corner had us jumping back on the sidewalk. The speeding car screeched to a stop. My heart dropped to my stomach as two men wearing dark hoodies, low-hanging jeans, and skeleton bandanas around their nose and mouths jumped out of the vehicle and headed straight for us.

A third man came around the front of the car, and I yelled, "Run, Jilly!"

Pivoting, I took off. My flats pounded against the concrete as my eyes searched for anyone who could help. I got halfway down the block before Jillian let out a muffled scream. Stopping short, I went to turn back, but was swiftly blinded by a dark hood thrown over my head. It smelled of fear and body odor, and the prickly material scratched at my cheeks. A strong arm wrapped across my chest. I couldn't breathe, and panic coursed through my veins. Luckily, adrenaline poured in with the panic, and abruptly my head cleared. The training kicked in. My opponent was bulky like Joshua, but shorter than me. As if Jin spoke to me via mental telepathy, I knew exactly what to do. I elbowed him in the gut, then reaching back, I grabbed a handful my opponent's hoodie, and part of an ear. Digging in with my nails and pulling with all my might, I dropped down to one knee, tucked my head, and he sailed over my right shoulder, landing with a grunt and hard thump on the concrete. Thankfully, I'd been able to take my attacker off guard. I also suspected he was not as well-trained as my J-squared buddies.

I ripped the bag off and drew in the warm, pollen-infused spring air. My assailant remained on the ground in front of me, bandana torn off. The landing must have knocked the wind out of him, for I recognized the silent fish-out-of-water gasping motion. His hood had fallen back, revealing a strange tattoo design on his cheek, and his dark eyes were wide with shock. A vicious snake tattoo around his neck flexed with the movements of his jaw. Jillian screeched, and I turned away from the breathless goon at my feet.

They'd covered her head with an army-green ski mask, only they must have put it on backward because I couldn't see any of her face. Two hooded men carried my thrashing sister as if wrestling an angry alligator. She got a foot loose and kicked the shorter assailant in the gut. He grunted and let out a string of Spanish invectives before recapturing her ankle in a cruel grip that made my sister let out a pained whimper.

They were too close to the SUV.

I rose to my feet, but it felt as if I was running upstream through a swift river. "Jillian! NO! LET HER GO! JILLIAN!" My voice came out in a high-pitched screech of terror.

To my horror, they tossed her into the SUV's back-cargo compartment. The one who she'd kicked climbed in with her. The other thug hopped into the back seat, and the car started to roll away before he closed the door. My sister grabbed at the knit mask on her head. The truck swerved. The thug who'd climbed in the back with her threw a wild punch and she went still.

"Jilly?" Her name escaped my lips as a broken whisper, and I stumbled to a halt.

My own assailant sprinted past me after the retreating SUV, galvanizing me into action.

"Oh, no, you don't!" I gave chase, but my cute little ballet flats couldn't keep up with the fleet-footed Hispanic in sneakers.

The SUV slowed enough to allow him to jump into the cargo bay, and my fingers missed his shoe by inches. The driver gunned the engine as I continued to stumble after them. I'll never forget the smug look on the criminal's face, holding up his middle finger as the back liftgate slowly descended. Then the vehicle peeled around the corner, out of sight. The entire incident happened over the course of a few moments.

"JILLIAN! JILLIAN!" My screaming was so high-pitched, it jangled in my head.

A horn beeped. A driver in a low-slung, dark sports car swerved so close, a whoosh of breeze dislodged my hair as he passed and sped around the same corner as the SUV. Another car screeched to a stop on my right, and a middle-aged, balding man in khakis jumped out, phone in hand. "Are you okay? Did you get a plate? I saw it from a few blocks back but didn't get a plate. It looked like a Chevy Tahoe. Was it a Tahoe?"

Chapter Seventeen

I stared blankly at the man's shiny head.

"What?"

The humming in my ears made it sound as if he spoke underwater, and my vision began to tunnel.

"I'm on the phone with 911."

"What?" *Why can't I get enough air?* The humming turned into a drone of bees. I couldn't comprehend what was happening. It felt as if my limbs detached from my body, and I couldn't force my legs to move. Darkness closed in, and all I could see was a pinpoint of white on his polo shirt.

"You don't look good. Whoa. Here, sit down. Put your head between your knees and breathe. In and out. That's right. In and out. Slowly. Deep breaths. In and out." His voice sounded as though it came from afar.

Eventually, the noise receded and my vision cleared. When I drew my head from between my legs, I found myself sitting on the sidewalk. The man who'd stopped to help was speaking into his phone, and two more cars had pulled up behind his. The rest of the traffic moved slowly along one lane, and in the distance sirens wailed.

A woman in a flowered purple dress hovered, crouching over me. "Here, honey, take a drink of water. You look pale."

Gratefully, I twisted the cap and gulped down half the bottle. "They took her," I said hoarsely. "Those men took my sister. I couldn't stop them. My feet—" I stared down at my ballet flats. "—my stupid feet. Why didn't they move faster?"

"Oh, baby girl, don't do that." Shaking her head, she sat next to me on the curb and placed a warm, comforting hand on my back. "This is not your fault. Those men are bad people."

"I'm her big sister. It's my job to protect her," I said, fidgeting with the cap.

The bald gentleman hung up and glanced down at me. "The police are on the way. Feeling any better?"

I shook my head and took another drink. The altercation spun around my head—those last few moments where my fingers just missed the man I'd thrown over my head. *Why didn't I kick him or incapacitate him when he was down? Why didn't I throat punch him or jump on his chest to keep him down? Why was he able to run faster?* Incapable of putting together some sort of action plan, I sat dumbly on the sidewalk.

"Do you have a phone, honey? Is there someone you can call?" The kind woman's round Mrs. Butterworth face peered at me with concern as she held out her iPhone.

I gaped at the phone. *A call. Of course, I could call someone. But who? Who should I call, or is it whom? I always have trouble with those two. Who and whom?* I pinched my lips together, silently mouthing the word. *Who. Who. An owl goes who. Just like Owl from Winnie the Pooh. 'Pooh' and 'who' rhyme.*

"Honey, you okay? I think there's something wrong with her. Are you sure she didn't hit her skull?" The latter question Mrs. Butterworth directed at the balding man.

Snap out of it! a voice in my head that sounded an awful lot like Jin's demanded.

Pressing two fingers against my temple, I finished the water, closed my eyes, and drew a breath, desperately searching for clarity of mind. I needed to get my shit together. With every second that passed, my sister moved further and further away. Mentally, I swept away Pooh's rhyme-time and my self-abasement. *What's past is past. The future is yet to be written.* Sounds of rubber tires swishing against the asphalt, the man's foot tapping, and the trill of a cardinal's whistle filtered into my brain, and with it, lucidity returned. My eyes popped open, and I pushed to my feet.

"Whoa, where you going, honey? I'm not sure you should be getting up yet." Ponderously, the woman at my feet began to rise.

"Thank you." I held out my hand to help her up. "Your name?"

"Shirley."

"Thank you for stopping, Shirley."

"Well, of course." She pressed a hand to her chest.

"And you are . . . ?" I asked the balding man.

"Paul, Paul Chowdery."

"Thank you. My car is parked just over there." I pointed. "It's got my phone and contacts. You're right, Shirley, I need to make some calls. Be right back." Initially a bit lightheaded, the sensation dissipated as I walked to the car, feeling the black tarmac firm beneath my feet.

First, I called Mike, but of course, he didn't answer. I left a message. Even though it felt as though I was thinking clearly, had I been, I never would have left that voicemail. He wouldn't appreciate getting another panicked SOS from me. I had no idea if my next call would produce any sort of help, but Silverthorne had been there for me in the past, and, at the very minimum, I hoped one of them could help me figure out what to do next.

Rick's number went to voicemail. Josh was next on the list.

"Go for Joshua."

"Josh," I said, my voice garbled. I cleared my throat, still raspy from the train whistle-style screaming. "It's Karina."

"What's the matter? You sound sick."

"I know you're on assignment, but I was hoping you could help me get in touch with Rick."

"What's wrong?"

"Oh, God." I pressed fingers to my temple. "I don't know how to say it. My sister's been kidnapped by, I think, a drug cartel."

He paused for a beat. "This isn't a punchline, is it?"

"I wish. We were in this scary neighborhood and a carload of Hispanic gang members jumped out of their SUV and snatched my sister. They tried to get me, too, but I was able to fight them off."

"Good girl," he mumbled under his breath. "Have you called the police?"

"Yes, some guy named Chowdery saw it and pulled over to help."

"Stay there. We'll be there soon." He delivered his command like an officer to a subordinate, in a manner that brooked no argument.

"Wait, don't you want to know where I am?" I spoke to a dial tone.

Paramedics wheeled onto the scene, followed closely by an Arlington County police car. Paul and Shirley flagged down the officer, and I returned to my coterie of Good Samaritans.

A handsome, black-haired gentleman with olive skin, dressed in a silvery suit, had joined Paul and Shirley while I was on the phone. "Hello, I'm Jamal," he said with a British accent.

"Karina." We shook hands.

"I apologize for the scare I must have given you earlier. But I was so focused on tracking down the men who took your friend."

"Scare?"

"Yes, with my car. I blew past rather close," Jamal

explained. "Shirley was telling me that you took affright and almost fainted."

"Oh, you must have been in the sports car. I didn't realize you were chasing them. Wait! Did you catch up?" My hope buoyed, and I'm afraid I clawed at his beautifully cut Italian suit. "Do you know where they went?"

He took my hands in his large ones and his face turned somber. "I'm afraid not. I was cut off three blocks down, almost causing an accident. By the time the traffic cleared, the vehicle disappeared. I drove around looking, but . . . I'm so terribly sorry." He shrugged regretfully.

My shoulders deflated along with my optimism. "Thank you for trying."

The officer reached our crew. "I'm Officer Benko. Someone reported an abduction."

"That was me," Paul said, then proceeded to explain what he'd seen from the stoplight a few blocks down the road.

Shirley interrupted a few times with her own recollections from sitting behind Paul at the light, and Jamal nodded along, infusing the conversation with what he remembered. I told them what happened and gave detailed descriptions of my sister's orange blouse and dark gray slacks. During my explanation, Officer Benko was joined by four more policemen. Two roped off traffic at the end of the street, detouring cars, while the other two canvassed the neighborhood, talking to the crowd of gawkers that had gathered—including, I noticed, hear no evil, see no evil from the lawn chair. *Hot Bench* must have ended.

"I think it was a Chevy Tahoe," Paul said.

"Lincoln Navigator," Jamal and I pronounced together.

Benko, who'd been taking notes, paused. "Which one was it?"

"It was a Navigator," I stated firmly, recalling the silver

word on the liftgate as it closed in my face.

"She's correct, it was a Navigator," Jamal agreed, backing me up.

"Did either of you happen to get a plate? Even a partial will help," Benko said.

"There wasn't one," Jamal and I spoke as one.

"They must have stripped it off," I continued.

Benko tapped his pencil against the pad. "Any other identifying marks you can remember from the vehicle besides make and color?"

"It had spinney wheels."

"Spinney wheels?" Benko's brows crunched in confusion.

"Yeah, you know those rims that keep spinning when you stop." I made a circular motion with my finger. "Spinney wheels."

"Spinning rims." He made a note on his pad. "Now you said you could recognize one of the assailants if you saw him again."

"Absolutely." I squinted into the middle distance. "I'll never forget that smug look as long as I live."

"Did he have any identifying tattoos?"

"Yes, a snake right here on his neck, and a strange design on his face. A pattern, like a Maori warrior, from his left cheek all the way around his ear. Here, maybe I can draw it." The officer handed over his notepad and I drew a curved shape and spiral-like pattern. "I'm afraid I'm not an artist, but kind of like this. If I saw it again, I'd recognize it. Don't you have a tattoo database or something I could look at?" Just then, I spotted a blond head as it detached itself from the crowd.

"Josh, you're here!" I shoved the pen and pad at the officer and pushed past him, throwing myself into Josh's muscled chest, and the warmth of his arms encircled me.

"Seems like you're in another pickle, Karina." His warm

breath tickled the top of my head.

I looked up into his concerned blue gaze. "Thank you for coming. I thought you were on assignment."

"The prince left this morning."

"How did you know where to find me?"

"You've still got our tracker in your purse."

I stepped back, holding on to his massive biceps. "Thank God you're here. They took Jillian. I've got to get her back. Can you help?"

"Of course," he said simply.

"Ma'am?" It was Benko, trying to gain my attention. I turned back to him. "These are Detectives Perez and Garcia. They're from the Arlington Gang Unit. They'd like to speak with you."

Detective Perez was dressed in worn jeans, running shoes, and a black T-shirt. He had brown hair, his own neck tattoo, and couldn't have been more than twenty-seven. On the other hand, Garcia's face was pockmarked and lined from years in the sun—or possibly on-the-job stress. His brows and goatee were thick with salt-and-pepper; I imagine his hair would have been the same, but he'd chosen to shave it. He wore a light blue button-down with black jeans and black work boots. Both wore guarded expressions, as though they weighed each word spoken.

"Benko said you saw one of their faces. He had a swirled tattoo and a snake on his neck?" Perez asked.

"That's right."

"Is this the man you saw?" He held out his phone.

Instantly, I recognized his face and tattoos. "That's him." Perez and Garcia shared a look. "Who is he?"

"I'm afraid your sister has been kidnapped by MS-13 gang members," Garcia stated.

His declaration held no surprise. I'd warned Jilly we were in their territory, but having Garcia confirm my fears did nothing to calm my current agitation; if anything, the boiling acid in my stomach churned up to hurricane level.

"The man you identified is Hector Cortez," Perez continued. "He's a soldier for Enrico Montoya, the head of the MS-13 gang around here."

"And I imagine he's got a rap sheet as long as my arm," I whispered with trepidation.

"Longer," Perez confirmed.

"So this guy Hector lives around here? You can get my sister back, right? I mean, you can hunt this guy down and raid his place. Right?" Desperation flowed through my questions.

Garcia spoke in measured tones, "We'll send officers to his last known address, but it's unlikely we'll find your sister there. MS-13 is well-organized and there are a number of places they could take her and hide Cortez."

"But you know his friends. Right? You can do a grid search and start kicking down doors of those guys too. Right? Like they do on television." I barely paused for breath as one idea flowed to the next. "Do you think they'll make a ransom demand? I don't have a lot of money, but I'm sure I could come up with something."

There was a distinct pause before Perez answered, "It would be unusual for this gang to make a ransom demand. We are going to do everything we can to find your sister, but we can't go around kicking in doors. If we go to the wrong house—they'll move her, or . . ." He didn't finish that thought.

"Kill her. That's what you were going to say, right?" I gritted out.

"Move her. Then we'll be that much further behind. We have to approach this methodically," Garcia explained.

I clenched my teeth. "Look, I'm not stupid. I know these

men are vicious. Do you think she's alive? Or do you think they took her to kill her somewhere else? Just tell me."

My gaze bounced between the two, but it was Perez who answered, "I can't speak for the mentality of the gang. There is a possibility they may have taken her for another purpose."

"What other purpose?" The question popped out, although I wasn't sure I wanted to hear the answer. I had a feeling I already knew the "other purpose" to which Perez referred.

"They may pass her along to gang members outside of the area and use her—"

Garcia forestalled his partner's explanation with a discreet elbow nudge.

I put a hand to my mouth and swallowed back the bile in my throat.

Josh slipped an arm around my shoulder and finished their thought. "Before they traffic her, you mean. Karina can handle it, and she's better off knowing."

The detectives gave me a pitying glance. I wasn't so sure Josh was correct. Ignorance is certainly less stressful and allows one to hope.

"Do you have a photo of your sister?" Garcia asked.

Swiping through my gallery, I found a recent picture. The pair of us stood in front of a local brewery. Her beautiful chocolate hair hung elegantly over her shoulder, and her smile lit up her face. Perez and Garcia each studied the photo; if anything, Garcia's frown turned fiercer.

"Can you text that to me?" Garcia asked.

"Yes, of course. Input your number here." After he typed in his number, I sent the photo along, and another for good measure.

While Garcia and I monkeyed with the pictures, Perez's phone binged with multiple incoming texts. The detective's studied response and deadpan features did nothing to calm my nerves. He looked up from his phone and searched the crowd, then his gaze swept the apartment rooftops. "Ma'am, can you and your friend come over here?"

He passed his phone over to Garcia and led the way to the back of the ambulance. Its doors were open wide, but none of the paramedics stood nearby. One was in the driver's seat and the other spoke to Benko, across the street.

"I'm not in need of medical assistance," I insisted.

"I understand, but why don't you sit down here," he said in a placating tone, and indicated I sit on the back bumper.

Garcia passed the phone back to Perez and eyeballed the surrounding area, much like his partner had just done.

I drew a ragged breath, and my heart fell to my knees. "Oh, God. You've found her, haven't you? That—that text you got. She's dead. Isn't she?" Josh's strong hand found mine, and I squeezed hard.

"We haven't heard anything," Perez assured me. "We wanted to get you off the street and give you some privacy."

I relaxed my grip. Josh released a breath through his teeth, and I mumbled an apology to him. By now the crowds had been pushed to the end of the block, and a man in dark slacks and blue button-down was taking photos of the skid marks left behind by the Navigator, while another detective bagged the bandana that came off Cortez's face.

"Please wait here. Detective Perez and I need a few minutes to speak with our FBI counterparts and make arrangements for you." The pair strode over to an unmarked black cop car and got inside.

I gazed up into Josh's concerned features. "Do you think they are telling the truth?"

His face softened. "I don't think they'd lie to you if they

believed they'd found her body."

"We've got to find her. Today," I said, determined. "She could be taken to God-knows-where in the next twenty-four hours."

"I don't disagree."

"Do you think they'll kill her?" I asked the question I feared the most, unsure if I wanted Josh to tell me the truth or lie to make me feel better.

Josh rubbed his cheek. "I couldn't say, Karina. She's a pretty girl. If they know they can make some money trafficking her . . ."

"I don't know which would be worse." I stared at the detectives. Garcia spoke into his cell, while Perez typed something into their vehicle's computer. "Is there any way Silverthorne can help?"

"Already on it."

I regarded Josh, surprised. "How?"

He pointed to his left ear.

"You on coms?"

"Listen to you—am I on coms?" His lip quirked. "Where did you pick up that lingo?"

My face burned. "Who's listening?"

"Hernandez. He's waiting in the car."

"I keep hearing that name. Do I know Hernandez?"

"You met him when we picked up Rivkin."

I recalled a stocky Latino with round cheeks and dimples who kindly handed my coworker a bandana to wipe his mouth after he'd become ill. "What about Jin?"

The quirk disappeared. "Jin is on a different assignment."

"Can't Hernandez be reassigned to do what Jin's doing?" I whispered.

Josh's frown deepened. "Hernandez is familiar with MS-13

and will be more helpful here. Jin is on duty following your jewel thief tonight."

"Oh. Sorry. Nothing against Hernandez," I said. "I'm just used to working with the J-squared team."

As I watched the police do their thing, an earlier discussion with Rick floated to the surface of my thoughts. So did a name I hadn't thought of in the past twenty minutes—Sadira. Sadira Manon. The probable reason why my sister was in this mess. What on earth did she have to do with MS-13? My car was now buried two cop cars deep, and, even if they moved, the ambulance blocked most of the street. I debated asking Josh to take me to the pokey where Sadira was incarcerated.

"Something's on fire in that head of yours," he commented.

I tapped my chin. "Does Hernandez have any leads on this Cortez guy?"

"He's searching the database right now for known associates."

I perked up at that. "You have a database?"

"We have access to lots of databases."

"More databases than the cops?"

"Possibly. We plan to start closest to the crime scene and work our way out."

"We?"

"Hernandez and I for starters. Rick is putting together a team to help search." In his element, Josh spoke in sure, clipped tones.

"What happens if we find her?"

"If we identify the location where she's being held, we'll assess and prep for a breach."

"A breach? That sounds dangerous. Can you do that? What about the cops?" I tilted my head to the pair of detectives still in their car.

"Rick will take care of it. He's got contacts in the FBI gang unit and can liaise with local P.D."

"Is Rick on assignment?"

"He's stuck on the beltway."

For some reason that struck me funny. "Wait a minute, you mean Batman doesn't have a special Batcopter to get him out of a mess as ordinary as rush hour traffic?"

Josh fought back a grin.

I suddenly had a bad feeling. "Is he on coms with you?"

The grin peeped forth.

"Crap. I'm sorry, Rick. My comments were thoughtless. Bad form on my part. Please don't give up. I need your help," I begged rather loudly in Josh's ear.

He flinched away. "You don't need to yell. We can all hear you. And Rick said to tell you, he'll find these motherfu—" Josh cleared his throat. "—criminals, no matter what it takes."

"You guys are the best." I threw my arms around Josh's neck and squeezed.

His face turned beet red. "Uh, no problem."

To his obvious relief, I let him go. "You know, Perez is right. If we go into the wrong house, it could put Jillian in further danger. Maybe get her killed," I fearfully whispered the last.

"So, we'll go into the right house the first time."

"You can't guarantee that."

"Sure, I can," he boasted, then flinched and put a hand to his ear.

"I don't think Hernandez agrees with you."

"Speaking of Hernandez, I need to rejoin him back at the car. You'll be okay here, with the police? They're probably arranging a safe house for you."

"Protective custody? No, I'm not staying with the cops," I

declared. Josh started shaking his head as soon as I began speaking. "I'm coming with you." I nodded in opposition to Josh's head shaking. "Oh, yes, I am. That's *my* sister." I thumped my chest. "And besides, *I* saw the vehicle, which means you'll need me to identify it."

"We can text you a photo if we find it."

"An extra pair of eyes couldn't hurt," I argued.

"I don't think it's a good idea."

"I'm coming."

"Karina . . . ," Josh said in a mollifying tone.

"No, don't 'Karina' me. Listen, it's not like I plan to be part of the raid. I'll wait in the car. But I *am* coming with you. And if you do find her, I want to be there. I *need* to be there," I said firmly in the same tones Josh had used with me on the phone.

Josh held up a finger and quirked his head, listening to the person in his ear. "Fine. You can come."

"Thanks, Rick." Hurdle accomplished, I dusted off my pants and hopped from the bumper. "Wait here," I said to Josh, "I'll tell Perez and Garcia that I need to leave." Striding over to the black car, I knocked on the driver's side window.

With a slight hum, the glass slid down. "We'll be a few more minutes, ma'am," Garcia said, chomping hard on a piece of gum. "Can you please return to the ambulance?"

"I need to leave. Here's my business card. My cell number is written on the back to contact me."

Garcia took the card without glancing at it. "I'm afraid I can't allow you to leave."

"Is there something else you need from me?"

"I don't think you understand the gravity of the situation. You can identify an MS-13 gang member, and they can identify you. Your life is in danger," Garcia explained. "Right now, we're working on setting up a safe house for you. In addition—"

"Yeah," I cut him off, "Josh said you'd be doing that, but I've made my own arrangements. You noticed the burly blond fellow with me?" They looked Josh's way. "He's private security. He and his buddy Hernandez will keep me company. So, you needn't worry about me. I'll be fine."

Perez leaned across the console. "Ma'am, my partner is right. MS-13 is not to be trifled with. There are hundreds of gang members here in northern Virginia. They're into drug running, sex-trafficking, and extortion. I doubt we'll get anyone on this street who saw what happened to talk to us. They are well organized, loyal, and violent. Last month we arrested three men who hacked their victim to death with a machete. One hundred and fifty-two cuts—"

"Thank you, Detective Perez, for that enlightening speech," I interrupted firmly with a curled lip of disgust, and waved Joshua over. "I understand these are very dangerous people. But, as I stated earlier, I have my own private security team to look out for me. Ah, Josh, could you please provide the detectives with your business card?"

Josh pulled a wallet out of his cargo pants and passed over his card. "Gentlemen, I'm with Silverthorne Security. We are qualified to protect diplomats and high-value targets within and outside of US territory. Additionally, we've had the pleasure of protecting Karina in the past. I can assure you; her well-being is our number one priority."

"So, gentlemen, unless you plan to arrest me, I believe I'm free to go," I added.

Garcia paused his chewing to glance at his partner, who shook his head. "We still have questions for you."

I sighed, knowing I hadn't provided the police with the full picture, but antsy to meet up with Hernandez and start *doing* something. "Okay, let's see if I can get you the answers you need. Since I don't see a body cam on either of you, how about we use the dash cam there. Can you turn it toward me?"

Perez twisted the camera to face me.

"We good? Okay, then. My sister came to this neighborhood today, asking questions about a teen she had a run-in with recently. The teen threw a milkshake at her car. In any case, Jillian found out the teen's name is Trudea." Perez opened his mouth. "Please don't interrupt, I'll try to answer your questions when I'm finished. Anyway, Jilly was concerned the teen was at-risk. Through further questioning of a local resident, specifically an eight-year-old boy, she found out this girl used to be a good student and has recently changed for the worse. She's skipping school, her grades have dropped, and she may have gotten into drugs. As a teacher, my sister felt she should try to reach out to this teen and help her. When I heard what she was doing, I didn't like the idea of her wandering this neighborhood. I came over to help talk some sense into her, suggesting she take her fears up the line to the appropriate people, like police, school officials, and youth protection services. She must have hit a nerve—asked the wrong question, or MS-13 thought she was an undercover cop or something."

Garcia's mouth dropped as I spoke, and the gum fell out.

"Does that help?" I asked.

"It certainly puts things into perspective." Garcia picked up the gum from his lap and wrapped it into a random receipt sitting on the dash.

"Does it change the situation?"

"It might," Perez responded.

"For better or worse?"

"I couldn't say." I didn't care for the look the pair shared, or Perez's hesitation in answering.

An urgency of intuition seemed to be pushing me to leave.

"Well, listen guys, you have our numbers. I'm going to head out."

Garcia shook his head. "We need your clothes."

My brows shot to my hairline. "I beg your pardon?"

"You said, in your statement to Officer Benko, that you threw the assailant over your shoulder," Garcia replied.

"I'm unclear why you need my clothing."

"DNA. Cortez may have left hair, blood, skin cells on your clothing."

"So? I've already made a positive ID. What do my clothes matter?"

"Court purposes," Perez chimed in.

I crossed my arms, considering his argument. I couldn't decide if this was simply a stalling tactic to keep me from leaving.

"We can take you to the safe house to change, then release you to into the custody of your bodyguard," Garcia said.

My shoulders straightened and I fixed him with a side-eye. If he hadn't used that precise language, "release me into the custody," I might have complied. However, I was not some child being passed off to her daddy for the weekend, and this felt like another way to stuff me into a safe house where I'd go batshit crazy pacing the floorboards. Josh didn't say a word, but I think I heard a snort.

"Fine. You got an evidence bag?"

"I'm not sure—"

"If you don't," I interrupted Perez, "I'll ask one of the forensic boys bagging and tagging everything."

"There are some in the trunk," Garcia answered, "but I don't have any clothes for you to change into."

"Well, it's a good thing I've got some. Josh, can you please grab the pink gym bag for me? It's in the trunk." I passed him my keys and waited for Perez to dig up an evidence bag large enough to hold my clothes. Josh stood guard outside the ambulance doors while I did a quick change into a pair of black yoga pants, a purple T-shirt, and sneakers. "I think that's everything, detectives." I passed the bag through Garcia's open car window.

He must have known when he was beat. He pointed to the cell number on Joshua's card. "We can reach you here?"

"That's correct. I will remain with Joshua," I assured him.

"We'd prefer it if you could stick around a while longer. There are more questions we'd like to ask. And FBI taskforce members will be here soon. They'd like to speak with you as well," Perez put in.

I forced myself not to wince when he mentioned the FBI. Mike would be furious if he found out what was going on from another colleague. Who was I kidding? Mike's blood pressure was going to be off the charts when he heard about this situation no matter what. And frankly, it should; Jillian was in a heap of trouble. To hell with Mike's blood pressure. "Have you heard anything new about my sister?"

Perez shook his head. "Not yet."

"Then if you don't mind, I'd like to get out of here. It's all so overwhelming," I said in a fadeaway voice and listed against Josh, clutching him. "I'm running on low. Can't we can arrange to meet at the station or via phone? The reporters have shown up, and I—I just can't face them. And what am I to tell Mummy and Dad?" I pressed a hand to my lips and worked to bring up some tears. To my dismay, I didn't have to work hard to manufacture them. The tears had been hovering just below the surface.

Josh put his arm around me and said, "Detectives, I can assure you she is safe with me."

Garcia frowned, but gave in. "I don't like it, but I suppose we can release you into your security team's hands."

I mustered a hitched, "Th-thank you for your understanding, d-detective."

"Where will you be?" Perez asked.

"We have a secure facility in D.C. I can take her to until more permanent arrangements can be made," Josh replied. "I'll need your contact information."

Both Perez and Garcia dug cards out of their wallets and passed them forth.

Josh shoved them into his back pocket. "I'll be in touch."

I leaned heavily against Josh as we headed away, but I paused upon the realization that I'd forgotten to mention one more person involved in this fiasco. I also realized I could send someone else to question Sadira while I searched for Jillian with the Silverthorne boys.

Tap, tap, tap.

Garcia's window slid down again.

"Sadira. Someone needs to talk with Sadira Manon." I pronounced her name clearly and concisely. "Current address, Fairfax County Jail. She is in this up to her neck."

"Wait—"

I ignored the request and trotted back toward Joshua.

Garcia got out of the vehicle. "Ms. Cardinal, wait!"

I paused a moment to let Garcia catch up to me.

"Sa-di-ra Ma-non," I repeated slowly. "Right now, she is my client so we can't discuss her further." I turned away, then quickly turned back. "But she may be in danger. Go talk to her." I left Garcia standing in the middle of the street, staring after me.

Chapter Eighteen

Josh was able to weave us through the throng of onlookers while avoiding the reporters that circled through the crowd, asking questions. Two blocks away, we stopped in front of a white panel van. Josh opened the passenger door for me. I hopped in and glanced over my shoulder. Through a safety grate, I found Hernandez sitting on a stool in the middle of a bank of electronics.

"Jeez, boys. Did you steal this from the FBI?"

Those dimples peeked at me. "Nope, it belongs to Silverthorne."

"Can all these electronics help find my sister?"

"You bet your ass they can," Josh said, climbing into the driver's seat. "Where to?"

"Did your sister have an iPhone?" Hernandez asked.

"Her phone! Of course, how stupid I've been." I smacked my forehead. "I can use the Track My iPhone app. Cripes. Why didn't anyone say anything earlier?" I logged into the app and waited. Sure enough, after a few moments, Jilly's phone number popped up on the map. "*There she is!*" I got so excited, I bounced in my seat. "Hernandez, you're brilliant. I could kiss you. It's not too far away! Go, go! Turn left at the light!" I shouted.

Josh cranked the ignition and the van roared to life.

"Hurry, hurry," I urged.

"Is the phone on the move?" Hernandez asked.

"Nope, it looks stationary. That's probably the house they took her to." The black knot of dread in my stomach flooded with the shine of hope. "Let's *go, hurry up*, Josh. You're driving like an old lady."

Josh leveled a stern look my way. "It doesn't do us any good to get pulled over by police, or into an accident. I can't just run over this guy in front of me."

Justly chastised, I sat back and bit my lip. My leg bounced nervously, but Josh didn't say anything further. "At the next intersection, turn left and then stay straight for a bit," I mustered calmly.

For the next fifteen minutes our silence was only broken by my directions and my own antsy shifting while we waited at the lights and behind traffic. The map led us to a middle-class neighborhood in Ashton Heights. "It's just up ahead, on the right."

Josh drew to a halt next to a playground. Half a dozen toddlers and elementary school-aged children squealed and climbed on the jungle gym while their caregivers watched from a bench.

"She should be right around here." I doublechecked the map. "I don't get it," I said, and opening my door, I bounded out, following the dot on my screen.

"Karina, wait! Hernandez, stay with the car." Josh slammed the van into park and jumped out after me.

"We're outside. The location should be accurate up to a few meters." My eyes searched the treed parkland for my sister's orange blouse as I approached the green dot, stopping when I arrived at the location indicated by my iPhone. I turned in a slow circle, searching the park.

"Found it," Josh said, about ten meters away.

I strode over to his location. "Do you think she's here?" I scrutinized the innocent-looking ramblers and cape cods across the street from the park.

"Doubtful. Don't touch it," he said, halting my movements. "They probably found it on her and threw it from the car." First, Josh photographed the phone and surrounding area. Then, pulling on a black rubber glove, he bent down, picked it up, and dropped it in a zippered plastic bag. He pressed the home button and the cracked screen lit up. "Do you know her password?"

I reeled off my parents' birth months and birth years. The home screen appeared. "Any activity? Maybe she tried to send us a text or something."

Josh scrolled around, but eventually shook his head in the negative. "I don't see any sort of movement on her apps since before the time of the abduction."

A feeling of panic crept over me. "I think we should look around. Check that building over there." It started as a fast walk and soon turned into a dead run, as if something drove me to the gray and white building that housed bathrooms and a water fountain.

"Karina?"

Ignoring Josh's calls, I burst into the women's bathroom, startling a mother and young son as they washed their hands.

"Jillian!" I yelled.

The woman hustled her toddler out the door as I checked each of the four stalls. Nothing. I spun around one more time before leaving. Josh exited the men's room the same time I came out of the ladies'.

"Anything?"

He shook his head.

"Nothing?" I said with desperation.

"Karina, I don't think she's here. It looks like they chucked her phone out the window."

"Well, what about street cameras? Does Hernandez have

access? Maybe we can follow the trail."

Hernandez had gotten into the driver's seat after Josh abandoned it, and the van pulled up to the curb where we stood. "You find anything?" he asked through the open window.

"No. Just the phone," Josh replied. "Did the boys at HQ get us hooked into the street cams?"

"They're in."

"Can they check this area?" he asked.

Hernandez shook his head. "There aren't any in this residential section. The closest ones are on Pershing and Wilson Boulevard."

"Dead end," I murmured, subdued. I had been so sure that we would find my sister before the police, FBI, and everyone else.

Josh's arm came across my shoulders.

"Don't lose hope, *pequeña ave*. We're just getting started. Come on, now, hop in," Hernandez said in a reassuring voice.

Resigned, I climbed into the passenger seat. Hernandez returned to his electronics in the back and Josh reclaimed the driver's seat.

"Now what do we do?" I asked.

"Rick wants to meet up and discuss strategy," Hernandez responded.

Twenty minutes later, we arrived at a fast-food parking lot and pulled alongside a black muscle car that must have dated back to the '70s. A cobra and the numbers 429 were displayed on the quarter panel behind the front wheel. The black paint was so polished and shiny that I imagined I would be able to see my reflection. Rick wore black slacks and a black button-down with the sleeves rolled up to his elbows, appearing as tough as the car he leaned against. Josh shut off the engine, and Rick opened the van door on my side.

"She wasn't there," I choked out. The drive over did nothing for my psyche, as I silently flayed myself over and over for my inability to save my sister when I had the chance.

"I know." He placed a black cowboy-booted foot on the running board. "We're working on it." He looked over my shoulder. "Hernandez, what have you got?"

Hernandez removed his headphones. "FBI is on scene now, working with the Arlington gang unit. I've reached out to my informant. He's got his ear to the ground, but he hasn't reported back yet."

"When do you expect to hear from him?" Rick inquired.

"He's a burglar and a drug addict—always looking for his next fix. If he can get money without having to steal it, he will. I imagine he'll get back to me as soon as he hears something or his latest fix wears off," Hernandez answered.

"Is he reliable?" Josh shifted to see his buddy in back.

"I'd say ninety-five percent of the time the intel is good," Hernandez said, then returned his attention to the monitor.

I scrunched my nose. "Really? A junkie burglar is reliable?"

Hernandez answered while continuing to type, "Yup. Burglars have got their ears to the ground. They know who shot whom and why, who jacked a car and where it got left, and who's passing around dirty drugs. He's quick on his feet, blends in, and as a junkie, tends to live in the shadows."

"Wow. I had no idea," I murmured.

"By the way," Rick said to me, "your jeweler is on the move with Jin tailing him. Jin's working with a D.C. detective from major crimes to make the bust."

"Do you think Tazim is going to sell the diamonds now?" I asked.

"Time is running out to pay his bill. He's already had a taste of what they'll do. I don't imagine he wants to test them." Rick's unusual gray eyes were as hard as slate.

"If they catch him, then Sadira will be released."

Nobody replied.

Twisting the ring on my middle finger, I continued, "I need to see her before they let her loose. I think she may have information. She's got to have something that can help us. Can someone take me?" My neck rotated back and forth as I waited for Rick or Josh to volunteer. "Or I can call an Uber, if you prefer."

"I'll take you." Rick's granite gaze focused past me on Hernandez as he spoke, "Why don't you and Joshua go in and get us all something to eat before we leave?"

I flinched at the thought of putting something in my stomach. "I'm not hungry."

"C'mon, Karina," Josh said, opening his door, "it may be a long night, and you never know when we'll get a chance to eat. Any special requests?"

"Burger, fries, Coke and a chocolate shake," Hernandez reeled off.

"Burger and a coffee." Rick stepped back and helped me out of the van.

I slung my purse over my shoulder and led Josh into the busy restaurant. "What's Rick talking to Hernandez about?"

"What do you mean?"

I slid him a slit-eyed glower. "Josh, the one thing you've never done is treat me like a fool. Please don't start now."

"It's nothing."

"Then tell me."

"You don't want to know."

"Of course, I do."

He cleared his throat and said softly, "They're discussing the likelihood of finding her alive."

The glowing menu wavered in front of me. "I need to go to the bathroom."

"What do you want to eat?"

"Nothing. Anything. You pick," I mumbled, stumbling out of line, past a handful of patrons. After locking myself in a stall, my stomach debated whether or not I needed to vomit. The moment passed, and I sat down on the toilet instead. Rubbing my temples, I rocked back and forth, humming quietly while drawing deep breaths and counting the black and gray floor tiles. *Keep it together, keep it together.* I had no doubt, if I lost my shit, Rick would pack me off and stash me in some sort of safe house until this was all over, just so he wouldn't have to manage a hysterical female on top of everything else.

My phone rang, and I fumbled, pulling it out of my purse. Rodrigo, grinning and holding up the peace sign, stared back at me. I tapped ignore. Twenty seconds later a text came across.

Are you okay?

Fine.

Are you coming to happy hour?

Don't think I'll make it. Friend in need. Drink one for me.

Ok. Let me know if there is anything I can do.

If only there was something he *could* do. Jessica's voicemail message blinked at me, but I couldn't face it. I washed my hands, splashed some water on my face, and rejoined the group back at the van.

Someone had opened the side door, and Hernandez was accepting a fast-food bag passed to him by Josh. He saw me and asked, "Everything all right, *pequeña ave?*"

"Fine." I produced a wan smile, absentmindedly accepting my bag of food and soda.

"Josh and Hernandez are following a couple of leads while

we visit Sadira," Rick stated.

I nodded. "Do you have one of those earbud thingies for me, so I can stay in the loop?"

Hernandez gave Rick the side-eye.

Rick didn't blink. "I'm afraid we don't have any more on hand. I'll try to arrange one for you."

"Sure." Somehow, I doubted I'd be seeing an earbud any time soon as Rick probably wanted the coms to stay private between them. I took my food and climbed into his passenger seat while the boys finished their pow-wow.

The leather bucket seat squeaked as I shifted around and checked out the old-fashioned dashboard with the original radio. The French fry I chewed held no flavor, and I had trouble forcing the bite down my throat. Giving up, I placed the bag at my feet. The diet soda wasn't much better. I might as well have been drinking battery acid. The classic car didn't have the convenience of modern day cupholders, so I placed the drink between my legs. Restless and edgy, I drummed my fingers against my thigh. The big silver glovebox button caught my eye. It dropped down to reveal some papers and a compact, semiautomatic Ruger. Fairly certain it was the same pistol Rick had offered to me a few months ago after Rivkin had broken into my home, I closed the compartment with a gentle click.

Doors slammed, Rick got in, and the van rolled away.

"I pictured you as a pickup truck type of guy," I commented.

"It's back at the house," he told me, then sipped his fast-food black coffee and placed it between his legs.

"Do you have a house? I thought you lived in a cave—with Alfred."

That comment received a single raised brow and the dry response, "I live in a loft-style apartment." The car rumbled to life and we rolled out of the parking lot.

"What kind of car is this?"

"Ford Torino four-twenty-nine Cobra Jet."

"That's kind of a mouthful. I'm assuming four-twenty-nine means a lot of horsepower," I babbled, trying to divert my thoughts from 'the bad place.' "What year is it?"

"Three-hundred-eighty horses, and it's a 1970." Traffic opened, Rick accelerated, and we rumbled down the road like an angry tiger, sucking gas as we went.

"Did you refurbish it? Or did you buy it this way?"

"It was my father's. He kept it garaged and in good shape."

"Ah, and he passed it along to you. Has he ever asked for it back?"

"He passed away ten years ago. Cancer."

I glanced at his stone-faced profile. Rick had never revealed personal information to me in the past, always speaking *en pointe*, in economical sentences. "I'm sorry to hear that. I'm sure you miss him."

"He was a bastard," he answered without emotion.

I could think of no suitable response. Checking out the rest of the vehicle, I found a black coat and tie in the back seat. I'd never seen Rick wear anything more formal than jeans or cargo pants. "What's with the coat and tie? Did you have court today?"

"Funeral."

I inhaled sharply. "That explains the black. Sorry for your loss. Who was it? Family? Friend?"

"Friend. We used to work together."

"In Afghanistan?"

He nodded.

"I'm sorry to drag you away from it. Couldn't Josh and Hernandez head up the team without you?"

Rick took a beat before responding. "Cardinal . . . Karina—" His voice noticeably softened. "—your sister's kidnapping . . ." He paused. His jaw flexed, and, for the first time since I've ever known him, he seemed to struggle in answering me. "When one of my clients is involved in an abduction, you can bet your ass I'm going to run point," he snapped.

"I see. Then I'm thankful to be one of your clients. But, if what you say is true, why aren't you back at the office running ops from the computer room? Why are you here? It seems obvious that you've taken on babysitting duty. I feel certain you think visiting Sadira is a waste of time." I don't know why I baited him in that snarky tone. Possibly, it was my pique at not getting an earbud. Or, maybe, I was so out of my mind with worry, I wasn't thinking properly. Or maybe I wanted to know what he had been about to say before he fell back on the obligation to his clients.

The car rolled to a stop behind a line of traffic sitting at a red light. Rick rotated to face me. "Three things. First, I don't believe anything that might help find your sister is a waste of time. Second, you have good instincts. Though, I'd argue, your impulsivity doesn't make the best decisions, they have led you to the right conclusions. Even if trouble lies around the corners of those conclusions. Finally—" He drew a breath. "—finally, it *is* my duty to make sure you're safe. Josh told the police Silverthorne would protect you, and I will do so to the utmost of my capability." The light had turned green and a blaring honk had Rick putting his foot down. The car roared forward. "I let you down once. I won't do it again," he spoke the last so quietly I barely heard it over the car's thundering engine, and I wondered if I'd heard correctly.

I sat in silence, chewing over that comment, searching my

mind for a time when Rick or his boys had *ever* let me down. I couldn't think of one. In reality, they'd provided intel, operational support, and saved my hide on more occasions than I'd like to admit. "You've never let me down."

"Remember how your shoulder was dislocated?" Rick stared ahead at the road.

"Yes. I also remember you saved my life. If it hadn't been for you, I wouldn't have gone to the hospital. I would've gone to the morgue."

"I should've cleared the stairwell. He never should have been waiting for you."

"You take too much on yourself. We can't predict the future. You couldn't have known. And we won't discuss it further," I stated with finality. The last thing I wanted was for Rick to feel that he "owed" me. If anything, I owed him. "I'm sorry you had to leave your friend's funeral early," I said softly.

"Don't worry. The funeral was over. I left the wake."

As we headed toward the county jail, a thought occurred to me. "Rick—can you pick a lock?"

"Yes."

"How are your safe-cracking abilities?"

"Depends on the type of safe, I've only done it once. It's not a skill I put on the resume. Where are you going with this?" He glanced at me.

"I'd like to stop at Sadira's apartment on the way over."

"Why? What are you looking for?"

"Leverage."

Chapter Nineteen

Rick and I scrutinized the in-wall safe. His lock-picking skills were Olympic-medal level, but the safe left him temporarily stymied. The black, steel box had a numbered keypad and three LED lights above the pad; much like a hotel safe, they likely turned green when opening and red when locking. There was a silver handle and a round knob, which seemed to serve no purpose.

"Can you crack it?" I asked.

He studied the little vault. "It's not like a dial safe. If I enter the wrong numbers more than three times, it'll lock up tight."

"Which numbers have fingerprints? Maybe we can look through Sadira's dossier and figure out dates that relate to them. Do you have a blacklight?"

"Not a bad idea, Cardinal. I don't have a blacklight but . . . be right back." Rick disappeared, and I heard rattling in Sadira's bathroom. He returned holding a blush brush and loose face powder. After tapping the excess off the brush, he tapped powder onto the keypad.

"Well, that can't be good for business. The only number that doesn't have a fingerprint is zero."

Rick placed the powder and brush on a shelf. "Either it's a long passcode, or she changes it often."

"What about one, two, three, four, five, six, seven, eight, nine?"

Rick drummed his fingers against the wall for a moment. "What the hell?" He tapped in the sequence to no joy. The red

LEDs flashed at us.

"What about backward?"

"Then we'd be down to one try."

"Yeah, I guess that's not a good idea. Hm." Stymied, the two of us scrutinized the safe, as if waiting for the answer to magically reveal itself. I tilted my head. "Those numbers light up. What happens when the battery wears out?"

"Good question."

"And what's this knob for? Do you push it in?" I pushed. It didn't move. I tried pulling on it. Nothing.

Rick twisted the knob left and right, and suddenly it popped off in his hand, revealing a key lock beneath. "You use the key when the battery dies," he stated.

"I think I know where the key might be!" I beelined to Sadira's desk. It only took a few minutes to find the small key taped to the underside of the second drawer I opened. "I found it!" I sang triumphantly.

I needn't have bothered. Upon entering the closet, I found the safe door open and Rick returning his lockpicks back into their brown leather case. "Do you always travel with those?" I asked.

"You never know when they might come in handy."

"Isn't there a Boy Scout motto about better to have it and not need it?"

He gave a snort. "It's 'Be Prepared.'"

"Of course, you were a scout."

"Indeed."

Sadira's passport and a few pieces of jewelry sat on the top shelf—a pearl necklace, emerald ring, and gold watch, but no loose diamonds. On the second and third shelf rested stacks of money rubber-banded together. "That's a lot of cash," I said with a whistle. Pulling out a stack, I shuffled through it.

Hundred-dollar bills flashed past. "It's all hundreds. How much do you think is in here?"

Rick's head tilted as he eyeballed the stack in my hand. "My guess, she's got them sorted into stacks of ten thousand each." I counted silently as he ticked off each stack.

"Seventy thousand. Would that go a long way in Argentina?"

"Undoubtedly. If she's got this much in cash, what's she got stashed in offshore numbered accounts?"

I returned the money to the pile. "You didn't come across any offshore accounts, did you?"

"We didn't look that hard, but nothing came up in our initial searches."

"What in the sweet hell have you been doing, Sadira?" I murmured, eyeballing the dough.

"Is this what you were expecting?"

"Not exactly. But it *is* my leverage." I pocketed her passport and closed the safe. The key I'd found fit perfectly, and the lock fastened with a discordant snick.

****

After signing in and placing the request to see my client in a private room, I turned to find Rick standing stoic at parade rest. "I think I'm safe in here. Why don't you take a moment to catch up with the team?"

"They're following a few leads, and Hernandez's informant set up a meet in half an hour."

"That's good news."

He crossed his arms and nodded. Behind him entered Detective Perez. The detective's face gave way to displeasure when he observed me. "What are *you* doing here?"

I gnashed my teeth. "Detective Perez, have you found my sister yet?"

"I thought that big blond guy was watching you. I *told* Garcia we couldn't trust you." He got in my face and lectured in angry low tones, "You should be at a safe house by now. Don't you realize the danger you're in? I'm going to have to insist on taking you back to the station—" He took my arm.

Rick stepped forward.

Yanking my arm away, I said rather loudly, "Detective, I'd like to introduce you to my security detail, the head of Silverthorne, Rick—" I suddenly realized I didn't know Rick's last name. I'd simply known him as Rick, or Batman.

"Donovan," Rick supplied and held out his hand. "I can assure you, Ms. Cardinal is safe in my care."

"Oh, uh, well then . . ." They shook hands.

"I'm here to see my client," I explained.

"Karina Cardinal," an officer called.

I acknowledged her, holding up a finger to give me a moment. "Following up on a lead, detective?"

He stared at me for a moment as if I'd gone insane. After all, I was the one who'd led him here. I tilted my head and winked.

Perez finally seemed to clue in. "Yes, uh, as a matter of fact, I am here to see your client."

"If you'll wait a few minutes, I need to see Sadira alone first." The detective opened his mouth as if to argue, but I cut him off. "Trust me, it'll go better if you wait."

Perez squinted, then nodded.

"Sign in and have them bring you up. Can you get my security detail in too? They were reluctant to allow him to join me."

Perez sized Rick up. "I'll see what I can do."

I waited ten more minutes before another guard ushered Sadira into our glass box. Rick and Perez had arrived and stood outside. Rick had returned to his stoic guard dog impression, not taking his eyes off me, while Perez paced the floor.

"Hello, Sadira," I enunciated.

Her hair was tucked behind her ears. The wild-eyed, angry fear I'd witnessed this morning seemed to have dissipated, or she was hiding it well. Without preamble, she asked, "Did you deliver my message to your sister?"

"As a matter of fact, I did. Are you still being threatened?"

Her eyes darted around, taking in the visitors in the hall. "Not lately, but I can't be sure."

"Have a seat." I indicated the metal chair across the table. "I have good news."

"Oh, yeah?" She sat. "What is it?"

"I found your passport." I removed the little blue booklet from my pocket, placing it between us. I watched her eyes widen in surprise.

She gulped. "Where did you find it?"

"Where you left it" —my lips pinched— "in your hidden safe. Along with $70,000."

Expressions flitted across her features—first anger, then wariness, finally settling on frightened mouse. "It's not what you think."

"Oh, I'm fairly sure it's *exactly* what I think."

Lots of headshaking. "No! You have to believe me, I had nothing to do with stealing those diamonds."

"I never said you did, Sadira." It was a difficult to speak with such coolness, but I knew I'd have to thread this needle carefully, or she'd fire me and refuse to talk. And I desperately needed her to talk. "We have a man following Tazim as we speak. I expect he'll be trying to pawn those diamonds within the hour."

"Then I'll be off the hook," she said with relief, and rose. "I can go?"

"*Au contraire*, I don't believe you had anything to do with the diamonds." I placed a hand on the passport. "The money didn't come from the sale of the diamonds."

Her butt plopped back down on the metal chair.

"I believe your money came from your courier jobs."

She swallowed and her gaze darted around the room. "It came from all my jobs. After all, I have three of them. I've worked hard for that money," she said defensively.

I knew better. "Really?" I tapped a finger against my chin. "You know, I went with my sister on one of those jobs. Tell me, Sadira," I said in a menacing voice, leaning toward her, "besides young girls, what else do you 'courier'? Drugs? Money? Weapons?"

Her face paled with each shot I delivered.

"You see, that's where *I* think the money came from."

"Never open the package, never speak to the passenger," she said as if by rote.

My mouth pinched. "Come off it, Sadira. You had to have known something wasn't right. Especially the girls."

Her expression shifted from fear to defiance. "So? Maybe I did, maybe I didn't. You're my lawyer. We have privilege. There's nothing you can do," she spat.

"No, ma'am." My fist slammed down on the table, making Sadira jump. "That is not how this is going to go. I'm your lawyer for an alleged diamond theft. I've signed no papers to represent you as an accomplice to major crimes. You see those two men standing in the hall?" Her gaze followed my pointing finger. "Police. I'm here because your gang friends kidnapped my sister. If she's still alive and you help me find her, I'll do what I can to work a deal for you. If you don't help us, and she winds up dead, I'll make sure they charge you as an accomplice to murder. Which carries twenty-five to life." Offhand, I didn't know the exact penalties for accomplice to murder, and I couldn't get her charged as an accomplice—the most she could be charged with was an accessory to murder, and even that would be a stretch—but I was betting she wouldn't have enough legal knowledge to know any of that.

Sadira turned white and tucked her chin. "They took Jillian?" she whispered.

"Look at me," I demanded, and I snapped my fingers in front of her face. Once I had her attention, I said in a low, menacing tone, "As God as my witness, Sadira Manon, if you do not help me *right now*" —I tapped the table for emphasis— "I will make it my mission in life to make your life a living hell."

"I don't know what I can tell you that will help," she whispered.

"Where did you deliver packages? Specifically, the girls," I snapped.

"Different places, and I don't have the addresses to all of them."

I pointed at Perez and Rick and crooked a finger. Perez opened the door.

"You got a pad and pencil?"

Perez nodded and pulled a small notebook and pen out of his pocket. I took it and closed the door.

"Write it down. Every rat house and hellhole you've ever been to on your courier job," I barked, tossing them on the table.

I paced like a caged animal as she muttered and sputtered, writing down half-addresses like, "There was this place off of 32nd Street, it had a gray door and green shutters." Her hands shook as she wrote, but I had zero capacity to feel pity. I could only imagine how angry Jessica would be with me. Again, I didn't care. All I cared about was something, anything that would provide me the smallest speck of hope in finding Jillian.

When she finished, I photographed each page and texted them to Josh and Rick. "The detective outside wants to meet with you."

She clutched at my hand with pleading, wet eyes, and whispered, "I'm sorry. I didn't know they'd kidnap her. I like Jillian. She's a sweet girl. You've got to believe me. I didn't know."

Disgusted, I pulled my hand out of her grasp. "I suggest you make a deal and spill your guts to the detective. I'm removing myself as your council."

I opened the door and handed the notebook to Perez. "She's all yours."

Chapter Twenty

On the way out to Rick's car, I listened to Jessica's message. Luckily, her voicemail from earlier was simply to check in. She'd been so swamped with the emergency at her own office, she had no idea of the chain of events that happened today. I texted, telling her I'd be removing myself from Sadira's legal team, and she'd better get someone down to the pokey, because although the diamond case would soon be cleared up, Sadira had fresh skeletons in her closet.

"Cardinal, we need to move." Rick's tone was curt. He took my arm and hustled me through the parking lot.

"What's the word on the street?" I asked, slipping the phone back into my purse.

"A lot." He opened the car door and I levered myself into the front seat.

"Don't keep me in suspense. Spill."

Rick got in and started the car. "The FBI scooped up a dealer and PJ. PJ is an addict and local snitch. He's squawking like a parrot. They've sent local PD to surveille a warehouse off Edsall Road, a home near I-495, two apartment complexes in Alexandria, one in D.C., and a massage parlor on Q Street. The dealer isn't talking, they're sweating him for a bit." Rick wheeled around a corner fast enough to make the tires squeal, turning onto Route 50. "Your jeweler tried to fence the diamonds and was caught up in the sting. Which means Sadira will be cleared of that crime soon. My boys back at the office have your sister's phone. She had her GPS on, and they are working on identifying the route the phone took through GPS and street cameras before getting dumped at the park." He delivered the news concisely but with an edge to his tone.

"How will that help? I would think we're more interested in where they went after losing the phone than before."

"We want to see if they switched cars. Also, Hernandez's contact gave him a neighborhood not far from where the phone was dumped." He sped through a yellow light that turned red as we drove under it.

"Wait. I think Sadira placed two homes in that area. Let me check." I pulled up the series of photos.

"She wrote down two, neither of which she had an actual address for," Rick stated.

"But she had a street name for one of them." I zoomed in on each picture, searching for the missing piece.

"Yes." Then, without effort, he reeled off the neighborhood and street name. "Hernandez and Joshua are headed there now."

"Where are they coming from?"

"D.C. Their meeting with the informant was in Southeast." He thundered up the entrance ramp onto the Capital beltway.

"Let's head over. We'll probably get there before they will." The sun dipped low; the fiery ball headed toward the horizon, leaving streaks of oranges and pinks reflected in the clouds. The minute hand on my watch approached ten 'til eight. "We don't have much daylight left."

"I'm not taking you there."

"What? Why not?" I gaped at his profile.

"I'm taking you back to HQ."

"Why? What's going on at HQ?"

"Your safety."

"No. I want to go back to the neighborhood with the park."

I crossed my arms and stared out the windshield. We blew past other vehicles as if they were standing still.

"It's too dangerous," he spoke in short, clipped tones.

"I'll stay in the car. I'll be safe in the car," I argued.

"I need to get you out of sight."

"Why?"

"You're not safe on the street."

"I'll be fine. Do you have a baseball cap I can borrow? Look, I'll tuck my hair up underneath like this—" I wrapped my hair in a low bun as I explained my plan.

"This isn't up for debate," he said in his no-nonsense manner.

I'm sure his former soldiers and current staff never would have considered arguing with his orders once delivered. I was neither. We arrived at the Springfield mixing bowl where three highways and a couple of local roads merged at once. If you weren't paying attention, it was easy to end up heading the wrong direction.

I waited for Rick to get in the correct lane and wheel us onto the I-395 highway heading north to D.C. before responding, "I'm the client. I want to go with Joshua and Hernandez. You can stick me out of sight in the back of the van." I delivered a firm look at his profile.

"Forget it. I'm taking you to the office," he snapped. His hands gripped the steering wheel so tight his knuckles blanched. Rick was usually more collected when dealing with my shenanigans.

My Spidey senses perked up and the hairs on the back of my neck stood at attention. "There is something wrong. What's going on?"

We decelerated behind a slower moving car, then Rick, seeing an opening, shot across two lanes, put his foot down and accelerated with such force it threw me back against the leather seat. He was on edge. I'd never seen him this way.

"Uh, Rick?"

"MS-13 put a contract out on your head," he gritted out.

"Charming," I drawled.

"This isn't a joke, Cardinal. Now we don't just have to worry about MS-13 gang members coming after you, any asshole with a gun in need of five grand will be looking for you. There are way too many idiots around here with guns for my taste."

"Five grand! That's all I'm worth?" I squawked.

"Dead. If you're brought in alive, the price goes up to ten."

My snarky confidence deflated, and my lips curled in as a queasiness filled the back of my throat. I desperately tried to block out the tortures they could inflict should I be captured alive.

Rick took his eyes off the road to flick a glance at my profile, which must have reflected some of my thoughts. "Exactly."

I swallowed. "When did this happen?"

"While you were with Sadira."

"Is it word on the street? Or did they put out a formal hit on the dark web?"

My question must have surprised him, because his head gave a little jerk. "On the street. Hernandez's informant mentioned it in passing."

I sunk down in my seat. "When were you going to tell me about this?"

"When we got back to the office. Relax." I didn't know if he was talking to me or telling himself, because his grip visibly loosened. "I doubt anyone knows you're with me. And it's not like they'll be taking potshots while we're doing seventy on the highway."

"They do it in the movies all the time. A sharpshooter could set up on an overpass."

He gave a derisive snort. "Well-planned stunts. And I don't think a mercenary sharpshooter is leaving his couch for five grand. But, if it'll make you feel better, check the floorboards of the back seat. There should be a ballcap."

Of course, it wasn't behind Rick. I had to climb halfway around my own seat, knocking Rick in the shoulder with my butt, to retrieve the black and orange hat. "I didn't know you were an Orioles fan."

"I'm not. Someone gave it to me."

"That explains why it's so stiff." I curled the brim and adjusted metal buckle in back.

We rode in silence for a time, but the further away we got from Ashton Heights and the closer to D.C., the more anxious I became. My fingers knit and unknit themselves and I chewed the inside of my cheek so much I tasted blood.

If I'm this freaky on the way, what's going to happen when we arrive at Silverthorne? An image of an old Bugs Bunny cartoon came to mind—Bugs finds himself on a rocket ship heading away from Earth, and the audience watches as he spazzes and screams hysterically in the window. My own mind was doing a similar impression, and I feared Bugs might escape through my mouth when we arrived at Silverthorne. I had no interest in making a fool of myself—or being sedated, which I wouldn't put beyond Rick.

I cleared my throat to be heard over the grumble of the engine. "Take the next exit."

"Why?"

It was coming up too quickly, leaving me no time for debate. "I'm going to be sick."

Rick tore across two lanes, receiving the beep-beep of a horn from an indignant driver, to get off at the exit. He found a shoulder and pulled to the side. I opened the door but didn't make a move to get out.

"You okay?" he asked.

I mustered my courage, drawing deep breaths to steady myself before turning to face him. "I can't go to Silverthorne right now. Maybe later. Now, I need to be in the field with the rest of the crew providing any sort of help I can. And, before you say it, I realize the risks. If you stick me in the bubble of your secure building—I. Will. Go. Nuts." I clenched my fists. "Seriously, I want you to think how you'd feel if you were in my situation. You're not a man of inactivity. Neither am I a man—" I shook my head "—woman who can sit around doing nothing. Helping *you* will help *me* keep my mind off the worst-case scenarios. It's the only reason you haven't seen me lose my shit. I *have* to be a part of this, keep moving forward. Get it? Some women could just sit back, wringing their hands while the big boys did their thing. That's not me."

Rick's scrutiny remained noncommittal as I spoke. As much as I would have loved to threaten to get out of the car and call an Uber, as I did earlier, I wasn't foolish enough to carry out that threat now. Nor did I believe Rick would allow me to carry out such a threat. If push came to shove, he'd probably cuff me and toss me in his trunk. I needed Rick. I needed his team. I needed him to understand and give me a chance. I tried my damnedest to maintain "interested neutrality," a look I'd perfected during law school, as we stared each other down. Every muscle in my body clenched tight. If I flinched first, I expected I'd lose the game. It's the first time I noticed flecks of green in Rick's gray eyes. My phone sang out the *X-files* theme. Neither of us moved.

Rick blinked and shifted. "Josh says I'd better let you come, or you'll figure out some other way to put yourself in danger."

I'd forgotten the team was in his ear. Normally, I'd deliver a smartass comment or a fist pump, but I refrained, the stakes were too high. Instead, I released the breath I'd been holding.

"Stay here." Rick took the keys out of the ignition and, after checking the traffic, exited the car. The trunk went up, and for a moment I feared he'd be putting me in it. A moment later he slammed it shut and came back carrying a bulky black thing. "Put this on."

"Is it Kevlar?" Rick helped me get the tactical vest over my head. The straps weighed on my shoulders and I think I felt my spine compress. "Oof. It's heavy. Why is it so heavy? I thought Kevlar was lighter than this."

"It's got armored plates inside." He pulled the Velcro straps as tight as they would go and tsked. "It's also too big."

"And unwieldly. What are all these pockets for? Lipstick?" I pulled open one at chest level and peeked inside. Empty.

"Ammunition, spare weapon, knife, cuffs, grenade, pepper spray—"

"Duct tape?"

"If your name is MacGyver."

My mouth quirked and my brow rose in shock. "Did you just make a funny?"

He adjusted a buckle at my shoulder, which wasn't easy with both of us in a sitting position. "Josh says he has a smaller one for you in the van. You can change when we get there."

"Thanks, Josh, always looking out for me."

With one more tug, he gave a satisfied grunt. "Let's go."

We got back on the highway, heading south toward our destination.

"When?"

"When what?" I asked.

Rick held up a finger and I realized he was listening to his earbud. "Okay. I'll tell her." The finger returned to the wheel. "Josh said you need to call your boyfriend."

"Crap. I forgot he phoned. I can't imagine the conversation with Josh went well."

"He's worried. You left a distressed message?"

"Ye-ah, I might have been a bit hysterical. My phone's in my purse." I went to reach for it and realized I couldn't. I grunted as I rocked back and forth, trying in vain to lean forward.

"What are you doing?" He flashed a glance my way.

"I can't move. I'm, like, in a hole in this bucket seat, and the vest is cumbersome. How do you function in these? I feel like an overturned turtle. Uh-uh-eouch. Don't you dare laugh at me." The hint of smile on his face disappeared, and grabbing the window handle on the door, I heaved myself forward. However, I could only bend so far in the vest, and it wasn't easy to see around the multitude of pockets on my chest. Sweeping my hand on the floor, it finally connected with the handle of my purse, and I pulled it onto my lap. "How did he know to call Josh?"

"FBI told him you were in our custody."

Great. That's going to go over like a fart in church. Mike's message blinked at me. I didn't bother to listen to it, instead, I dialed him directly.

"K.C.? Are you alright?" He sounded more concerned than angry which boded well.

"I'm fine. I'm with Batman."

"You're not at home, are you?"

"Nooo—"

"Good. You'll be safe at Silverthorne." He actually sounded relieved.

My lips rolled in. I couldn't outright lie to him. But, I knew, if I told him where I was headed, it wouldn't go over well and only worry him more. Instead of disabusing his assumption, I sidestepped by telling him, "Rick has me in an armor-plated vest. It's really heavy."

"Well, that's good . . . I guess. Don't take it off unless they tell you to."

"Yeah, it's kind of cool. It has places for my stuff. It's a purse vest." I dropped a lip gloss in one of the pockets and slid my sunglasses in another.

"I've spoken with one of the agents on the case. The FBI and local PD on the joint task force are top notch folks. They're doing everything they can to find your sister," he said in his reassuring voice.

However, the mention of my sister was a punch to the gut. Not that I'd forgotten, but for all of, what, five minutes, it had been pushed to the periphery.

"I know," I breathed.

"You need to stay strong and be positive. Have you spoken to your family yet?"

The thought had crossed my mind that I should tell my parents, but I had no idea how to break the horrifying news. So I'd shoved the task aside. I'd had a notion that I could tell the entire story in retrospect—after we'd found Jillian—when life was back to normal. In my head, I'd already had the conversation, it would go something like, "Hey, Mom, so you won't believe this crazy thing that happened today. . . ." Only, the further we got from the incident, the less and less it seemed everything would be normal.

"I-I don't know how to tell them." To my dismay, my voice hitched.

A moment of silence hung between us.

"Do you want me to call them?" he asked quietly. "I can have an agent sent out to their home."

"Do—do you think we have to?"

"Yes, Karina." He rarely ever used my name, and even more rarely used it with such concern. Usually when he used my name, he barked it at me in frustration or anger. "She's their daughter. They have a right to know. And it's better they hear it now, before they hear it on the news."

"Oh. My. Gawd." I put a hand to my mouth. "Is her name on the news?"

"Not her name or picture, the task force is keeping it under wraps and the FBI has clamped down on local press, but the story is out there. It's only a matter of time before it gets leaked."

I was not normally one to shirk a duty that had to be done, but for the life of me, I simply couldn't picture myself getting the words past my mouth with my mother on the other end of the line. "Can you do it?"

"Of course, sweetheart." Mike also rarely used endearments. His compassion was almost my undoing. "I'll be in touch. I'm catching the first flight out."

I swiped at a stray tear gathering in the corner of my eye. "But your training isn't over until tomorrow."

"It ended today. Normally, the team goes out for one last hurrah. You know, drinks and dinner. Obviously, I'll be skipping that."

"Text me the flight details when you know."

"I will. Be safe, stay strong. Before you hang up, can you put Batman on the phone?"

"Uh, why?" I asked warily.

A sigh blew at me. "Just put him on the phone."

"Fine. Here, he wants to talk to you." I held the phone out, covered the microphone with my thumb, and whispered to Rick, "Don't tell him where we are going."

He took the phone. "Rick here. Uh-huh. That's correct. Yes, we are. I've got men following a few leads. Yes, we're in touch with them. She'll be safe. Yes, I understand." Rick gave the phone back to me.

"You want to tell me what that was about?" I asked Mike.

"Don't worry. I'll see you soon. Love you." He hung up.

"Is he flying home?" Rick inquired, flicking on the headlights as the steely dusk descended upon us.

"Yes. He'll talk to my parents too. What did he have to say to you?" I asked warily.

"He wanted to know if we were doing our own investigation, and he warned me to keep you safe. If you get hurt, he's holding me personally responsible."

"Good times," I said drily.

Rick remained silent for a moment, his jaw clenched and eyes narrowed. "He's right. If you get hurt, it's on my head."

I turned to stare out my window. "If *she* gets hurt, it's on mine."

We'd left the highway and came to a stop behind a line of traffic. Rick, perhaps sensing my urgency, peeled off to the right at the next turn and wove his way through neighborhood streets to get to our destination. Finally, he pulled up behind the white panel van parked next to a lot overgrown with weeds and a house that appeared vacant.

With arms crossed, Josh leaned coolly against the back bumper. He must have been waiting for us and came to open my door.

"Good to see you still alive, Karina." I held my hand toward him, and he hoisted me out of the seat. I didn't say anything, but I'm pretty sure I wouldn't have been able to get out on my own.

"Let's get you into some gear that fits."

I followed Josh to the side of the van. He knocked twice and Hernandez slid open the door.

"Lift up your arms," Josh commanded.

"Wait a minute, let me get my stuff out." I'd been squirreling away my handbag's worldly goods while we drove over. I pulled out the lip gloss, wallet, phone, sunglasses, pen, hand sanitizer, tissues, and a compact, laying them on the floor of the van. "This vest is really handy. I can see why y'all use them."

"A compact? Really?" Josh picked the offending item off the floorboards, holding it between two fingers, as if it might bite him.

I snatched it back and answered defensively, "It's got a mirror, might come in handy if you need to see around a corner."

His head dipped and slowly shook back and forth, and I'm fairly sure it was accompanied by an eyeroll. He peeled off the bulky vest—a relief to my shoulders and back—and passed it to Rick. "This will be more comfortable. Arms up."

The new black vest descended over my head, and Josh helped guide my hands through the armholes. When it was on, I twisted and rotated, getting a feel for the bulletproof armor. The lightweight Kevlar fit more comfortably, if a bit snug. It kind of squished my breasts, forming a uni-boob. A small concession I was willing to endure for safety.

"Hey, this one doesn't have pockets." I patted the front and sides.

"It's not a tactical vest," Josh said, tightening the Velcro straps on the sides.

"But what about all my stuff?" I pointed to the pile.

"Here, she can have the belt." Hernandez held out a nylon

belt with all sorts of pouches and pockets.

My eyes widened. "Oh-ho!" I snatched it out of his hand. "Look at that, it's got a gun holster. Like the old west." I wound it around my waist and tightened the buckle, but to my disappointment it was too big. If I let it go, it would have fallen to the ground.

"Here." Josh undid the buckle and slid off some of the pouches, including the one for the gun.

"So, no gun?" I asked.

Josh paused, but it was Rick who answered, "Do you want one?" The man had to walk on cat feet because I hadn't heard him return from his car. It took every effort not to jump.

Staring at Rick, I recalled a conversation we'd had, not so long ago, when he'd encouraged me to learn to handle a gun. I didn't want one then, but today I gave that Ruger some serious thought. Perhaps it was because back then, the threat had been less tangible. Today, I'd been physically attacked, and my sister taken. The need for vengeance was more palpable. I glanced between Josh's frowning mien and Rick's blank face. Rick was perfectly willing to arm me, Josh clearly had reservations.

"Perhaps not. I might end up shooting one of you accidentally," I replied with resignation.

Josh continued removing the gun holster, then tightened the belt so it fit snug beneath the vest. "By the way, where is your stun gun?"

I grimaced with regret. "It's in my drawer at the office. I forgot to put the damn thing back in my purse." Something I did regularly. I couldn't take it into any of the buildings on the Hill, so it often got left behind in a drawer or the glovebox of my car.

"You can have a taser if you want," Hernandez said distractedly.

A taser? How I wished I'd had a taser a few hours ago. "I'll take a taser."

Rick retrieved the little black device, explained how it worked, and stuck it into one of the holsters on my right hip.

The belt didn't have a good pocket for my sunglasses, so I put them on my head. "Okay. Now what?" I planted my feet shoulder-width apart and put hands on my hips. "What are you grinning at, *Joshua*? Don't I look like a badass?"

"Get in the van," Rick intoned.

I climbed in and peeked over Hernandez's shoulder to see what held his attention on the monitor. "What are you watching?"

"Drone footage." His hands manipulated a joystick and buttoned controller. The drone circled a red brick rambler.

"I don't think that's our house. Sadira said it had dark green or black shutters. This one doesn't have shutters," I said.

Hernandez raised the drone over the roof and moved on to the next house, with mustard siding and brown shutters.

I shook my head. "Huh-uh."

The drone turned catching a glimpse at the home across the street before rotating back to the mustard home.

"Hold up, stop." I gripped his forearm. "Go back to the house across the street." The camera shifted. "Right there. Zoom in on the car in the carport." The back of a black Lincoln Navigator came into focus with a license that read, RTZ-333. "Guys! Get in here!"

Josh and Rick had moved away from the open van door; they now clambered in to see where I pointed on the screen. Their invasion made for tight quarters, which got even tighter when someone shut the door.

"I thought you said there were no plates on the car," Josh stated.

I ignored him and grabbed Hernandez's forearm. "Can you get closer and show me the hubcaps?"

The drone flew downward and one of the back tires came into view. "Spinney wheels," I breathed. "Show me the back bumper. There was a scratch to the left of the license plate holder." The SUV flew out of sight. "Your other left."

Hernandez zoomed in and slowly moved the camera across the back bumper, halting on the wiggly scratch that marred the shiny bumper's surface. "That's it! That's it! Hernandez, you found it!"

"Your nails," Hernandez bit out.

"Oh, sorry." I released him, leaving behind little halfmoon indents on his russet skin.

"Run the license plate," Rick directed at Josh, who reached past me to grab a tablet. "Hernandez, check the backyard for signs of a dog."

The drone zoomed up over the roof of the house. Light from inside spilled onto the back patio, where a man stood smoking a cigarette and talking on a phone. A bistro table with two chairs and an umbrella sat on the concrete, but the man didn't use the seating, instead, he paced back and forth.

"Do we have audio?" Rick asked.

"No. This isn't the MAV," Hernandez replied.

"What about infrared?" Rick peered closer.

"Switching to infrared." Hernandez pushed a button and the screen suddenly turned into a rainbow of colors and outlines. The man on the back patio lit up blood orange and the tip of his cigarette burned a deep cranberry red.

"Looks like we've got two people in the room off the patio. Someone is lying down in the back bedroom. There's something, wait—" Hernandez hovered near the front entrance. "I can't tell— maybe a pet in a crate or closet? It's not moving, whatever it is." He spun the drone in a different direction. "There is probably a basement, but I can't get infrared down there."

"Why not?" I asked.

"Concrete block is too thick," Josh replied.

"Check the structure in the back," Rick recommended.

The drone flew past the smoking guy to hover over the back shed. "No heat signatures in the rear structure."

"The license plate doesn't exist." Josh held out the tablet for Rick. "It looks like it was on a list of plates to be destroyed two months ago."

Rick's eyes scanned the information, then turned to me. "Are you sure about the scratch on the bumper?"

"I was this close" —I held my hands six inches apart— "to that damn bumper. Believe me, it's the car." I may have exaggerated, but I wasn't mistaken about the squiggly line. It stood out against the black paint, and I remember reaching for Hector's foot as it was hanging directly above the scratch. "Don't forget, the spinney wheels too."

The drone had returned to the house; after flying over the carport and finding no red-blooded humans, Hernandez returned to hover over the unmoving heat signature in the back bedroom.

"Do you think that could be my sister?" I asked to no one in particular. When I didn't get an answer, I peeled my gaze away from the screen. Rick pinched his lip and looked stern, Josh noncommittal, Hernandez just continued watching the screen, moving the drone slowly around the house, trying to get a peek in the window. He flicked a switch and the drone feed returned to normal. The window was blocked by a mish-mash of black and hot-pink poster board duct-taped together, filling every gap.

"Can you get a clear shot of the subject on the back deck?"

Rick asked.

"Not without coming level and risking discovery," Hernandez replied. "Do you want me to try?"

Rick shook his head. "No, bring it back. We'll send in the MAV. I want audio. If the back door is open, we can get inside."

The drone rose high above the rooftops, flying at a fast clip back to the van. Hernandez's mastery with the drone impressed me. My brother received a drone for Christmas a few years ago. We all had fun taking turns with it in an empty field. I ran it into the only tree in the field, and my sister crash landed twice. It wasn't as easy as it looked. However, Josh diverted my attention from Hernandez's skills when he opened a miniature box that he'd pulled out of a small metal briefcase. Inside lay a dragonfly-looking insect.

"What is that?" I pointed.

"The MAV. Micro-air vehicle," Josh replied. Gently, he removed the dragonfly from its protective nest of foam and laid it in his palm. "Robotic bug. Literally the fly on the wall."

"It has camera and audio?"

"Yes."

I swallowed. "That's so disturbing. I saw one of those in a movie. I thought they were a Hollywood myth. Can anyone get a hold of one of those?"

"Right now," Josh said as he placed the fly back in the box, "the US government holds the patents on MAVs like this."

"So how did you get it?"

Nobody answered. I should have known. "Don't tell me, a gift from the CIA?"

No response. A gentle tap on the roof of the van had me starting in fear. "What was that?" I whispered.

Unconcerned, Rick slid the door open and retrieved a black,

four-rotor drone about the size of a turkey platter. He tucked it into a box next to the console. Hernandez placed the drone's remote controller alongside it. From the dragonfly's briefcase, he retrieved a USB drive and stuck it in the computer. Rick and Josh were moving around the limited space of the van, while Hernandez loaded the dragonfly's software onto the computer, and I realized everyone was doing something except me.

I was in the way.

I should have offered to go sit up front, but I didn't want to miss anything to do with the drone.

Finally, Josh drew open a hatch in the ceiling of the van, hereto unnoticed by me, and placed the dragonfly on the roof. "She's ready when you are."

With a soft flapping sound, we had liftoff. Hernandez put on the headphones with one earpiece halfway off and stared at the screen, manipulating the MAV with the mousepad and a couple of keystrokes. The camera angle was a bit different from the other drone, but Hernandez seemed to have no problem adjusting to the new viewpoint. A few minutes later, the MAV landed gently on the umbrella. The man was still smoking and pacing, but no longer on the phone. He turned and paced toward the drone. He had a teardrop tattoo beneath his eye, short, dark hair, and a scar along his chin. I caught my breath, fearful the drone would be discovered. The boys in the van, however, seemed so sure of the technology that they didn't even blink.

"Do you know him?" Rick asked. I shook my head. "Get a still frame. Once we get a good shot, Josh can run it through facial rec," Rick ordered.

A phone rang loud in the small space, and I let out a startled yelp.

"Sorry," I mumbled.

With a scowl, Rick slid the door open and exited the van to take his call, closing the door behind him.

The MAV's view was limited, but up in the corner, I noticed the screen door had been left open about a foot. "Can the MAV get through that opening?"

Hernandez shifted the bug to get a better shot. "Yes."

The scarred man put his phone to his ear, grabbed a cigarette out of the pack and lit up.

"What's he saying?" I asked.

"He's talking to his girlfriend," Hernandez said with a glance back over his shoulder, and our noses almost touched. "Some space, *pequeña ave*. There's a stool over there," he said, pointing.

"Oh, sorry." I stepped back. "Why do you keep calling me little bird?"

"Your name is Cardinal," Josh said in a flat tone.

"Oh, right." I pulled the stool over and took a seat. "What are we waiting for?" I whispered. "Why aren't you going inside?"

"I'm waiting for him to turn away," Hernandez said in a normal voice. "They can't hear us, you know."

My face turned hot. I glanced at Josh. "Do you have a hit on facial rec?"

Josh shook his head. "Not yet."

"How long does it take?"

"It could be hours."

"Hours? But—"

"This isn't television. When the computer is done running, it might give us a dozen possibilities," Josh said drily.

"A dozen?"

"Or more, then we'll go through them one by one."

Disillusioned, I returned my attention to Hernandez's

screen. Smoke wafted past the bug's camera, and finally, the man moved away from the table. I spotted the gun tucked in the back of his pants as he turned away. Hernandez's face tightened and he grunted before moving the MAV skillfully through the narrow opening.

I held my breath. "Don't you worry the people will be alerted by the noise?"

Hernandez shook his head and flipped the closest headphone out toward me. Gunfire and booms blasted through the earpiece. The couple on the brown couch were watching an action movie on a large flat screen television at full volume. Hernandez landed the dragonfly on a nearby, dying plant. A girl lay half-reclined on the couch, her feet in the man's lap. Her long black hair hung stringy around her shoulders, and she wore a white sweatshirt that read *Juicy* and a pair of white capri leggings. Cellulite rippled through the thin material. Her black eyeliner was smeared, giving her the look of a panda, and she seemed to be watching the show in a daze. The man wore a dark T-shirt and jeans, and one black-booted foot lay perched on the glass coffee table, which was littered with a half empty pizza box, four sodas, paper plates, a bag of white pills, and a big silver gun. Tattoos scattered up the visible parts of his arms, but none displayed across his face or bald head.

"I've got two more to run through facial rec," Hernandez remarked.

The action sequence continued, and the couple's attention remained riveted to the screen. Hernandez lifted the MAV upward and headed down the hall to the back bedroom. The door was closed.

"We can't get in," I whimpered.

"Just a minute." He lowered the MAV to the floor. "There should be enough clearance."

We held our collective breath as the MAV inched forward beneath the door. Centimeter by centimeter, it crept forth. I fiddled with my ring as it advanced, until it finally reached the other side.

Rick slid the door open, startling all of us. Luckily, Hernandez automatically removed his hands from the keyboard, so the MAV wasn't disturbed.

"Where are you?" he asked.

"In the bedroom." Hernandez returned his attention to the computer. The drone flew up and over the sleeping figure.

She wore underwear and a light T-shirt. Mottled markings of bruises dotted her arms and legs. Her long dusky hair spread across her face, and she had one arm above her head—cuffed to the iron bedpost. I sucked wind.

"Is that your sister?" Hernandez asked.

"I don't know, it's so dark." I chewed my lip. The small shimmer from around the door and filtered streetlight through the pink poster board on the window provided the only illumination. "Can you get any closer?"

The MAV descended, the girl groaned and shifted, and her hair fell back, revealing a cut lip and swollen black eye.

Air whistled through my teeth and I rubbed my temples. "It's not Jillian. I believe that might be Trudea."

"Hector Cortez is dead," Rick announced, the revelation dropping like an anvil in our cramped compartment.

"What? Where? How? Was my sister with him?" I twisted around and peppered my anxious questions at Rick.

"He was trying to get on a flight to Mexico, out of Dulles. He had a false passport, but the FBI sent out a BOLO and airport security recognized him. Hector ran, they gave chase. He pulled a gun, they shot him down." Rick delivered the news in an emotionless tenor.

I rubbed my temples harder and closed my eyes. "She isn't here. Hector is dead, which means we can't capture and interrogate him. What do we do now?"

"How's it going with facial rec?" Rick asked Josh.

"Nothing yet. Still running."

"We got two more to run through the system," Hernandez put in.

"That's good," Rick said confidently, "more leads. Don't give up hope, Cardinal." He squeezed my shoulder.

"With Cortez dead, do you think the gang will remove the contract on my head?"

"Possibly." Rick squinted at the monitor. "Where are you now?"

"Closet in the front hall. Look at this." The MAV pulled back and Hernandez pointed at a latch with a padlock on it.

"What do you think they're hiding in there?" Josh pondered, arms crossed.

"Drugs. Probably a whole closetful to go with the ones on the coffee table." I stated the obvious.

Rick didn't respond and I noticed Hernandez squinting at the monitor as he slowly moved the MAV around the lock. "I don't think it's for keeping people out," he said, "I think it's for keeping something in."

That got my attention, and I leaned in. "What do you mean?"

"There was a heat signature here." Hernandez moved the MAV closer to the door. "I thought it was a dog. You don't put a pet in with your drug stash. It's also not a smart idea to keep it in the front hall. That's a rookie move. Something a dime-bagger would do."

"What kind of sick fuck locks their dog in the front hall?" Josh muttered.

I pulled one of Hernandez's earphones closer and heard nothing but movie noises. "Why isn't it barking?"

Josh and Rick turned to me.

"The dog. Why isn't he barking in a frenzy? I can't imagine he likes being locked up in there. Unless you think they've drugged or beaten it into submission."

Hernandez put the MAV on the floor and crept toward the crack under the door. Unfortunately, the older house must have shifted, because there wasn't enough room for the MAV to get very far.

"There's more space at the other end, near the door hinges," Rick pointed out, and the dragonfly flew its way to the opposite side of the door.

I held my breath as it slipped beneath the crack . . . into utter blackness. "I can't see a thing," I said. "Doesn't this drone have a light source?"

"*No,*" Rick and Josh answered at once.

"Can you tell your CIA friends to put one on?" I suggested.

Hernandez shushed me, put the second headphone on, and pushed them tight to his ears. "Something's . . . breathing."

"Dog?" Rick shifted closer and squinted at the dark screen.

Hernandez's face pinched in concentration, but he shook his head. "I can't tell. I'd better get out, in case it wakes up."

He backed the MAV under the door, into the light. A finger followed it. The nail was broken and ragged, but it wore a distinct bright neon-pink fingernail polish, and it reached toward the camera.

Holy shit! I gasped, reaching out my own hand.

Hernandez backed the MAV further, and the finger followed as far as it could.

I jumped up and grasped Rick's arm, shaking it with the might of a wolverine. "It's her. She's in the damn closet. My sister. It's her. *That*" —I pointed— "is her fingernail polish." I looked back at the screen, but the finger had disappeared. "Go closer. Do it again." I pounded Hernandez on the shoulder.

Hernandez did as he was told, and the finger reached out again.

"It's her. I knew it. Let's go! Move! Get out of my way!" I tried to push past Rick to the door.

"Slow down, Cardinal. Slow down." Rick gripped both of my wrists, forcing me to a halt. "Calm down. We are going to get her out, but we need a plan first. We can't go running out of here with our pants on fire. Someone's going to get killed."

I stopped trying to pull away as his words penetrated my excitement. "You're right. I'm sorry. What do we need to do?"

He released me. "First, *you* aren't doing anything. Remember our deal? You. Remain. In. The. Van."

I opened my mouth to argue, but at his stern look, I thought better of it and nodded instead. "Okay. Yeah, I get it. Now what?"

"I need to make a call. Then I want to review the footage. Hernandez, I want you to check the rest of the house. Make sure we know what we're dealing with. See if you can get into the basement. I don't want any surprises."

"On it, boss."

Rick exited the van; Josh laid his tablet on the counter and followed Rick, slamming the door shut behind him. In the meantime, I chewed a hangnail as I watched the bug fly throughout the rest of the house, getting the lay of the land. My knee bounced in nervous anticipation, which probably annoyed Hernandez, but he was gentleman enough not to comment on it. Another bag of pills, yellow this time, lay on the kitchen counter, and dishes piled up in the sink, but there were no other human beings. He ran into an issue trying to get into the basement. The door was closed, and the gap at the floor was simply too small for the MAV to get through. Dim light shone through the cracks, and Hernandez grunted with frustration.

"Is that going to be a problem?" I asked.

"The boss is not going to like it."

"Any other way of getting down there? Maybe a peek through an outside window?"

"I'll give it a try." He navigated his way out through the back screen door, which luckily had not been shut, and winged the MAV over to a deep window well. We encountered more darkness. Not a speck of light shone through the dirty glass.

I chewed my lip as Hernandez checked the well next to it, and then the two in front of the house with the same result. "Does this mean Rick won't go in?"

"Not necessarily. It just means we don't know what's down there."

"Which will make it more dangerous for you."

He didn't respond. The dragonfly flew out of the well, and Hernandez returned it to the umbrella to observe our smoking man, who was still wandering the back porch. His conversation with his girlfriend must have ended. He now concentrated on his phone, as if reading a deep philosophical debate espoused by Plato or Socrates. The cigarette hung out the side of his mouth, forgotten.

The van door slid open, drawing our attention away from the monitor.

"Christoph is here," Josh said.

Hernandez removed his headphones and hopped out. I watched the footage for a few moments, but our smoker did nothing of interest. Giving up, I trailed Hernandez, curious to meet this Christoph. I found the four men standing in back of a green SUV parked behind Rick's car. The rear liftgate was open, and they spoke in quiet tones.

I stationed myself next to Josh and whispered, "What's going on?"

He must not have heard my approach—I was learning from Rick—because he gave a slight jerk. "You should be in the van," he hissed.

My arrival caught the eye of the fourth man, a thin guy with stringy, light brown hair that fell in his eyes. He wore ripped jeans, a dark windbreaker, and was in need of a shave.

"Hi, you must be Christoph." I held out my hand. "I'm Karina."

He stared at me for a moment, taking in the vest and utility belt. "Is this who I think it is?"

My hand dropped.

"Tell me you didn't bring the witness here." He glared at Rick.

"Don't worry, I stay in the van where it's safe," I assured him.

"You know there's a contract on her head?" He continued to ignore me and address Rick.

"Hey!" I snapped my fingers in front of Christoph to get his attention. "I am well aware there's a contract out on me. As you can see, Silverthorne has taken precautions." I pounded my vest.

Christoph seemed to finally focus on me.

Rick sighed and shifted his weight. "It was either bring her, or handcuff and forcibly detain her. Not exactly protocol for a client."

"That's why you should have left her in FBI custody," Christoph admonished, taking off his windbreaker and pulling his own bulletproof vest out of the cargo area.

"She wouldn't stay. Besides, she's been helpful in identifying her sister," Rick said in a deadened tone.

Christoph replaced the windbreaker, zipping it over the vest. "So you have confirmation?"

"Well—" Rick hesitated.

Josh answered on behalf of his boss, "We've got a partial identification."

"What does that mean?" Christoph pushed his long hair back and placed a baseball cap on backward to keep it out of his face.

"I recognized her hand," I provided.

Christoph's attention returned to me. "Her hand? Does she have some sort of identifying tattoo? Birthmark? Scar?"

I shook my head at each question. "I recognized her nail polish."

"You're shitting me. Her nail polish?" he snorted derisively.

"It—it is very distinctive," I supplied defensively.

Christoph crossed his arms and surveyed the other men, one by one. Hernandez stared down and kicked at a pebble. Josh stuck his hands in his pockets. Rick watched me with a slight curl to his lip. I couldn't tell if he was amused or disgusted.

"Whether it's her sister or not, there is a woman locked in a closet, and another imprisoned in a bedroom, cuffed to a bed," Rick explained.

"And the drugs?" Christoph asked.

Rick's scrutiny finally left me to return to Christoph. "Don't worry. They'll be there."

Christoph clipped a holstered gun to his belt. "They better be. It's my ass on the line if there aren't any drugs."

"Charming." The sarcasm oozed out of my mouth. "And rescuing two women from human trafficking isn't good enough?"

"Look," he informed me as he hung a badge around his neck. "I'm DEA, not FBI. And while I want to get these girls released just as much as the next guy, I'm in it to bust the dealers and confiscate the drugs. Trafficking isn't exactly my bag."

"DEA! What's DEA doing here? I thought you called your FBI friend!" I turned on Rick angrily.

"The FBI is" —Rick coughed— "rather busy at the moment."

"So, what? We get the B-team today?" I flung my hand at the DEA agent.

"I can see why you brought her," Christoph drawled. "She's a real barrel of laughs."

I itched to slap him, but refrained, instead delivering a glare that could stop a charging water buffalo.

"Cardinal, can I speak to you a moment?" Rick gripped my bicep almost painfully and led me back to the van.

I pulled my arm away and snapped, "Why did you invite him? I don't understand why the three of you haven't gone in already. There are only two guys with guns." I held up two fingers for emphasis. "What's up with bringing the DEA? If you were going to bring someone in, why didn't you get one of the cops, like Perez, or someone in the FBI? Don't tell me you don't know some more law enforcement who would help in this situation. I mean, c'mon, who is that Christoph guy, anyway? He looks like he's been sampling some of the product he confiscated, and he needs a damn haircut." Okay, maybe I was being a bit harsh, but lashing out came from concern about my sister, and I didn't appreciate this Christoph guy's laissez-faire attitude about two prisoners in a gang den.

Rick remained silent during my rant and took a beat before answering. "Christoph is one of the best undercover DEA agents on the force. He recently came off a job and had some time on his hands. And, to answer your question, no; my friends at the FBI are busy chasing down PJ-the-snitch's leads."

"What about Sadira's leads? My sister *is here*. I bet if I called Perez and Garcia, they'd get themselves on over right now."

"It's my understanding that your friend Perez and his partner are following a few other leads from Sadira. Additionally, last I heard, the joint task force has got viable intel at the warehouse site, and there is a raid about to go down. It's all hands on deck."

"But, she's *not* at the warehouse. Why didn't you tell them what we found?"

"And how would I explain how we found a woman locked in a closet who we *think* might be your sister because we saw a finger?" His brows rose.

"Oh, c'mon, you're the King of Crap. You could've made something up."

"And what if it's not her? What if she's in the warehouse where they think she is?"

I paused. He made a good argument. What if Jilly wasn't here? Still— "I don't see how diverting a few cops over here would make a difference."

He rubbed the five o'clock shadow on his cheek. "There's another reason I don't want to bring the force down here. A full-on SWAT raid will take time and put those girls in further danger. The moment we call police or FBI, we're in a holding pattern until they come up with their own plan. This is a precision extraction, anything else can lead to collateral damage. Bringing in a DEA agent for the drugs gives the raid legitimacy and keeps it small."

What he said made sense. I knew military spec ops were highly trained to make maximum impact with a small team and minimum body count. "Christoph has the DEA's blessing to raid this joint?" I asked.

"Something like that," Rick hedged.

"Do I want to know the exact story?"

"Let's just say, the pills on the coffee table give him probable cause."

I sighed, rubbing my arm where Rick had held me. "When are you going in?"

"Soon. Since Hernandez can't get in the basement, I'd like to have one more on the team. We're waiting for Jin to get here."

"Can I be on coms while you execute the raid?"

He gave me one of his analytical hard stares. His eyes narrowed and he finally said, "Tell you what, I'll put a body cam on Josh, and you'll be able to hear the coms through the computer. I'll also leave the MAV up. You can watch and hear it all from the comfort of the van, but it'll be one-way. You won't be able to speak to us. I can't have you interfering in the raid or throwing the team off balance with an ill-timed comment, or smart-ass remark. Deal?" He held out his hand.

"Deal." I shook his hand and climbed back in the van to wait.

The boys suited up in tactical gear while I watched the MAV's footage.

Rick directed his men to use nonlethal force unless absolutely necessary. "That means beanbag rounds and tasers. I'll need someone to interrogate in case our target isn't in the house." Rick, along with Christoph, returned to the trunk of his car to retrieve more gear. Josh and Hernandez were in the rear of the van, loading up on weapons and body armor.

Smoking guy got a call, jumped up and started agitatedly pacing. I listened in the earphone, but Spanish spurted from his mouth far too quickly for my poorly trained ear to follow.

"Hey, the guy on the back porch got a call. Something's up."

I held the headphones toward the boys.

Hernandez snatched them from my hand and jammed them on his head. "FBI raided the warehouse." His brows turned down into a glower. He stuck his head out the door and barked, "Boss!"

Rick came around to the van. "What is it?"

"They're moving the girls."

"Shit. When?" Rick hopped into the van.

Christoph arrived. "What's going on?"

"They're moving the girls," I threw over my shoulder.

"They know about the warehouse raid, and the fact that Hector is dead. Someone's coming to get them now." Hernandez shook his head. "Sounds like they'll be here in fifteen minutes."

Expressions of irritation, anger, and frustration swept across Rick's features in quick succession. "We can't wait for Jin. Are you ready?" He glanced around at the team.

"I'm ready," Josh answered.

Christoph nodded. Hernandez gave a thumbs up while continuing to listen to the one-sided phone conversation.

On the monitor, I watched smoking man hang up, toss his cigarette to the ground, and return to the living room. Unfortunately, he slammed the screen door with a quick flick of his wrist, effectively shutting off the MAV's access back into the house. He then shoved the large sliding door closed, but it bounced back open about two inches. Hernandez moved the bug to observe through the window and hear better.

The two men seemed to get into a heated discussion. The girl curled up into the corner of the couch, her eyes wide and fearful. Her boyfriend lifted the gun and brandished it in the air, while smoking man shook his head, and I distinguished the words *tranquilo* and *cálmese*.

"What's going on?" I whispered.

Hernandez held up a finger, listening intently.

I didn't like the looks of the hothead on the couch. Of the two, I assumed smoking man was the leader because he'd received the call. However, a hothead with a gun could quickly shift the balance of power. I couldn't hear or understand what he shouted, but I had a bad feeling he was suggesting that getting rid of the girls with a bullet to the head would be a lot easier than smoking man's plan.

Hernandez's jaw hardened and instead of answering me, he dropped the headphones and turned to Rick. "We need to go. *Now.*"

"Josh and Christoph, you take the front. Hernandez and I will take the back. Go on my command," Rick said, delivering the orders. "Hernandez, bring up Josh's body cam, and coms for Cardinal on the computer—listening only. You—" He speared me with his intense gaze. "Do. Not. Leave. This. Van."

"Wouldn't dream of it." I rocked, rubbing my hands up and down my thighs against the soft knit of my yoga pants.

"Try not to worry," was Josh's parting shot before he slammed the door.

Far easier said than done. The risks had just gone up for everyone involved. The warehouse raid put our suspects on alert, and any moment, their backup would be arriving.

The MAV's footage was probably still rolling, but, in his haste, Hernandez didn't put it up on a split screen, so all I could see was Josh's footage. I watched as they jogged the two blocks to the house. Josh's body cam bounced up and down in a jarring manner that made me nauseated, and I had to look away.

I tuned back in when I heard Rick whisper over the coms, "Subject One has returned to the patio."

From Josh's camera, I saw the back of Christoph. Both were

hunched down in front of the house, near the door.

"Do we breach?" someone asked.

"Negative. Wait for my signal. Hernandez, take care of Subject One," Rick said.

There was a grunt, some scrabbling sounds, and then Hernandez uttered, "Subject neutralized."

I heard a loud *bang!* and then Rick yelled, "*Go now, breach, breach, breach!*"

Josh and Christoph busted in through the front. Chaos ensued, the noise of the breach, shouts, and then a buzzing came over the coms. Josh ran into the family room with the television.

Hernandez tasered the guy on the couch, while the girl sat screaming with her hands around her ears. "*Cállate!*" he barked at her.

Someone muted the noisy movie.

"Clear the other rooms!" someone shouted—Christoph, I think.

"Hernandez, cuff him. I'll cover you. Then we'll take the basement," Rick said.

Josh followed Christoph down the hallway, busting down the bedroom doors one by one, checking closets, under beds, and behind large pieces of furniture. Each yelled "clear!" when they found nothing.

"*Dios mío*, would you look at that," Hernandez whistled across the coms.

"Joshua, are you done clearing the rooms yet?" Rick asked.

"Almost." Josh took the room with Trudea. He put a finger to her neck. "Pulse is steady on the girl in the back room."

"Chris, you better get down here," Rick said.

Josh returned to the narrow hallway, and Christoph pushed past him. "On my way to the basement."

Josh paused as he entered the TV room. The two men were handcuffed with zip ties and lay face down on the floor. The girl sat on the couch, also cuffed, looking frightened but no longer screaming. Hernandez stood at the top of the staircase.

"What's in the basement?" Josh asked.

"You need to see it." Hernandez jerked his head. "I'll keep an eye on them."

At the bottom of the stairs sat a folding table surrounded by two empty chairs. A deck of cards, two empty beer bottles, a half bottle of tequila, two shot glasses, and a half-eaten slice of pizza were scattered across the table. Josh turned the corner, and it took a moment to process what I was seeing through his grainy body cam. Six cubes, two-by-two-feet square each, wrapped in light blue plastic, sat in the middle of a makeshift counter created by a pair of saw horses and an old door. It was cash, and a lot of it. Running a fifteen-foot length of the back wall was a shelving unit filled from floor to ceiling with industrial-sized bottles of pills—enough to fill a pharmacy—and wrapped white packets. Kilos of drugs, I assumed. Christoph counted the packages on the shelves.

Josh stood in front of the cash. "How much do you think it is?"

Rick, on the other side of the counter, shrugged. "Depends on the denominations. Could be millions."

"Why weren't there more guys guarding it?" Josh asked.

Rick's brows turned down, as if wondering the same thing. "No idea, but if there is this much money and drugs in here, they'll be sending an army to retrieve it. Is the rest of the house clear?"

"Yes."

"Let's go get the girls, we don't have much time." Rick turned to Christoph. "Have you called it in?"

"There's got to be at least fifty kilos," Christoph mumbled almost reverently.

"*Chris,*" Rick barked to get his DEA pal's attention, "you need to call it in. *Now.*"

"Oh, yeah. On it." Christoph pulled a cell phone out of his pocket and dialed.

"Get a couple of teams down here," Rick ordered. "We don't know how many men Montoya will be sending."

"Yeah, yeah." Christoph put the phone to his ear and returned his attention to the drugs.

Rick frowned, regarding his DEA pal.

As if reading his boss's mind, Josh said, "You stay here, I'll go get the girls."

Rick gave a brusque nod.

Josh returned to the front hall. After two whacks with the butt of his shotgun, the lock broke off. The door opened and my sister rolled out at Josh's feet. An empty water bottle fell from her lap. Her wrists were cuffed with zip ties and her ankles were duct taped together. Josh bent and scooped her up.

I didn't wait for more. Abandoning my post, I climbed into the front seat and cranked the key that the boys handily left in the ignition. The engine noise sounded loud in the relatively quiet neighborhood. The van jerked forward as I planted my foot to the floor and peeled away from the curb. Things in the back slid around, dropping to the floor with bangs and clanks. I cringed. I hadn't taken the time to secure the equipment. Braking, I wheeled around the corner at a slower pace. Only a few items dropped to the floor as the van wobbled back and forth, returning to its center of gravity. I hoped they weren't expensive electronics bouncing around back there. Hernandez might not forgive me if I broke his toys.

Creeping around the next turn, I saw a dark sedan pull into

the driveway. A man got out of the driver's side, carrying a gun at his side. Hunched over, he approached the busted front door hanging drunkenly from its hinges.

"Damnit, Rick. *This* is why you should have given me an earpiece," I grumbled.

Working with what I had, I pinned the guy with my high beams. Blinded, he fired off a couple of wild shots. One hit the side mirror and another, the windshield, dead center. Ducking down, I gunned the motor, jumped the curb, and blared the horn. His body made a *whap* as I hit it, and he flew forward into a hedge of boxwood. Hernandez and Josh were at the door in an instant. Hernandez leapt over the body, aimed his weapon, and nailed another man—who had gotten out of the sedan and was running away—with a beanbag round, square to the back. The guy went down, howling.

I turned off the ignition but left the lights on. Their brilliance bounced back at me off the white siding as I hopped out. "Where's my sister?"

"You were supposed to stay in the van," Hernandez admonished over his shoulder.

"I did," I replied, indicating the guy moaning in the bushes.

"You broke my leg," he cried.

Pushing past Josh, who was pulling the guy out of the hedges with cuffs ready, I found my sister laid across a flowered couch beneath the window. The van's high beams lit up the front room, bright as day.

Josh had removed the cuffs and tape. Her wrists were rubbed raw, and I gripped her clammy hand. "Jilly? It's me, Rina. I'm here, c'mon, you can wake up now." I shook her gently, but her head lolled back, revealing a dark bruise across her left cheek. I pressed a hand to her cold forehead. "Jilly? Wake up, hon." Her breath seemed shallow. Calming my own breathing, I felt for a pulse and found it slow and sluggish. "*JOSHUA!*" I yelled over my shoulder, to find him striding through the front door, carrying a black duffle bag with lots of zippers and pockets. "Something's wrong," I cried.

"She's been drugged." He unzipped the duffle, revealing gauze, bandages, and other medical paraphernalia.

I tucked a lock of hair behind her cheek. "Is there anything we can give her? Like an epi-pen or Narcan? Do you have that in your bag?"

He shook his head. "Not until we find out what's in her system. I think it's a tranquilizer, maybe valium or similar, but I can't be sure. There's an entire pharmacy in the basement. If I give her the wrong medication it could send her into cardiac arrest. Hernandez!"

Hernandez came in through front door. "Yeah?"

"See if you can find out what they gave her," Josh said.

He disappeared into the TV room and I heard a spate of angry Spanish.

"Here, put this resuscitation bag over her nose and mouth." Josh handed me a balloon-shaped bag attached to a mouthpiece, the likes of which I'd seen on a variety of medical shows.

I put the cup over her nose and began quickly squeezing the bag.

"Hold on, not like that. Here, cup your fingers around the valve and draw her chin up to make sure the airway is open. Use these fingers to keep it anchored." He put his hands over mine and positioned my fingers properly. "Squeeze and allow the bag to refill fully before administering another breath. See how her chest is rising. That's good." He returned to digging around in the duffle.

"What are you doing now?" I asked, ignoring Hernandez's increasingly loud shouts at the two suspects and the unmistakable sound of flesh hitting flesh.

"EMTs are on the way. Since you conveniently brought the van, I can start her on an IV drip." A minute later, my sister had a needle in her arm and Josh hung the IV bag on the nearby lampshade. I thanked the stars he'd been a Navy corpsman before joining Silverthorne.

"Keep doing what you're doing, I'm going to check on the other girl." He scooped up the duffle and headed down the hall, leaving me alone with Jillian.

Hernandez continued spewing Spanish, but he didn't seem to be making headway. I didn't like the looks of Jillian's coloring.

Rick came in from the kitchen. "SWAT and DEA are on the way. The ambulance is eight minutes out."

One of the men yelled out in pain, and I flinched.

"This isn't working," I growled. "Here, take over with the bag."

To my surprise, Rick complied. I walked in to find Hernandez with the butt of his gun in the air, ready to bring it down on the bald man's hand, which he held down with his foot. The girl had backed herself into the corner between the sliding glass door and the wall, and her frightened eyes were as big as baseballs.

I went over and got in her face. "You speak English?"

She nodded.

I jerked her upright, pulled her into the front room, and pointed at my sister. "What did they give her?"

Her eyes darted to the room's doorway, where her boyfriend lay. She shrugged. I realized she wouldn't talk as long as he was within hearing distance. She stumbled as I dragged her down the hall into the empty bathroom. Slamming the door, I pushed her down onto the toilet seat.

"Listen up," I hissed. "If we don't get the antidote to the drugs you gave her, she might not make it. If she dies, whether or not you gave her the drugs, you'll be an accessory to murder by virtue of being in this house. You got me? That's murder one." I held up my finger in her face. "Murder with intent. And here in Virginia, we don't just lock you up. Oh, no, in Virginia, we like to give you the chair." My mouth spread into an evil, Grinch-like grin. "You know, fry you up like a *churro*. Zzzztt."

She flinched.

"Now, I'm going to run some water in this bathtub." I turned on the taps. "Then I'm going to have my big blond friend put you in. And then, I'm going to take this taser here and shoot it into the water to give you a taste of what it'll feel like in the electric chair. You understand?"

I had zero plans to actually carry out the threat, but I must have been convincing enough because she shied away from the tub and started talking. "Roofies. They gave her roofies. They put it in the water bottle."

My sister must not have realized they drugged the water. "How much did they give her?"

She shrugged. "I don't know."

"Anything else?" I shook the taser at her.

I must have looked vicious enough to carry out my threats because her frightened face paled and she pulled back further. "I don't know. Flaco told me to go to one of the bedrooms and wait while he and Leon took care of business. That's all I know."

"What about the other girl? In the bedroom? Same thing?"

She shook her head. "Trudy's drug of choice is heroin, but Flaco might have given her roofies too. I'm not sure."

I opened the door. "Joshua!"

He stuck his head out of the bedroom right next to me.

"They gave my sister roofies. Sounds like Trudea may have a heroin cocktail going on."

I closed the door again and assessed the girl in front of me. As much as I wanted to return to Jillian, this girl gave me answers, at the risk of taking a beating, or worse, getting killed. "Are you Flaco's girlfriend?"

She produced an ugly look and wouldn't meet my eyes. "He chose me. I didn't choose him."

"Are you one of the gang? Do you want to be here?"

Her toes curled inward, and she stared down at the floor with the slightest shake of her head.

"Would you be willing to testify?"

Her head started shaking violently.

"The police can put you into witness protection," I explained.

The shaking continued. "I've got a grandmother and brother. They'll kill them before I walk out the front door," she declared.

"What if I have you arrested with Flaco and his pal? The FBI can get your family members to safety, while they take you in."

Her eyes narrowed as she assessed me. "You can do that?"

"I can make that happen, but they'll want you to testify. The drugs, guns, prostitution rings, everything you know. I realize this is a big leap, but it'll get you out of here. How old are you? Eighteen? Nineteen?"

"Sixteen," she whispered.

I drew breath through my teeth. "You can go back to school and be safe. Away from here."

She scowled and stared at the running water.

I shut off the taps. "You need to make a decision now. Once I walk out this door, I'm done helping you. In or out?"

"In," she murmured.

"Then play along." I pulled her to her feet.

"What are you doing?" she asked in a panic.

"Come here, lean over the tub, I need to get you wet." There was a plastic cup on the counter which I filled with water and poured over her head, soaking her stringy hair and face. The water was ice cold and she squealed in protest. "That's good, make some more noise." I poured a few more cups on her before dragging her back down the hall and shoving her to the floor next to Flaco and his pal. "This one's no use to us. She's drugged up. Doesn't know shit. Worthless," I said with disgust.

Flaco sported a swelling middle and pointer finger, while Leon's eye was darkening to purple. Hernandez must have showed some restraint. I'd expected ripped-off fingernails and waterboarding from these guys.

Returning to my sister, I took over the bag from Rick. "What's that?"

Josh stood above her, pressing a syringe of clear fluid into the IV. "Flumazenil, it's the antagonist to the Rohypnol, a.k.a. roofies."

"Thank you," I said with feeling. Twisting back to Rick, with a jerk of my head, I indicated he come closer. "The girl wants to testify for immunity and WITSEC. She's got a grandmother and brother who need to go with her. Can you arrange it?" I murmured.

Rick nodded and left the room, putting a cell phone to his ear.

Jin stepped through the front door just then. "Looks like you started the party without me."

"You're late." Josh adjusted the IV bag. Sirens wailed in the distance.

"Paperwork." Jin shrugged, hooking his thumbs in his

pockets. To me, he said, "I heard you bounced someone off the bumper."

I squeezed the bag before answering. "I would have used my taser, but they said I had to stay in the van."

"Nice," he said with a smirk. "Told you she could be an asset to the team."

Josh shook his head and commented, "Warned is a better adjective."

Rick reentered the room. "Actually, she was an asset. We had no idea the pair of them had shown up. We were spread too thin. I was in the basement with Christoph, Hernandez was watching the three in the back, and Josh was attending the girls. If it weren't for the racket out front . . ."

"Alright, alright." Josh held up a hand and sighed. "I owe you one, Karina."

Jin grinned.

Embarrassed, I stared at the inflating bag.

The sounds of the sirens grew closer and closer until they arrived on scene. With them came my own relief, for it meant the nightmare had come to an end.

Chapter Twenty-One

At the hospital, they wheeled my sister into a treatment room, gave me a pile of paperwork, and pointed me in the direction of an empty lounge. It wasn't empty for long. Jin must have followed the ambulance and soon joined me for the interminable wait.

"I guess you drew the short straw," I said, scribbling my way through the intake form.

"Nah, I volunteered."

My brows arched in surprise.

He shrugged. "I've had my fill of paperwork for one day."

I smirked. "Well, thanks for coming."

"Someone had to. I found that in the ambulance," he said, holding up the Kevlar vest. "You need to put it back on."

I'd removed the vest on the ride over. While I'd ditched the vest, my stocked utility belt remained wrapped around my waist. It was probably a good thing I'd been wearing it, because it's unlikely I would have remembered to grab my purse on the way to the ambulance. I was starting to see the draw in wearing cargo pants—like the pair Jin wore—or a utility belt. They kept your possessions close without the burden of a heavy handbag.

I stared at the vest with the pen poised above the clipboard. "I'm not keen to put it back on," I admitted. "Don't you think we're safe here in the hospital?"

"No, as a matter of fact, I think you're vulnerable." He held it out to me.

With a put-upon sigh, I tried to wrestle my way back into

the vest. My arms got stuck in the upright position, and I couldn't seem to get the vest to go up or down. "Uh, Jin, a little help."

Jin wasn't as tall as Josh, but his hands were strong, and with a tug and a yank, the vest slid into place, once again squishing my boobs.

I struck a pose. "Sexy, huh?"

"It's not supposed to be sexy. It's supposed to be safe," he replied in a monotone voice while adjusting the Velcro straps.

After I finished the forms, Jin carried them to the appropriate paper pusher. He returned to find me absently picking at nonexistent lint on my yoga pants.

"Is there someone you need to call?" he asked.

"Probably a million people," I muttered, pulling my phone out of a pocket on the utility belt. I'd turned the sound off after talking to Mike, and to my displeasure, I found dozens of voicemails and texts. Dropping the phone in my lap, I rubbed a hand across my face. Mike was on a plane, so I couldn't call him. On the other hand, my parents deserved a call. I dialed their number.

Mom answered before the first ring completed. "Hello?"

"Mom? It's Karina, we found Jilly and she's going to be okay."

My mother immediately began sobbing, and I paced the floor as I consoled her.

Twenty minutes later, it had been decided my mom would fly out on the first flight she could get. My father had been teaching classes at the local community college and the upcoming week was finals. Grades would be due afterward, so we determined he would stay behind for the time being.

Not long after I hung up, Mike walked into the waiting room wearing jeans and a black hoodie, wheeling a suitcase. I stumbled into his open arms, so incredibly thankful as his warm embrace curled around me.

"I thought it would take you longer to get home," I mumbled into his shoulder.

"You can thank your friend Rick. I don't know who he called, but it must have been someone high up the food chain. I couldn't find a direct flight, and the next thing I know, an Air Force pilot is knocking on my door with orders to fly me into Andrews Air Force Base. From there I was choppered to the Pentagon, where I got a taxi. I guess you haven't seen my texts."

Sheepishly, I shook my head. "Things have been a little . . . chaotic."

"That's what I understand." The deep crease between his brows spoke to hours of worry.

I rubbed a thumb along that furrow and found myself pulled into his embrace again. I welcomed the comfort it brought.

A little while later, he released me enough to allow proper breathing to return. "I spoke with your parents," he told me.

"I know. I called them just before you arrived. My mom is getting a flight out tomorrow morning."

"Let me know when she's supposed to arrive. I can pick her up."

I smiled weakly at his thoughtfulness, realizing I'd probably have my hands full with Jillian.

A thickset man with thinning brown hair, black-rimmed glasses, and wearing green scrubs entered the waiting room. "Who's here with" —he glanced at the clipboard in his hand— "Jillian Cardinal?"

"That would be us. I'm her sister, Karina." I took Mike's hand in mine and stepped closer to the doctor. I felt Jin's presence on my other side. "How is she?"

"I'm Dr. Kanter." We shook hands. "Your sister is in stable

condition, but we are going to admit her, and keep her under observation overnight."

"Can I see her?" I asked.

"After we get her a room, you can go on up. Only family." He eyed the two men. "Wait here, and someone will direct you once we get her settled. Officially, visiting hours are over, so the nurses won't allow you to stay for long. You can return tomorrow at nine."

While we waited for Jillian to get a room, Rick arrived, his gaze alighting on Mike and me. "You made it," he stated in greeting.

"Thanks to you." Mike rose and shook Rick's hand, slapping him on the shoulder with his other one. "I don't know what favors you called in, or how you knew where I was, but I appreciate it. I owe you one."

Rick gave him a calculating look as he replied, "One day, I'll collect." Then he moved past Mike to me and gestured to the vest. "You can remove that."

"Oh, thank goodness, it's making me sweat." I loosened the straps and Rick helped wrench off the bulky vest.

"Did the hit get called off?" Mike frowned as I readjusted my shirt.

"The hit was put out by Hector Cortez." Rick tossed the Kevlar onto nearby bench. "Since he's dead, no one has offered to pay the bounty."

"Are you sure everyone knows?" Skepticism filled Mike's question.

Rick nodded. "Cops have put word out on the street that there's no money in it. The gang took a big hit tonight."

"You mean all the drugs and money in the house?" I asked.

"That, and the warehouse the taskforce raided. Drugs, cash, guns, and military weapons."

"Military weapons?" I exclaimed.

"M252 mortars, MK19 grenade launchers, cases of M-16s, XM25 Counter Defilade Target Engagement System—" Rick listed half a dozen more weapon systems that was all military Greek to me.

Jin crossed his arms with a deep frown. "That sounds a lot like a shipment to Afghanistan that went missing last summer."

Rick stuck his hands in his pockets. "Looks like they'd already sold off some of the larger equipment."

"How'd they get ahold of it?" I asked.

"Inside job," Mike and Rick answered at once.

All the men exchanged looks that made me feel left out.

"They also confiscated a computer system." Rick tilted his chin at Mike. "Your people will have a field day."

Mike rubbed his jaw and held back a yawn. "Maybe we can identify our Pentagon arms dealer with it."

"I believe that's the hope." Rick rocked back on his heels. "Whatever the case, MS-13 took a big hit tonight. It's my understanding they arrested two of Montoya's top lieutenants along with a dozen soldiers at the warehouse. Nine more were killed on site, and four went to the hospital. Cops rounded up over a dozen more gang members tonight. Word on the street— Montoya's on the run and a rival gang is already positioning themselves to move in on his territory."

"A productive evening," I murmured.

"Jin—" Rick addressed his subordinate. "You can go. I'll want to see your report tomorrow, but you can clock out tonight."

"Wait, Jin, before you leave—" I placed my hand on his sleeve "—what happened with Tazim?"

"He went to fence the diamonds. Once the police entered the picture, Tazim crumpled and was more than willing to squeal on anyone he could think of." He gave a knowing grin. "They didn't even offer protection, he was spouting names as they put him in the squad car. Gambling ring bosses, loan sharks, even some guy who deals in counterfeit cash."

"So, Sadira had nothing to do with the original diamond theft?"

He gave a head shake. "Doesn't look like it. She was an easy target for Tazim."

"Why did he do it? Was it just the money to pay for his gambling habit?"

Jin's scar elongated as he frowned. "They threatened his wife and kids. The mix-up with the manager at the jewelry store simply made Sadira an easy target."

"Hm, just think," I mused, "if Tazim had pinned the theft on another one of his employees, all of this never would have happened. MS-13 would be selling those weapons to the highest bidding military *junta*."

"Most likely," Jin agreed.

"Huh, my sister, in her quest to help an at-risk youth, brought down a little gang empire."

Mike put an arm around my shoulder and squeezed. "She deserves a medal."

A nurse came in, breaking up our little coterie, to direct me to Jillian's room. She reiterated the doctor's orders that only family would be allowed. I gave Jin and Rick a hug, thanked them for everything they'd done for me tonight, and told them I'd contact them tomorrow.

"I'll wait here," Mike said, "and take you home afterward."

I squeezed his hand, then followed the nurse's directions to Jillian's room.

The room held two beds, but Jillian was the only one in it. IV tubes and wires monitoring her heartbeat snaked out from beneath the covers. They'd intubated her, and the breathing machine wheezed quietly. Her left eye was swollen angry red and her cheek, a mottled purple. She slept.

I took her cool, limp hand in my own and murmured a prayer. The nurses kicked me out, in the kindest tones, after what seemed like five minutes, but checking my watch, I found I'd stayed with my sister for more than half an hour.

Rick had remained behind with Mike and drove us both to my condo. Utter exhaustion took over as I sat in the back of his car.

The next thing I knew, Mike was in my face, shaking my shoulder. "K.C., we're here. Do you want me to carry you?"

I made it to my apartment on my own volition. Kicking off my sneakers willy-nilly, I dropped the utility belt as I walked to the bedroom, where I collapsed on my bed. I'm not even sure if Mike followed. At that point I didn't care. All my body craved was rest, and my mind, the blinding numbness of sleep.

Chapter Twenty-Two

JILLIAN

A high-pitched beeping drew her out of the depths of a strange dream where she'd been at school, grading a stack of papers that kept growing and growing no matter how fast she graded. She tried to open her lids, only she couldn't seem to get her left eye to open properly, and as she came to, aches and pains in her arms, back, hip and legs announced themselves, but they were overshadowed by the grinding headache, sore throat, and dull throb in her left cheek.

Where was she? Her right eye rolled in the socket, taking in the industrial ceiling tiles and the fluorescent lighting. She lifted her left hand to touch her tender cheek and found gauze wrapped around her wrist and a plastic clip-like thing with a cord attached to her finger. Lifting her right arm, she found more gauze around that wrist, a needle and IV tube taped to her hand. She studied it in confusion and heard an indrawn breath.

"Jilly! You're awake." Karina came into Jillian's line of sight and touched her forearm. "Hey, sleepyhead."

"Karina?" she croaked, cleared her gritty throat and tried again, "Where am I?"

"You're in the hospital, sweetie. Is your throat sore? I've got some water. Do you want me to raise you up a bit?"

The hospital craft-o-matic bed hummed as it levered Jillian into an upright position, and she took in the rest of the room. Sunlight striped through the partially open blinds, a muted TV was turned to the HGTV channel, where a burly man sledgehammered kitchen cabinetry. The walls were painted seafoam green, and an ugly pink recliner squealed shut as Karina got up to retrieve a green-lidded cup with a bright yellow straw for Jillian.

"Here, the nurse said your throat might be sore. They had to intubate you." Karina put the straw between Jillian's cracked lips.

Jillian greedily sucked down the cool water, a balm against the tenderness. After gulping half the glass, she released the straw. "What happened? Was I in a car accident?"

Karina's face pinched with concern. "What's the last thing you remember?"

Jillian concentrated, trying to recall her last memory. "I was at school, grading papers."

"What day was that?"

"Wednesday? Thursday?" Jillian chewed her lip. "It's kind of hazy. Why? What day is it?"

"It's Saturday."

Jillian could only seem to get her left eye to open halfway, and it hurt when she tried to use the muscles to get it opened wider. She lifted her fingers to explore the pain, but Karina, with the gentlest pressure, pushed Jillian's hand aside.

"Don't touch. It's swollen. You're going to be sporting a shiner for a few weeks. I think we should let the nurses know you're awake. They'll probably want to take your vitals and do . . . nurse things." Karina pressed a little red call button wrapped around the bedrail.

"You haven't told me what happened. Was it a bad accident?" Jillian's mouth trembled. "Was it my fault? Did I kill someone?"

"No! No, good lord, no. There was no accident, Jilly. You were kidnapped." Karina drew the rolling table up closer, so the water was within Jillian's reach.

"Kidnapped? But—by who?" Jillian drank some more water, searching her memories for anything that happened in the past forty-eight hours. "Did it have something to do with Sadira?"

A petite African-American nurse with bright blue eye shadow and wearing yellow and white polka dot scrubs entered. Jillian turned her head and noticed the empty bed on her left for the first time.

"Good morning!" The nurse erased the name Kim from the chalkboard beneath the TV and wrote down Destinee. "That's me, Destinee." She smiled, removing a clipboard hanging at the foot of the bed. "Let's get some of your vitals." She glanced at the machines beeping behind Jillian and scribbled something on the clipboard, then she attached a Velcro cuff just above Jillian's elbow to check her blood pressure. While the cuff squeezed, the nurse ran a thermometer across Jillian's forehead. "Good, good." She nodded, releasing the cuff and writing the information in the chart. "How's your pain on a scale of one to ten, one being none and ten being excruciating?"

"Uh, maybe a six or seven. My cheek hurts. My throat is starting to feel better, but I kind of ache all over and it hurts when I take a deep breath," Jillian said.

Destinee nodded, her pen scratching away. She peered at Jillian, checked the IV, and clicked her tongue. "You've got some bruised ribs. They'll take a few weeks to heal. I can get you an ice pack for that cheek, and we'll get the doctor in to see you," the nurse said, hanging the chart back on its hook.

"She can't remember anything," Karina said.

Destinee paused. "Anything?"

"Nothing about what happened to her."

"What's the last thing you remember, hon?" Destinee directed her question to Jillian.

"Being at school in my class . . . a few days ago."

"Is that unusual, the amnesia?" Karina asked.

"It can happen." The toothy smile returned. "Don't worry, we'll get the doctor in soon." Her thick white nurse shoes squeaked against the beige tiles as she exited the room.

Jillian found her sister staring at the empty doorway, her face tight. She seemed to come back to herself and morphed her expression into a jolly smile. "Well," she said in a chirpy falsetto, "the doctor will be able to tell us what's what. I'm sure it's nothing." She adjusted the blanket around Jillian and checked her watch. "If her flight is running on time, Mom will be landing in about thirty minutes. Mike offered to pick her up and bring her to the hospital."

"Mike? I thought he was out of town. Wait, Mom is coming?" Jillian's world spun unexpectedly, and she squeezed her eyes shut until it passed.

"Well, she and Dad were both going to come, but Dad has finals next week. And I thought you might not want everyone converging at once," Karina continued with the upbeat tone that put Jillian's teeth on edge. "But it only takes one a call, and he'll hop the next flight out." She waggled her cell phone in the air.

"No. Mom's enough," Jillian grumbled, and tried shifting into a more comfortable position.

"Do you want me to adjust your pillows for you?" Karina crooned.

"I want you to stop with this false chirpy act," Jillian groused. Karina's face fell. "And yes, can you put that pillow behind my head?"

Karina helped her sister in silence.

As she did so, Jillian noticed the tightness around her mouth and the circles beneath her eyes. She wore no makeup. It was unheard for Karina to be in public without her war paint, and her ponytail was still damp from her morning shower. Whatever demons haunted her couldn't be hidden from the sharp eyes— well, eye—of the sister she grew up with. "Jesus, Karina. What the hell happened? You look like hell."

Karina glanced away. "The past twenty-four hours have been . . . hard. But I don't know if I'm supposed to burden you with the details. We'll talk more after the doctor visits. In the meantime, what would you like to watch?" She picked up the TV remote and turned up the volume. "I was watching *Flip My House.*"

"That's fine."

They hadn't gotten through the commercial break when two men walked into the room. The first was a man of Vietnamese descent with a scar down his face so prominent that it looked like Dr. Frankenstein had sewed him up. Jillian recognized the face, but she couldn't recall how or where she knew him. She searched her mind for a name. The other, a tall, handsome blond wearing a navy-blue T-shirt so tight it revealed a set of six-pack abs, followed the shorter man, carrying a posy of flowers. Jillian seemed to remember seeing him in her sister's building a few months ago.

Karina rose stiffly from her recliner and limped over to give each man a quick hug. "Hey, guys, what are you doing here?"

"Checking on the patient." The blond set the vase on the table in front of Jillian and winked. "How are you feeling?"

"Jillian, this is Jin," Karina said, pointing to the Asian, "and that's Joshua, also known as the J-squared team. They're with Silverthorne Security, they helped locate you. And now that you're all in the room together, I can call you J-cubed—Jin, Jillian, and Josh." She grinned at the poor quip.

One side of Jin's lip lifted while Josh ignored the pun and

picked up Jillian's chart to scan the material. Jillian's mouth dropped at his hubris.

"Josh used to be a Navy corpsman," Karina supplied, returning to her chair. "He put in your IV last—"

"What's with the limp?" Jin interrupted.

"Oh, I banged up my knee yesterday when I threw that guy over my shoulder. Concrete is a lot harder than the mats we work on. I remember a sharp pain when I hit the pavement but didn't really notice it last night. However, it's a little stiff this morning." Karina waved a dismissive hand. "Oh, don't give me that look, Jin. You're probably right, I did something wrong when I threw him. I was working more on instinct and panic," she said defensively.

"What guy? You threw a guy over your shoulder?" Jillian stared at her sister in shock.

"Let me look." Josh went down on one knee in front of Karina and patted his leg.

"It's no big deal." Karina laid her left foot on Josh's thigh and he pushed her jeans up. She sucked air through her teeth as he pushed the denim past her knee. "Just a little tender."

Jillian leaned forward to get a gander. Her sister's knee was purpled with an angry bruise and swollen to the size of a small grapefruit. Josh's brows crunched together. He poked and prodded, asking if this or that hurt. Karina denied it all, but Jillian could tell the spots Josh touched that caused her sister pain by the flexing of her jaw and wincing of her eyes. From Josh's expression, Jillian was fairly sure he could tell when Karina was lying as well. He straightened the leg, then rotated it. There was a clicking sound and Karina jerked involuntarily with a yelp.

The perky nurse returned, squeezing and shaking a blue and white instant ice pack. "Here you go, dear. And look, you've got company." Destinee wrapped the pack in a pillowcase and showed Jillian how to hold it against her face. "Ten minutes ought to do it. No longer."

Josh peered over the bed. "Can we get another one of those?"

"Another ice pack?" Destinee cocked her head, observing the tableau.

"She hurt her knee." He indicated Karina.

"I'm sure it'll be fine," Karina stammered as she tried to push her jeans past his hands.

Destinee came around the bed and gave a low whistle when she saw the injured knee. "Ouch, sugar. Why didn't you say something?"

"It's not that bad," Karina tried valiantly to assure the medical personnel, but no one listened to her.

"I'll be back with another pack in a jiffy," Destinee said, hustling out of the room.

"I don't need it," Karina said through gritted teeth.

Josh regarded Karina. "Are you a glutton for punishment?"

Jillian snorted, and Karina's mouth flattened. "I don't want to be a bother."

Jin threw his head back and let out a shout of laughter. Jillian grinned, which made Karina's face squeeze up even more as if she'd sucked on a lemon. It was in that moment of jocularity that another man walked in—someone Jillian had never seen before. His hair was short, cropped military style, brown with a bit of pepper mixed in, and his eyes were a mesmerizingly silvery blue-gray. In one hand he carried a brown bag, in the other a pair of aviator glasses and a cup of coffee. He walked with incredibly erect posture, reminding Jillian of the guards she'd seen at the Tomb of the Unknown Soldier at Arlington Cemetery.

"What's Cardinal said now?" he asked without preamble, placing the brown bag next to the flowers.

"She said she doesn't want to be a bother," Jin provided.

The military guy came around the bed to see what was going on, concern written plainly across his handsome features. "Damn, when did that happen?"

During the guffaws, Karina seemed to have given up and placed a hand across her eyes, her face crimson with embarrassment. "When I threw Cortez over my shoulder."

Destinee bustled back in with another ice pack. "Here you go. Place it on that knee for ten minutes. And you ought to have someone check it out. Get an X-ray."

Karina popped the footrest up as Josh moved out of the way, and placed the pack on her knee. "Thanks, Destinee."

"No problem. And the doctor should be here soon to see you." She pointed at Jillian. "Your color's looking better, sugar. Must be the attention of all these handsome men." With a wink and a wave, Destinee's curvy backside swished out with a sway to rival Betty Boop.

Stymied for conversation, nobody spoke and the only sound was a loud commercial promoting erectile dysfunction medication.

"What's in the bag?" Jillian asked.

The new guy reached inside and pulled out a to-go container. "Ghetto soup."

Jillian pushed back against the pillows, distaste written across her features. "I'm sorry, did you say ghetto soup?"

"Best soup in D.C." He pulled out a plastic spoon, removed the lid, and placed it on the tray in front of her. "Comes from this dive in a questionable section of Southeast called Big Mama's. Best chicken noodle soup in the area. I thought you might be hungry."

Jillian had no idea when she'd eaten last and her stomach grumbled as she whiffed the delicious scent of the warm broth. Pulling it closer, she scooped up a spoonful of noodle and chicken, and tentatively slurped. "Yum, this is good, and the chicken tastes delicious. It's not too salty. Sometimes restaurants make their soups too salty. You know what I mean?"

"Not Big Mama." His features softened as he said her name. "Thanks—uh . . ."

"That's Rick," Karina tossed over her shoulder. "A.k.a. Batman."

"Ah, the elusive Batman. So we finally meet." Jillian and Rick shook hands. "It sounds as though I have your team to thank for rescuing me last night."

"No problem," Rick replied.

"I wish I could remember something of what happened."

Josh returned to Jillian's chart. "You don't remember?"

Jillian squinted in concentration. "Nothing since Wednesday or Thursday, I think."

He grunted but said no more, and Jillian tucked into Big Mama's soup.

"What's the story with the money at the . . . uh, pharmaceutical house?" Karina asked Rick. "Did your DEA friend . . . uh . . . clean things up?"

Rick nodded and sipped his coffee. "DEA finished counting and cleaning out the stash around five o'clock this morning."

"And Christoph? Did he get credit for the bust?"

"He did. He needed a win. The undercover job he returned from last month went bad. He accidently led his team into an ambush. Four perished and Chris barely escaped with his own life." Rick stared at his feet and gave a head shake.

"I didn't realize. . . . Is that why you called him in?"

Another sip of coffee accompanied Rick's nonchalant shrug.

"I figured it couldn't hurt."

Karina stared at the TV with an ashamed expression. "Apologize to him for me. I was . . . distraught."

Rick's features softened as they rested on Karina. Jillian held a hand to her mouth to cover the gasp at the unexpected tenderness she read in his expression.

"Everyone understands. Don't worry about it." Josh patted her shoulder with brotherly fondness.

Rick took another sip of coffee, and his countenance returned to its natural detachment. Shifting her gaze, Jillian connected with Jin's dark, unreadable eyes. He pulled his ballcap lower and glanced away.

A woman with long, curly brown hair wearing a white lab coat over green scrubs arrived. "Good morning, I'm Dr. Balaban. My, you have quite a crowd this morning." Josh passed the chart to the doctor. "I understand you're having difficulty remembering what brought you here."

Jillian nodded.

"It's not unusual to experience short-term memory loss after trauma, but it's more likely from the drugs that were pumped into your system. You were given a cocktail that is known on the street as Goodnight Cinderella. It's a combination of GHB, Ketamine, and Flunitrazepam, also known as Rohypnol. Unfortunately, you were dosed with enough to knock out a two-hundred-and-fifty-pound man and suffered some complications." The doctor went on to explain the drugs they'd found in Jillian's blood last night and how it depressed her system, especially her breathing, and the steps the ER doctors took to stabilize her condition. "You're lucky the medical personnel found you when they did. The cheek is not broken, but bruised, and will be painful for a bit. Same with the ribs. It'll hurt to take deep breaths and laugh for a few weeks. I'm going to send you home with a script for the pain, but there will only be enough for four days. When you run out, you can use over the counter pain relievers, Tylenol or Ibuprofen, and ice to alleviate the swelling, which will dissipate in the coming days."

"When will I be able to leave?" Jillian asked, voicing her main concern. She hated hospitals and just wanted to recover in her own bed, surrounded by her fluffy pillows and down comforter.

"We're going to run some more blood tests to make sure the drugs are out of your system." She scribbled something on the chart. "If it looks clean, I can probably release you by the end of the day. Do you have someone who can keep an eye on you at home?"

"I can." Karina waved from her chair. "And our mother is flying in today, she'll be staying with Jilly for a while."

"Is there anything else you need?' Dr. Balaban asked.

Karina raised her hand, as if in elementary school. "Should we tell my sister what happened to— you know, jog her memory?"

The doctor frowned. "Let's wait and see if it comes back to her." She exited a few minutes later, passing Jillian's boyfriend, Tony, on his way in.

"Babe, whoa, what happened?" His sneakers squeaked against the floor tiles as came to her side.

The Silverthorne guys backed up to give him space.

"Tony! How did you know I was here?" The tension in Jillian's stomach relaxed as his warm, mahogany gaze rested on her. Tony came by his tanned skin through his Guatemalan ancestors and his athletic body from playing soccer. He worked as an EMT in Alexandria. He and Jillian had been dating since Christmas.

Jillian reached for him, and he cupped her uninjured cheek

and gently kissed her forehead. "A strange number texted me and said I'd find you here."

"That would have been me," Josh said. "I found his number in your phone. It seemed like you had a—*cough*—personal relationship." He reached into his back pocket and tossed Jillian's phone on the bed.

Jillian could only imagine some of the sexy texts Joshua had culled through. Her face turned beet red, and she snatched up the cell. "Hey, the screen is cracked."

"It was thrown from a moving vehicle," Karina explained in a deadpan voice.

"A moving vehicle? What on earth happened?" Tony asked the crowd.

No one spoke. The guys suddenly found the HGTV channel fascinating, and Karina stared down at the ice pack on her knee and massaged her temple.

"Hello? Anyone? Bueller? Bueller?" Tony glanced around the room, his gaze coming to a rest on her sister. "Karina!"

She started guiltily but glanced up with innocence written across her face.

"What happened?"

"Well—" She released a big sigh. "Jillian was kidnapped last night and drugged, and these guys" —she indicated the Silverthorne crew— "helped locate her. They're with Silverthorne. The big blond here is Joshua, Jin's the guy in the corner with the ballcap, and that's Rick, their fearless leader. And—that's all."

"That's all? Are you kidding me?" Tony's tone turned belligerent. "Who kidnapped her? What the hell is a Silverthorne? Why is her face all beat up? What's going on?"

"Silverthorne is a security firm. I'm not sure I'm allowed to divulge further information," Karina told him as her phone dinged twice. "Well, that's it for my ice pack." She tossed it aside. "I could use a cup of coffee. Boys, why don't we give Jillian and Tony some time alone?"

Jin helped Karina out of the recliner and slung her arm over his shoulder. "We can take you down to the ER to get X-rays."

"Good idea," Joshua said, backing him up.

"The ER? What's wrong with you?" Tony asked.

Karina grimaced as she put weight on her injured knee. Nobody bothered to answer Tony.

Jillian snorted. "You'd better escort her, or she'll slip away and let it fester. She's terrible about seeing doctors when she's sick."

Karina limped past the bed and mumbled, "I don't know what you're talking about."

"Remember the walking pneumonia? And the infection from your braces bracket? How long before you told Mom about it?" Jillian needled her sister.

Karina grunted. "You better be nice to me, or I'll call Dad and Tyler and invite them to descend upon you too."

"Don't you dare," Jillian called to her sister's retreating back.

Rick slid his aviators on. "I'll make sure she's taken care of."

"I'm sure you will," Jillian said beneath her breath.

Once Karina and her escort were out of earshot, Tony said, "That was a loaded comment. Who are all those people?"

Jillian scooted as far to the right as the bed would allow and patted the blankets. "Climb up here with me, and I'll tell you what I know, and what I think I know. Some of it might be coming back to me. I'm fairly sure it has to do with Sadira."

Chapter Twenty-Three

I hobbled down the hall, leaning on Jin and trying to loosen up my knee. It was strange, although it kind of hurt last night, the pain was nothing compared to today. And the swelling—I didn't remember it looking like that when I fell into bed.

As our crew approached the elevator, the doors slid open and Detective Perez stepped out, carrying Starbucks cups in each hand. "Ms. Cardinal, I see you're still wandering around with your protection detail. I'm not sure if anyone told you, but the hit was called off."

"Yes, I had heard that. We just left my sister's room. Are you here to see her?" I asked as our group moved to the side to allow others passage through the hallway.

"I did plan to stop in. We need to get a statement from her if she's awake."

"That's going to be tough," Josh said. "She has memory loss from the drugs they fed her."

Disappointment spread across Perez's features. "Nothing?"

We shook our heads.

Josh continued, "The doc said her memory may return, but they don't know when."

The detective gave a troubled squint. "Well, Trudea remembers. She can provide us information. *If* I can convince her to testify."

"Is she here?" I asked, feeling guilty that once we'd found my sister, I'd barely given poor little Trudea a second thought. I knew Josh had taken care of her before she was carted off in an ambulance, but I'd been so focused on Jillian and her health, inquiring after Trudea's condition slipped my mind. "Is she going to be okay?"

He nodded. "She's in room 507. MS-13's been trafficking her as part of a larger prostitution ring."

The news wasn't surprising, but hearing Perez confirm my suspicions still packed a punch. "I was afraid of that. Why didn't she tell the police?"

The detective shook his head. "She's grown up in a life where she doesn't trust the police. Her mom is an illegal. They threatened to have her deported and kill some little boy she babysat in the building."

I thought of the kid who gave Jillian the skinny on Trudea's recent changes.

"That house you took down last night—" Perez tilted his chin toward Rick "—they'd just moved all the money from the warehouse two days ago."

"Into that neighborhood?" I said, astonished. "But it seemed so—"

"Middle-class? Unassuming?"

"Yeah." I nodded.

"Officially, it's not in MS-13 territory. That's why it wasn't on anyone's radar. It's off the grid, so to speak," the detective explained. "The home is owned by Ahmed Akbar. Guy lives in California. He works for a tech company. Apparently, he's got nothing to do with the gang, just an unsuspecting landlord. Leon rented it three months ago. Paid for the first year's rent in cash."

"And that didn't send up any alarm bells for Ahmed?" I asked, astonished. "Didn't he run a background check on his new tenants?"

"Apparently not." Perez shrugged. "It's lucky Sadira had

been there; or your sister might not have been found."

He was right, we had to give Sadira credit, but no one seemed to want to speak the words out loud, least of all me. Instead, I changed topics. "Can you offer Trudea's mom citizenship in exchange for her testimony?"

Perez grinned and held up the cup he hadn't drunk from. "Why do you think I brought her some hot chocolate? To celebrate. FBI cleared a package for her testimony with the A.G.'s office. Immunity, citizenship for her mom, and WITSEC."

"Has someone told her mom? Is she coming?" Jin asked, shifting my weight.

I'd begun to hang on him as we stood around talking, so I straightened, putting more weight on the injured knee.

Perez flashed a smile that softened those hard cop features. "Garcia is bringing her over now."

I shifted again, trying to find a more comfortable position to stand. "What are you doing with Sadira? Did you get more out of her? By now she should be cleared of the diamond theft. Did you have enough to keep her?"

"We did. Her other lawyer showed up and played a bit of hard ball, but an anonymous tip came in that Sadira had a safe in her closet. Behind a shoe rack. It held a bundle of money and jewelry. Interestingly, the safe was open." He directed an inquiring look around our half-circle.

I knew the tip off didn't come from me. *And* I remembered locking that safe back up. Either Rick picked it again after I exited the closet, or he sent one of his guys to do it. I flashed a glance over to Rick, who stood stoically aloof, with a hand in his pocket while sunglasses covered his eyes, sipping coffee. The man was a vault. Nothing indicated he'd made the call or reopened the safe.

Either oblivious of the look I'd just shot Rick or choosing to ignore it, Perez continued, "We made an offer to Sadira, and she took it."

"Will she serve time?" Rick asked casually, tossing his empty coffee cup past Perez toward a trash bin about ten feet away. Of course, it arched beautifully and dropped straight in.

"Twelve months. She'll be kept at a black site under twenty-four-hour guard. After she testifies and serves her sentence, WITSEC will put her in a new life."

I thought she'd gotten off lightly, but didn't comment.

"How did she get drawn into this mess to begin with?" Josh asked.

"A kid from her past, Marshall Ellison. We picked him up last night at his apartment. She knew him in juvie. He goes by a couple of different names. Lately, Trevor."

I whistled. "Blond hair that needs a cut, kind of lanky with bedroom eyes? Dull as a butter knife? About twenty?"

"That's him. He's actually twenty-five. And he's not as dumb as he portrays. His job is to find the girls. Ones with low self-esteem, usually poor, often living with only one parent. He befriends them, finds their weaknesses. Makes them feel special. May start a sexual relationship or introduce another 'friend' to start up a sexual relationship with the mark. He'll usually introduce drugs, if the girls aren't already taking them. It's a long process working them into the fold. Traffickers will often entice the girls to do things they wouldn't normally do. Trevor uses a scheme by telling the girls he's got connections in Hollywood and he can set up a meeting with a talent scout, usually it's acting, or modeling."

When he mentioned the modeling, I got woozy and leaned harder against Jin. He spread his legs further apart to take my weight.

Perez must not have noticed my consternation because he tsked and plowed on, "Their lives aren't the best, and they always think they can be the next 'it girl' and get out of the poverty they live in."

I thought of Jillian at that age doing her high school plays; she wanted to be the next Reese Witherspoon. "It's not just their living situation, it's also the age," I mused. "Girls are so self-conscious at that time in their lives. They want to be admired. Hollywood is glamourized on TV, magazines, and even social media."

The men around me nodded in agreement.

"True. Ellison preys on whatever 'dream' they've confessed to him," Perez explained. "This is how she's introduced into the sexual part of things—convincing her it'll get her out of the dump she lives in. If they start to refuse, by now Ellison's found the girl's weak spot, and he'll push that button. Often that's when the gang members are brought in to scare the girls into cooperating and keeping their mouth shut. Your friend Sadira was a part of the introduction to the high life. She's attractive, drives a high-end vehicle, she looks safe. She'd pick up the girls from Trevor and drive them to the 'talent scout.'"

"Is that why she changed her name?" I asked.

He shook his head. "We think she changed her name to get away from her life back in Oklahoma. Ellison ran into her one day when she was eyeing a pair of Prada shoes she couldn't afford on her teacher's salary. He bought them for her. Then bought more designer clothes and bags for her."

"Sadira does like her designer fashion," I drawled with antipathy.

"He started small, with seemingly benign packages for her to courier. She got hooked on the easy money. When she started to transport girls, she initially didn't know what was going on. It was about that time Ellison paid off her college loans and she was able to buy the condo. As she got further into it, she began to realize something wasn't right about driving the girls. She says she tried to get out, but the gang knew her. . . ."

"And they're like the mafia, you don't just walk away," Rick supplied.

"No," Perez said with a scowl, "you don't."

Conversation stalled as we digested the detective's information and he digested more of his coffee.

"So MS-13 had their hooks in her." Rick removed his glasses and squinted thoughtfully. "How did she keep them from turning her into something more? One of their prostitutes?"

"She drew a line in the sand. She told Ellison in no uncertain terms that there was a safety deposit box. A lawyer somewhere in the city has the key. If she doesn't check in with him on a regular basis, or if she contacts him and uses a certain phrase, he opens the box and sends the envelopes to the police, FBI, DEA, and the press."

Rick whistled through his teeth. "Did she really do it?"

"She says so." Perez shrugged. "We get the key once she's relocated to the place where she'll serve time under house arrest."

"Damn, that chick outsmarted a vicious gang. She's hardcore," Josh commented.

"Oh, there's nothing dumb about Sadira. Shrewd, I think, is the word that best describes her," I commented.

"You're not kidding," Perez agreed. "Well, this hot chocolate is getting cold, and Garcia should be here any minute with Trudea's mother. I'd better head back to her."

"Take care, detective." I gave a finger wave as he walked off. While we'd been standing, my knee's dull ache had turned into a throbbing pain. "Okay, Joshua is right. I need to go to the ER."

Rick took my other arm, and between the two men, I was able to hobble onto the elevator, but, as we turned, a pain shot down my leg. I couldn't suppress a groan. Rick lifted me up into his arms as if I weighed no more than a sack of flour.

"This really isn't necessary, is it?" I groused.

He stared straight ahead, watching the numbers count down to the first floor. "If you prefer, I can throw you over Joshua's shoulder and he can carry you fireman style?"

Josh turned and delivered a wicked grin.

"Never mind." I put an arm around Rick's shoulders. "It's all good."

Josh's grin disappeared and Jin adjusted his hat.

"What do you think it is?" I asked Josh.

"Torn meniscus," he replied.

"Is that bad? Will I have to have surgery? And why didn't it hurt like this last night?"

"Oh, now you're full of questions," he replied wryly.

I reached out to slug him in the shoulder. Only he was standing at an odd angle, and I barely connected.

"Weak, Karina, weak." He shook his head sadly.

I tried again, he stepped aside, and I almost fell out of Rick's arms. "Damnit, Josh. Don't egg her on," he grunted, struggling to rebalance me.

"Children, children." Jin shook his head at us like a disapproving father. "Joshua, you should tell her what you know. It is unkind to keep it from her."

Josh gave in. "Depends on how badly you've torn it. It may not need surgery. The doc will probably need an MRI to determine a diagnosis."

"Great."

The elevator bell dinged. My entourage and I traipsed

halfway across kingdom come to get to the ER.

Mike found me in a treatment room an hour later and my entourage reduced to one. Josh abandoned me first when he left to take a date to a National's baseball game. Rick got a call from the office and left to put out some sort of fire with an angry client. Jin had kindly remained behind, although I'd almost wished he'd gone with Rick. Jin held my full respect, and I appreciated working with him in self-defense class and on a case. However, I found that when we weren't working, it was very hard to make small talk. Twice I told him to go, not to worry about me, and enjoy his day off. Twice he refused, as if some sort of obligation required him to remain by my side. Our conversation was stunted, with long pauses in between my questions and Jin's brief answers. Jin seemed oblivious to the awkward silences.

I was so grateful to see Mike, if I could have, I would have launched myself off the table when he arrived.

Instead, he came to me, hugged and kissed the top of my head. "Now what have you done to yourself, K.C.? I swear I can't leave you alone for a minute," he teased. "Jin, it's good to see you. Keeping an eye on her for me?"

"Making sure she doesn't leave before the doctor finishes," Jin deadpanned.

"Is *that* why you wouldn't leave?" I cried.

He nodded in confirmation. "Rick also told me to stay."

"Oh, for the love of Pete."

Mike grinned. "Probably a good idea. I'll take over guard duty now if you'd like to go."

"Be off with you." I shooed Jin away. "It's a gorgeous day out. The weather is supposed to be in the upper seventies. Go jogging . . . or whatever you do on a day like this."

Jin shot me one of his rare smiles. "Cycling. Take care,

Cardinal."

"You too, Jin. And—thanks for—well, everything. You know . . ."

He delivered a two-fingered salute on his way out.

"Now, where were we?" Mike asked.

"You were about to give me a kiss. A real one." Mike leaned in and gave me a kiss that made my toes curl. It also had the effect of making me forget about the throbbing pain in my knee for a few moments. "Wow, that was a good one."

"I missed you."

"Me too." I stared into his handsome face and my stomach fluttered. "I'm glad you're back. I'm assuming you picked up Mom. Everything okay?"

"Yes, I left your mom fussing at Jillian after she told me where I could find you. So, what's the story? When did you hurt your knee?"

I explained my over-the-shoulder toss, and how I tore the meniscus (Josh was right) doing that little move. "The doc says I don't need surgery, but I'll need to rest, ice, and elevate it. I'm waiting for someone to return to outfit me with some sort of brace. The doctor wants me to follow up with an orthopedist next week. If I'm a good little girl, it should heal properly, although there might be some physical therapy involved."

"Good times." Mike pinched my chin. "I can't leave you alone for a second, can I? Between you and your sister, you've got disaster written all over."

I rolled my eyes. "I'm surprised you're not yelling and pacing in front of me with your mean face."

He sighed heavily and pulled me close. "Right now, I'm just glad that you and your sister are going to be all right."

I laid my head against his chest and listened to his steady heartbeat.

"Where is your mom staying?"

I pulled back to answer, "With Jillian. Mom can fuss to her heart's content over my sister. And if you ever want sex again," I said, pointing a finger at Mike's grinning face, "you will not disclose to my mother how bad the knee is. We are downplaying. It's sprained, and I must wear a brace for a few weeks. That's it. Period. You got me?"

"So, I shouldn't have mentioned that a gang member put a hit out on you yesterday?"

I sucked wind so hard it turned into a coughing fit. "You didn't," I choked out.

Mike rubbed my back. "Calm yourself. I didn't tell her. I'm not a fool."

"Why does everyone like to yank my chain?" I wiped the tears out of my eyes.

"Because it's easy to rile you up and fun to watch you spin your wheels."

"Ha-ha."

A nurse walked in carrying a black knee brace with Velcro straps.

After they released me, Mike and I headed back up to Jillian's room. I have to admit, the new brace provided excellent support and made walking easier. It was also ugly as sin, and my mind was sorting through work outfits, trying to determine which ones would fit comfortably over the brace and still hide it.

I forgot everything when my mom wrapped me in her loving embrace. The sweet scent of her perfume enveloped me. Even as an adult, occasionally we need the love and security of mom. It brightened my outlook, like the rising morning sun over the Potomac, knowing she was here now. It meant that everything was going to be okay.

Afterword

One of the most asked questions I receive from readers and interviewers is: where do you get your inspiration? For each Karina Cardinal novel, inspiration came from different avenues. In *Isabella's Painting,* catching the last fifteen minutes of a documentary about the 1990 Gardner Museum heist provided the seed which grew into an international bestseller. In *Fatal Legislation,* a recall ad for pacemakers provided the kernel of creativity. For *Diamonds & Deception*, it was the underbelly of the human trafficking storyline that came to me initially, not the diamond theft. During a Back-to-School event at my son's high school, I learned from the health teacher that the students would be discussing human trafficking in their ninth-grade year. One of the issues they would discuss—safety at a local mall where human trafficking, unbeknownst to me, apparently runs rampant.

Days later, I ran across an article about the *Just Ask Prevention Project,* an initiative in Northern Virginia. The mission of the project is to educate and mobilize communities to end human trafficking. What I read, when I visited their website, surprised me. Like many folks, I've seen the *Taken* movies with Liam Neeson, where a young girl is abducted in a foreign country and auctioned off to the highest bidder. The reality can be very different. Not all girls are abducted and trafficked outside of their hometown. Girls who have been manipulated, groomed, then held hostage through money, drugs, and threats of bodily harm are used and abused right where they live. Some go to school and are trafficked in the afternoons and evenings, cooperating out of fear for their lives or their family's lives. According to the FBI's website, "human trafficking is the third largest criminal activity in the world." The International Labor

Organization estimates that there are 4.8 million people trafficked into forced sexual exploitation globally, and 99% of victims in the commercial sex industry are women and girls. A moving testimonial on the *Just Ask* website reveals how a young girl was trafficked for three years starting at the age of fourteen. She lived at home and was seeing a counselor. She says, "If someone had cared enough to JUST ASK what was going on, maybe I would have never been a victim." I incorporated MS-13 into the story, because they are one of the worst human trafficking offenders in the Washington, D.C. metro area.

Diamonds & Deception has been the most difficult Karina Cardinal mystery for me to write because of the solemn and weighty topic of human trafficking. To learn more about human trafficking, how you can identify and prevent it, I encourage you to visit any of the sites listed below.

Just Ask Prevention Project: *justaskprevention.org*
Saved in America: *savedinamerica.org*
National Association for Missing and Exploited Children: *helprescuechildren.org*
Human Smuggling and Trafficking Center: *www.ice.gov/human-smuggling-trafficking-center*
FBI Human Trafficking and Involuntary Servitude: *www.fbi.gov/investigate/civil-rights/human-trafficking*

Acknowledgements

This Karina Cardinal adventure wouldn't have come to fruition without some input and help from so many. First, thanks to David Swinson. Your advice as a retired police officer is always intriguing and helpful when I'm storyboarding. You'll see I incorporated your information regarding burglars. Andrew Billings, thank you for sharing your stories as a paramedic and knowledge about drug interactions and medications. Matt Fine, your professional knowledge is always helpful, and thinking about how you will react when reading my stories keeps me honest. You always provide sage advice and encouragement, which is much appreciated. The FBI museum provided valuable information as did the retired FBI agents who are docents at the museum. Additionally, I deeply value the information I received from the *Just Ask Prevention Project*. Their website, along with others, was a fount of knowledge and provided me an accurate reality of the human trafficking tragedy in Northern Virginia.

Being an indie author can be daunting, as all aspects of publishing are on my shoulders. Over the past few years, I have surrounded myself with a team that helps me put out both an entertaining and competitive product. I couldn't do without my editor, Emily Junker and my cover artist, Rebekah Sather. Finally, to my blurb wizard, Carolan Ivey.

As always, I appreciate the support from my loving family and friends. They have listened to my crazy ideas and supported my dream.

About the Author

Ellen Butler is an international bestselling novelist writing critically acclaimed suspense thrillers, and award-winning romance. Ellen holds a Master's Degree in Public Administration and Policy, and her history includes a long list of writing for dry, but illuminating, professional newsletters and windy papers on public policy. She is a member of International Thriller Writers, Sisters in Crime, and the OSS Society. She lives in the Virginia suburbs of Washington, D.C. with her husband and two children.

You can find Ellen at:
Website ~ *www.EllenButler.net*
Facebook ~ *www.facebook.com/EllenButlerBooks*
Twitter ~ *@EButlerBooks*
Instagram ~ *@ebutlerbooks*
Goodreads ~ *www.goodreads.com/EllenButlerBooks*

Guided Reading Questions for Book Clubs

Available on Ellen's Website
EllenButler.net

Novels by Ellen Butler
Suspense/Thriller
Isabella's Painting (Karina Cardinal Mystery Book 1)
Fatal Legislation (Karina Cardinal Mystery Book 2)
The Brass Compass
Poplar Place

Contemporary Romance
Heart of Design (Love, California Style Book 1)
Planning for Love (Love, California Style Book 2)
Art of Affection (Love, California Style Book 3)
Second Chance Christmas

Made in the USA
Middletown, DE
17 February 2020

84806644R00172